HIDDEN STEEL

Hidden Steel

Doranna Durgin

FIVE STAR

A part of Gale, Cengage Learning

GALE
CENGAGE Learning

Detroit • New York • San Francisco • New Haven, Conn • Waterville, Maine • London

GALE
CENGAGE Learning™

Set in 11 pt. Plantin.
Printed on permanent paper.

LIBRARY OF CONGRESS CATALOGING-IN-PUBLICATION DATA

Durgin, Doranna.
  Hidden steel / Doranna Durgin. — 1st ed.
    p. cm.
  ISBN-13: 978-1-59414-681-7 (alk. paper)
  ISBN-10: 1-59414-681-0 (alk. paper)
  I. Title.
PS3554.U674H53 2008
813'.54—dc22   2008010693

First Edition. First Printing: July 2008.

Published in 2008 in conjunction with Tekno Books.

Printed in the United States of America
1 2 3 4 5 6 7 12 11 10 09 08

DEAR READER—
Usually when I start a book, my characters know who they are. And because they know, I know. I can plan the book around them and how they'd handle things, and mostly I'm pretty close. But this time . . . both of us were in the dark. Boy oh boy did that mean a fast learning curve along the way. And outlines? We don't need no stinkin' outlines! Once Mickey began to trust herself, it was all I could do to keep up with her. I have the impression that Steve felt the same way. And as for those bad guys? Ha!
So I've decided to take a page from Mickey's book. More trust in myself, and full speed ahead!

Ritual Disclaimer:

This book is set in San Jose and Palo Alto . . . if you've been there, you might recognize a thing or two. But I made up some stuff, too, so it won't all be familiar. So take a drive past that big brick warehouse, but don't expect it to be a pottery co-op. . . . After all, making stuff up is my job!

Doranna Durgin

CHAPTER 1

Sound first invaded her cocoon of awareness. Beeping. Really annoying beeping. Something tightened snugly around her upper arm . . . and when it went away, so did she.

When the beeping returned, it came with odors. Astringently offensive odors of new plastic and antiseptic, and the earthier odors of unwashed hair and barely washed body. It came with the trickle of a thought: *hospital.* And the more worrisome question: *What am I doing here?*

Nothing hurt particularly, aside from the ache of being too long in one position. No pain in her limbs, her torso, her head . . . although every thought came surrounded and obscured by thick mist. So then . . .

Why?

Voices came from beside her bed. Murmurs, just barely loud enough to make it through the mist. A demanding question. Something beside her head gave a plaintive beep, and with a hiss, the snug feeling returned around her arm. Blood pressure cuff, she realized. And again—*What am I doing here?* She tried to say the words out loud; her dried lips didn't so much as twitch.

The voices rose again—a man and a woman. Something-somethingsomethingMICKEYsomething.

Mickey.

Must be her.

★ ★ ★ ★ ★

Mickey opened her eyes. She hadn't thought about it, hadn't planned on it . . . just suddenly found herself awake. Chaotic images struck her with the force of a physical blow; she flinched and closed her eyes. As she tried to sort out what she'd seen, she realized she wasn't alone. At least, not quite. Two voices hovered in another unhappy discussion, far enough away so they might not notice her new awareness, close enough so she couldn't discount them.

Hmm. What a suspicious way to think.

She cracked her eyelids open again, keeping it slow. Abstract shapes resolved to objects, most of them white in tone. Over there, the slats of closed blinds. The walls. The ceiling, sound-absorbent tiles pocked with little holes. Her skin, lightly tanned and freckled arms emerging from a gown of definite hospital vintage. *Hospital.* Made sense, with the woozy pounding in her head and the mist that loomed not far away, threatening to close back in on her. The black blood pressure cuff wrapped her upper arm, stark against her skin. A boxy blue monitor on a pole sat beside the bed. It gave a familiar plaintive beep and the cuff automatically inflated.

Hospital.

Why?

She couldn't see the man and woman who conversed; they seemed to be just outside the door. She considered opening her still-dry lips to ask, suddenly overwhelmed by the taste of morning mouth. Ick. And as she hunted the room for any sign of ice water or maybe even randomly placed toothpaste—because hey, one could *hope*—other details impressed themselves upon her.

She lay on a fancy cot of some sort, not a hospital bed. There was no television in the corner, no privacy drapes around the bed. A stethoscope and a brand-new box of latex gloves sat on a rickety fake-wood table not far from the bed—no sign of a hospital bed tray in sight. None of the ubiquitous identical supplies one seemed to find in a hospital room—no dull pinkish-rose plastic emesis basin, no matching pitcher, no box of scratchy generic tissues. A flattened, empty IV bag sat on the floor beside the table, along with a battered box of vials and syringes.

And then there were the handcuffs.

Handcuffs.

She'd had reason for her suspicious thinking.

She just had no idea what it might be.

Mickey took a sharp breath as the fear hit, a great wash of *unknown* that flooded through her body in a jumble of panic and adrenaline and goose bumps. Acutely vulnerable in the oversized but still immodest gown, handcuffed to this aluminum-frame cot, and . . . no idea why.

No idea what she'd done, how she'd gotten here . . .

Who she was.

Mickey.

But only because she'd heard them say so.

Right on cue, their voices rose again.

"You *said* it was a sophisticated form of a Mickey Finn!" the woman snapped, the indefinable trace of an accent barely evident in her voice.

Mickey Finn. It hadn't been her name after all. But at the moment it was all she had, so she thought she'd keep it.

"It *is.*" The man responded with a combination of deference and annoyance. "She had a reaction to it. That happens even with the old-fashioned chloral hydrate—it's not predictable."

"She's not of any use if we can't question her. That was the whole point of acquiring her, was it not? Of using the 'sophisticated delivery timing' of your absorbable drug?" High heels landed on thin carpet with a muted firmness of tread.

The man remained placating. "I have no doubt you'll be able to speak with her soon. I'd be more certain of her recovery if I had real facilities for her treatment."

The woman responded with a genteel snort. "We were lucky to have arranged this much without attracting attention." And then her voice dropped back to a murmur, though it still held command.

Great. Whoever Mickey really was, whatever she'd been up to, she'd attracted the attention of this woman and her people—and they'd gone to great effort to get her here so they could *question* her. That didn't sound like fun, not at all.

But it was more than she'd known just moments before, and it was enough to give her some goals—to find out who she was . . . who *they* were . . . why they'd imprisoned her here. To escape.

In any order she could get it.

She realized the hallway conversation had ended and the man—a doctor, perhaps—stood in the doorway shuffling through papers. Mickey quickly closed her eyes. The longer they thought she was out, the more time she had to gather information before the unpleasant-sounding *questioning* began. The more chance she could plan her escape.

Escape. Just what kind of life did she lead when she wasn't cuffed to a cot awaiting a meeting with a woman who'd had her drugged so as to conduct a conversation?

"I know you're awake," the man said, quite conversationally. Somehow he'd made it to her side to fiddle with the machine while her mind wandered the edge of the still-lingering mist. He tapped the machine. "You've left behind a very revealing spike in your pulse and blood pressure."

"Bother," Mickey said crossly. She opened her eyes to regard him with unconcealed interest. He turned out to be a sallow little man in turquoise scrubs with bags under his eyes and a sagging jaw line. He took a step back at her immediate and direct response. Maybe he'd expected her to flutter her eyelids and ease into the situation with some demure decorum. Instead she met his washed-out brown eyes with a demand. "What did you do to me?"

"You're fine," he said.

"I'm not," she told him. "I obviously haven't been for . . . what? Days? Weeks?" She flexed her unsecured arm and eyed the tight, lean muscle there. Thin, but . . . "Not weeks, surely."

"No." Startled all over again, he still managed to shake his head. "A few days. You had a bad reaction to a drug."

"*Your* drug."

By now he seemed to have given up on being surprised. He pulled a chair in close to the bed, an ancient office chair on wheels. If he tried to touch her, she could literally send him flying. *Hmm. Do I do that sort of thing?* But he gave her no such excuse. "I'm helping to test it, yes."

"Was I allergic to it? Should I get a little bracelet to warn all future kidnappers?"

"I—that is—" He took a breath, pressed his lips together. "Literally speaking, you weren't allergic to it. But it was a serious reaction, and I'm relieved to see you so coherent."

Mickey nodded wisely. "It'll get *her* off your back, anyway."

"Among other things." He leaned forward, propping his elbows on his knees, his sheaf of papers—notes and records about Mickey—threatening to spill from his grip and scatter. Did he have a key to these cuffs somewhere? He wasn't the jailor, but surely he'd have it in case of a patient crisis. Something to think about.

Something to think about. Good God, how could she be so cool? Kidnapped, handcuffed, no idea where she was or *who* she was . . .

Then again, what did she have to go on but instinct? She'd

have to trust it . . . to trust herself. And when instinct told her to panic, she would.

He hadn't followed her train of thought—had she hidden it so well? He narrowed his eyes and nodded at the door behind him, presumably indicating the woman who'd just been standing there. "Don't play these games with her."

She took the warning to heart. He might be working for the enemy, but he'd evidently not intended to hurt her. He seemed genuinely concerned that he had. The realization, the awareness of such sympathy in this cold, frightening situation . . . it released her fear in a sudden burst, turning it into a burning impulse to ask the most important questions of all—the *who am I* question and the *when will I remember myself* question and even the most frightening of all—the *will I* ever *remember* question.

But she didn't. The woman wanted her for something. A *discussion.* That meant that Mickey had information . . . and it was the information that had made her valuable. If she'd lost the information . . . then she'd lost her value.

She didn't want to think what that owner of that cold, angry voice would do to an acquisition who had lost her value.

"Jane A. Driedler."

The voice woke Mickey. She hesitated long enough to identify it—the angry woman—and to realize that there had been an odd tone attached to the words. As though they were being said in quotes. As though it weren't a real name at all. So when she opened her eyes, she held the puzzle of it there.

The woman nodded with some satisfaction. "Yes," she said. "We know your station name."

"You—" Mickey started, baffled—and then realized she couldn't ask that particular question, although she instantly accepted that Jane was no more her name than Mickey. She frowned and looked away, trying for the dismay that such a pronouncement seemed to deserve. When she glanced back from beneath a downcast brow it was to soak up the visual details of this woman, hunting for familiarity. She found only the nondescript—a woman of average height with a shapely and well-padded figure, dressed in conservative corporate with a tailored grey suit over a black silk shirt, her hair dark brown and her complexion a light olive that left Mickey no clue as to her originating culture. Her features offered no help; they, too, were non-committal, pleasant on an oval face. But her eyes . . . they were the darkest brown, perhaps even black, and they were just as cold and angry as her voice.

Mickey quailed before those eyes. Whoever she was, whatever she'd been up to . . . this woman was harder than she. Crueler.

"Tell me," the woman said, in a purr so false it made Mickey wince, "about Naia."

Mickey shifted her wrist within the handcuff, looking for freedom and finding only the loose but perfectly secure fit. Slender, she was . . . but not so slender she could simply slip their restraints and run for it.

All the same, she wasn't about to lie here with this woman looming over her, so she awkwardly levered herself around the stationary wrist to sit. "I have to go to the bathroom." No doubt it wasn't the first time, but she didn't care to think about the details.

"How inconvenient for you." The woman sat—on a new chair, padded and highly adjustable and obviously her own.

She thinks she'll be here awhile.

"Naia," the woman said. "How compromised is she?"

If I'm supposed to know Naia, then she must know me. Maybe if I find her . . . "I wouldn't know." Mickey tugged her gown around her thighs and decided she must be a jogger. Or a cyclist.

The woman gave the same genteel snort Mickey had heard upon first waking. "You've been cultivating her for months. Don't think you can save her with your silence. You can only save yourself, by giving me the information I need."

Mickey dared to look into those cold black eyes. "Can I?" she said. "Save myself?"

The woman's lips curved in smile made stark by the deep red of her lipstick. "You can certainly save yourself some trouble. How much? That would be up to you."

The skin tightened across Mickey's spine and arms and lower belly; an instant of disorienting panic gripped her so tightly she couldn't move, couldn't think. *Who am I who is she what am I who is Naia* . . .

The woman smiled.

Instincts. They were all Mickey had. She'd trust them. She'd damn well *cling* to them.

"Really," she said. "Just woke up . . . small bladder . . . how about that bathroom?"

With a flicker of irritation, the woman leaned back in the chair and crossed her stocking-covered legs. "I don't understand your reluctance. Naia is still at liberty only because we're playing her like a plump little fish. As I said, your silence won't save her."

Mickey hid her instant skepticism, looking at her bare toes, wiggling them slightly. If they were so sure about Naia, why play her? Why would they need any additional information from Mickey?

Perhaps the woman read Mickey's mind . . . or maybe she'd just done this too many times before. "We do, however, need to follow up on the damage Naia has caused us—and since it isn't convenient for us to reveal our knowledge of her activities just yet, you will be our source. It's only fair, don't you think, since you corrupted her in the first place?"

Corrupted her to do what? And who *was* Naia? Sister, friend . . . or some clueless mark of whom Mickey had taken advantage?

She winced at the thought, and hoped—hoped hard—it

wasn't that last. And then thought . . . *if it bothers me to consider it now, would I have done it?* Surely her personality had remained intact.

Except she immediately recalled the head injury cases she'd heard of, people who'd had to relearn themselves—and the frustration of their family members as they turned out to have new personalities along the way. New likes, new dislikes, new responses.

Damn. Self-doubt . . . this wasn't the time or place. Whoever this woman was, she had the money and backing to employ her own unscrupulous doctor, and access to the building Mickey found herself in. And one look at the woman's eyes let Mickey know she was used to getting her own way.

In fact, aside from that mild frustration, she didn't seem particularly upset with Mickey's reticence. She simply regarded her captive with a raised eyebrow. "You do realize, I hope, that the good doctor is hardly here just to hold your hand? His primary purpose was to help us acquire you—and then to make sure I get the information I want. He has a creative collection of chemicals to help you feel talkative—but he did suggest that, given your recent reaction, it might help avoid scrambling your brain for good if I simply talked to you first. So far, I don't find this approach very rewarding."

And if Mickey talked? If she admitted she was of no use to the woman at all? What were her chances then?

Her voice sounded strained even to her own ears, a whisper fighting its way out to be heard. "And hey," she said, somehow finding the strength to lift her gaze back to meet those cold black eyes. "How about that bathroom?"

"I'm not an orderly!" the doctor insisted, standing just inside the doorway, offended and not trying to hide it.

"And I don't want her exposed to anyone else on staff now

15

that she's awake." The woman didn't bother to get angry . . . mostly, Mickey realized, because she truly didn't care. "Don't waste my time arguing. Take her to the bathroom, or clean up after her when she wets herself. Your choice." And she looked over at Mickey to say, "This is my gift to you, Jane A. *Dreidler.* Time. Think over our discussion. When I come back, it'll be your last opportunity to preserve your mind, such as it is."

Oh, ha ha. Clever. *And if she only knew . . .*

Disgruntled and still a little disbelieving, the doctor fished in the pocket of his white lab coat. No name over the pocket of that one, nope. Still . . . he had the key. She waited expectantly as he came in to free the cuff from the cot frame, and then helped her to her feet when she found herself wobbly.

More wobbly than she'd expected. Not a good thing when those instincts she now relied on so heavily screamed for escape. Escape *before* that woman came back for another chat. When the doctor took her elbow in a supportive hold, she didn't hide her flinch . . . but she accepted his help, shuffling like a little old woman.

Then again, maybe she *was* a little old woman.

No, she knew that much. Her skin wasn't old. It didn't tell her much, but she wasn't elderly. Her voice told her she spoke English as her native language. If she had a regional accent she couldn't detect it, but she didn't set much store in that. Who heard an accent in their own speech? Maybe she'd find a mirror in the bathroom. . . .

She'd been here at least once before, but it was no more than a hazy memory; she'd barely been awake, and she'd had two people at her side—both of them big and husky and male. She thought they'd left her alone in the bathroom stall. She *hoped.* Then again, if that had been her first self-powered visit to any facilities, no doubt other arrangements had been made before that point. Maybe she'd been wearing adult diapers for days.

She certainly wasn't wearing any undergarments *now*. Just this damn drafty gown.

She hesitated in the doorway, looking both directions down a hallway that could have been in any low-rent corporate building. Stained carpet of a variegated dark blue, off-white walls, fluorescent panels set into more of the sound-dampening tile. No noise to speak of—as far as Mickey could tell, she and the doctor were the only ones occupying this area. Her room was in the middle of the hall; there were exit stairs at one end of the hall and a corner at the other.

The doctor gave her an impatient nudge, directing her away from the exit. Mickey stumbled when they reached the carpet, but straightened herself out and offered up a good impression of a woman moving upright. Each step she took seemed like an opportunity wasted—another step in which she hadn't escaped. Hadn't even thought of a way to escape. Really, couldn't think of anything other than getting closer to the bathroom.

To her dismay, the doctor followed her right through the door marked *Ladies*. At her incredulous expression, he said, "The stall is privacy enough. Did you really think I'd leave you alone in here?"

Mickey glanced around the room—bad linoleum floors, pale yellow tile on the smooth walls, an empty towel dispenser beside them and . . . and nothing. Just a row of three stalls, one with a missing door. "Just what kind of trouble do you think I could get into?"

He remained unmoved. "I haven't the faintest idea, but I'm not taking the responsibility for it."

Mickey made a face at him. She checked the first stall, gave thanks for the presence of toilet paper, and made use of the facilities without giving his presence much additional thought. If he wanted to listen to her pee, then let him.

And still she hadn't come up with any great escape. Nothing

clever, nothing diabolical. Maybe she just wasn't any good at this even when she had her memories intact. Maybe that's why she'd been caught.

Whatever she'd been doing.

Whoever she was.

She emerged from the stall to give the doctor a sweetly insincere smile, and went to wash her hands as he all but tapped his foot in impatience. And there. A mirror. Her chance to learn just a little more about herself without revealing how little she knew.

Whoa.

Hard to sort those first impressions. *Too pale, face strained and unwell. Lanky, dirty hair, falling around her shoulders. Collarbones too sharp, a thin look accented by the oversized gown.*

But otherwise, she was the girl next door. Caramel brown hair, very straight, cut in layers to curve around her cheeks and a jaw on the long, sharp side. Tiny little smile parentheses at the corners of her mouth. A faint mole, not next to that mouth, but right on the plump curve of her lower lip. Eyes blue enough to grab her attention even though she knew it was her own reflection.

"Forget what you look like?" the doctor asked, all sarcasm.

Mickey cast him a little wrinkle-nosed *ha ha* expression and turned the water on; the loose handcuff clattered around the sink until she caught it up, shoving her fingers through so it rested above her knuckles like . . .

Like a pair of brass knuckles.

Ooh.

But it had to be done here. Here, where no one would see them. Or find the good doctor.

Mickey hesitated, testing the thought. *Reality check. Just where does this fit on the scale of stupid?*

And a little voice answered, *How stupid would it be if you didn't even try?*

Mickey ducked her head, splashing water on a face that hadn't been washed in far too long. No soap here, but the cool water chased away a remaining cobweb or two. And then, somehow before she'd even thought it through, she clutched her hand to her eye and made a startled noise.

"What—?" the doctor said, moving closer. Responding automatically to his years of training.

"Something in my eye," Mickey said, and frantically splashed more water at her face.

He huffed with impatience, moving close enough to take her head in his hands and lift it with a casually proprietary air that removed any trace of regret she might have been harboring for what she hoped would happen next.

For what *did* happen next. Because as the doctor planted a thumb and finger to force her watery eye open, Mickey brought up her cuffed hand in a swift, precise punch that had more than desperation behind it.

Training. *I know how to hit people.*

Her blow landed right on the bridge of his nose; she felt the give of it—and heard the crunch. The doctor cried out in astonished agony and clapped his hands over his nose; blood flowed freely from beneath them, dripping off his chin and onto the lab coat and turquoise scrubs. He staggered backward, cast her one disbelieving look, and turned to bolt.

She reached the door before him, and she turned him casually over her hip to land hard on the cold, dirty tile.

He was a slight man, no bigger than she. He was no athlete. And still, she found herself startled when he looked up at her in fear, his hands leaving bloody tracks on the floor as he scooted back away from her.

"Oh, relax," she snapped, not happy to have even this

unscrupulous and harmful person look at her in such a way. "I'm not going to hurt you. I mean, not *really.*" But he froze as she dropped down over his legs, knees digging painfully into his thighs while she swiftly searched the lab coat pockets and found the handcuff key with one hand, the other cocked to do damage.

"My *nose,*" he said, disbelief evident, all signs of fight lost in his pain. "You broke my—"

"Shut up," she growled. She backed off slightly, releasing the remaining cuff and rubbing her fingers where the improvised weapon had cut into skin. "And take off those scrubs." He hesitated, and she whirled the cuffs in a not-so-idle threat, nerves and muscles buoyed by sudden adrenaline. "You're just aching for a swirly, right?"

In moments he was down to boxers and white socks, and she wasted no time cuffing him to the plumbing. It took only a moment to slip into the scrubs, still—*ugh*—warm from his body heat. They smelled like him, too, and having his scent close to her skin made her feel even dirtier than before. She jammed her feet in his sneakers—they were too big, but better than going without. She managed to tighten the laces enough to keep the shoes from flopping around. She gave him a quick, critical squint of a look, ignoring his flinch, and then took up the hospital gown. The thin, old material ripped easily even in hands growing trembly—the adrenaline rush hadn't lasted nearly long enough. She jammed the pieces in his mouth and wrapped the ties tightly around the gag, avoiding his gaze. It was his own fault.

It's just that she was used to helping people, not hurting them.

Wasn't she?

As a final touch she dropped the lab coat over him, a strange little touch of modesty.

And then she stuck her head out the door, saw no one and nothing between her and the exit door, and ran.

She ran with her luck, and expected it to run out at any moment. Expected to hear a shout of alarm, to feel a rough snatch at her arm. She found the best combination of stealth and speed she could as she hit the stairs and headed down, but every step brought her closer to stumbling in those big sneakers and every moment drained what little energy she had. The spray-painted letters beside each door told her she'd started on the fourth floor; by the time she reached the first, those letters swam in her vision, a fey enticement to freedom. She flattened herself up against the wall to catch her breath, but only waited until she'd quieted it enough so it didn't roar in her ears—or anyone else's.

She pushed on the heavy door bar with trembling hands and excruciating care, trying to ease past the *clunk* when the latch engaged, and peered out into a hallway that mirrored the one she'd just escaped from.

This time, she heard voices.

She let the door close.

The stairwell promised one more level down. The basement. Surely they wouldn't be in the basement, and even if she couldn't find an exit, she could get a better handle on the building layout.

Unless she stayed here, crept out to where she could hear, and tried to understand more about the odd situation into which she'd woken.

Mickey looked at her shaking hands, and down at her wobbly knees and the oversized sneakers. Her heartbeat came fast and thready and the grey mist edged in around her thoughts and her vision. Could she even remember what she heard, if she wasn't caught?

Be smart. Run away.

Mickey ran. Down to the basement, where the lights seemed dimmer—or the grey mist crowded closer. She bounced around the hallways, past pipes and electrical boxes and phone relays and inexplicable blocky structures jutting from wall and ceiling, and then eventually—she wasn't quite sure how—she found herself a way out. Out into the bright daylight.

She should have been paying more attention. She might not have run into the over-muscled, neckless man in his perfectly tailored suit. As it was, she didn't see him until she slammed into him, finding out for herself just how hard those muscles were and just how well that suit hid the gun that dug into a soft, tender spot she had to keep herself from reflexively grabbing in public. But luck stayed with her—because she bounced right off him, and she had the space to turn on her heel and bolt.

She heard his curse—and she heard him bark something into a hand-held radio. If they hadn't known about her escape before . . .

Mickey ran.

CHAPTER 2

Heat. White hot summer sun in dry air. Mickey ran into someone, blurted an apology, and ran onward, unsteady and drawing offended shouts. No doubt people stared. At some point she crossed a river, clutching the railing of the bridge pedestrian lane and fighting the impulse to simply jump right in, embracing the cool wetness. The chest pocket of her stolen, blood-spattered scrubs yielded a few folded dollar bills and she lurched past a gas station vending machine, hesitating long enough to buy an iced tea. Somewhere else she got an apple . . . she wasn't sure she'd paid for it, but she ate it to the core.

She didn't know if she'd been followed. She thought not, that she'd grabbed that instant of opportunity between discovery and enemy mobilization and actually made it. But she didn't know. They could be using teams, they could be hanging back, they could simply be waiting for an opportunity to snatch her up when no one would notice.

When she hesitated, knowing she'd hit the end of her limited resources, she found herself beside a high, ratty chain-link fence. She laced her fingers through the diamond links and held herself steady. In the distance, long hills rippled up into mountain ridges, parched brown formations that made her long for that river. More immediately, she found herself surrounded by city formations—buildings of brick and block crowded together in a variety of tired store fronts, their line-up broken only by narrow alleys and fenced, junky lots like the one she'd stopped beside.

A few cars parked along the curb, most of them looking as though they'd stopped here only because they couldn't go any further. *Just like me.* Broken glass seemed to be the major decorating theme, but in this particular lot, used condoms ran a close second. Garbage crowded into the corners of the fence, blown there and left to decompose at its own rate. Rather like the stiff, flattened body of the rat sticking out from beneath a crushed six-pack carton.

Mickey swallowed hard against a sudden faintness. All that running . . . *I went in the wrong direction.* She should have gone the other way. *Any* other way.

A silver-grey tabby looked out an apartment window, paw poised to snag the lilac-colored curtains stirring in the breeze.

Mickey blinked. What—?

She blinked again, hard and deliberate, and refocused herself on this grey-edged street. At the end of the block, a signal light went from yellow to red. A shop door swung open with the chime of bells, then slammed shut in a way that spoke of a malfunctioning automatic closer. Scanning to find it, her gaze fell on the building across the street. Glass storefront with a giant hand-printed schedule of some sort, a few flyers spotting the glass, but nothing in the way of professional lettering. Above the door—which was blocked ajar, and couldn't have been the sound source she hunted—a plain, unassuming sign declared *Steve's Gym.*

A gym. Relief tugged at her; she frowned when she realized it, and realized she couldn't say why. A gym. *Safety. Refuge. Strength.*

In the end she quit trying to understand the *why.* What did it matter? Where else did she have to go? And if nothing else, a gym always had a drinking fountain.

Indoors. Out of the sun. Out of sight.

Mickey extricated her fingers from the chain link fence and

aimed her big clunky sneakers across the street.

"Big isn't always better." Steve Spaneas held his arms wide with the declaration, a *Hey, look at me—What could be better than this?* gesture that always made the students of this class laugh. Some of them even pointed. "*Prepared* is better. *Smart* is better. You stick with me, and we'll make those nights on the street feel a little safer."

And at this they always nodded. Fear crept in around their eyes—weary eyes, wary eyes, and often just a little bit unfocused eyes.

They weren't on drugs. The problem for this bunch was that they couldn't or wouldn't take the drugs they should. Local street folks, dressed in old and scavenged clothing, always needing haircuts and shaves and a good solid application of toothpaste and deodorant. During this class, the old gym . . . well, it smelled like a gym, all right.

But it didn't mean they weren't *people*. That they didn't deserve to feel safe in the little niche of this world they called their own. The self-defense skills he taught them were basic, but the very fact that he held these free classes let the local toughs know they'd find no easy prey in this section of town.

A tribute to his brother, who might not have died so young if someone had done the same for him.

His other classes were more typical. Young men and women, drawn to the discipline and fellowship his classes offered—nondenominational, he thought of them, and culled from all fighting disciplines to cater to a street-fighting method. Low-cost memberships that also drew them to the free weights, and friendly competitions that gave them the motivation to follow-through. Kickboxing for those who wanted to get serious.

It didn't add up to a lot. But it was steady, and it was enough to cover his gym and the apartment above it in this low-rent district. And the neighbors liked having him here. Casseroles and brownies and tomatoes grown in pots outside back doors . . . there was always some kind of offering on the store front counter just inside the doorway, just beside the open-topped barrel where he kept the donated hotel soaps, tooth-pastes, feminine supplies and disposable razors.

A doorway he'd propped open for this tangibly odorous class, in spite of a day hot enough to keep the cranky old air condition-ers working hard. Unusual for the San Jose climate, but it always happened a couple times a year.

He didn't need the class reaction—ten of them today, all frequent flyers—to let him know someone had come to that open door, and hesitated there. He didn't read anything into their suspicion, either—many of them survived on suspicion. But he wasn't expecting what waited for him when he turned around.

Bright scrubs, splattered with . . . yes, blood. Bright eyes to match. Utter exhaustion on that face, and a personable haircut that didn't match the filth factor dulling the honey-brown color. Too thin on a slender frame—and too exhausted to stay upright for long. An old, old story . . . she'd walked out of a clinic somewhere, wasn't on her meds, had forgotten to eat . . . and someone else on the street had sent her in Steve's direction with the misguided notion he could do more than hand out soap and teach free self-defense. But . . . surely her feet weren't really that big?

"I just—" she said, and her voice was hoarse and weary, barely reaching him. "I need—"

And then her eyes rolled up and she folded to the ground in an absurdly graceful faint, just missing the barrel with her head on the way down.

No panic. Not like he hadn't been here before. *His brother's face, curly black hair damp with sweat, that same dazed and somehow surprised expression* . . .

Steve gave the class a reassuring word and left them long enough to scoop her up—oh yeah, way too thin—and deposit her on the cot in the office. He left a cool damp washcloth on her head, a tall plastic cup of water on the desk, and checked his watch. He'd take just a moment to give the class some familiar warm-up exercises, and then he'd make sure his assessment—that she just needed rest—was on the mark.

He hesitated at the door, looked back at her. Small in those scrubs. Her face wan and pale, her eyes deep with shadows. For the moment, peaceful.

For the moment.

Here we go. . . .

Chapter 3

Naia Mejjati stopped in the act of placing demure diamond studs in her ears, swamped in a wave of homesickness. It stopped her breath short.

Not because of the depth of her feelings. No, because she'd had them at all.

She quite deliberately slipped the back over her earring before thinking or feeling anything else. Then she gave herself a critical eye in the mirror. *Foolish girl,* she told her reflection—classically Irhaddani, those features. Olive skin, big dark eyes, generous lips and a long nose, delicately shaped. In her own country, she was a beauty. In the United States, she was yet another ethnic set of features not quite conforming to the standards of beauty set by Hollywood and advertising.

At least in this country, other people could actually see those features. They could see the sparkle of her earrings, the expression of a mouth lightly glossed with color. They could see by her clothes that she was a conservative young woman, but one who understood quality. The composed, appropriate daughter of President Sayid Mejjati.

None of those things were true in her homeland, where she went veiled outside the presidential household, and where her own people knew only that she existed. The Irhaddan princess in a tower . . . but it was no fairy tale. It was any woman's life in Irhaddan.

True, she hadn't initially been excited about the prospect of traveling overseas to attend Stanford—her father's grand gesture to prove that Irhaddan was indeed modernizing its attitudes toward women. Not after her initial schooling was entirely handled by tutors in an extravagant indulgence . . . a gift from her father to her mother. Not when she was used to the relative anonymity of the veil and chador. Here in the States, anyone could see her—*everyone* could see her.

But once she'd gotten used to it . . .

She dreaded her graduation, and the inevitable call back to Irhaddan. She'd come here as a symbol, and she'd learned to embrace a different kind of life. She'd even learned to see the corrupt nature of her father's regime—not her father himself, but his advisors and cabinet members. Her father might be old-fashioned and inflexible, but he honestly strove to lead his people through a tumultuous time in a tumultuous region. Others . . . had their own agendas.

And it was for the sake of her father that she'd allowed herself to be drawn into Anna's world of espionage. She'd quickly understood the value of her contributions—how easy it was for her, a practically invisible member of the presidential family, to pass along details of secure building structures, of overheard conversations. Things that would help the States to keep on top of the corruption her father refused to see.

Even if Irhaddan intelligence suspected they had a leak, they'd never look to Naia. Not proper, demure Naia, loyal and obedient to her father. They simply neglected to understand that she could distinguish between her father's efforts and their own.

And still, it had taken all her nerve to leave the recent notes at her first dead drop exchange. They weren't even terribly significant notes, not for this practice run. The real intelligence still burned in her memory, acquired during her most recent visit and festering there, waiting for an outlet.

She could only hope she had the nerve to pass it along. Even now, another wave of homesickness washed over her, and she recognized it for what it truly was.

Fear.

Red blooming Christmas cactus, a silver tabby cat in a bay window, a Bristol Blue Nailsea vase on a serpentine mahogany chest of drawers with a dressing slide above graduated drawers and fluted, canted corners—

Mickey's eyes flew open to the view of yellowing acoustic foam ceiling panels. Bristol Blue Nailsea vase? What the—?

Me. Something about me.

Not a very useful something, but useful nonetheless.

"Feeling better?"

She didn't startle, because some part of her had known he was there all along. She merely turned her head on a somewhat lumpy pillow, identifying her bed as a narrow cot and the smell in the air an unexpected combination of stringent sweat and old gym mats. She found him sitting in a folded chair beside an old metal desk, ankle propped on one knee, T-shirt snug across his chest. Day-old stubble framed striking lips, the set of which suggested that his lower jaw didn't quite fit neatly inside the upper. Curly black hair gone beyond the need for a haircut topped off deep, expressive black eyes. *Greek god.*

Except this wasn't heaven *or* Olympus. Just a gym she'd stumbled into. A tiny office in that gym, complete with the old desk and its computer monitor perched at one corner, the kickboxing awards and photographs, and a corner coat rack holding colorful satin workout gear and a brown belt tangled in lightweight boxing gloves.

He didn't seem bothered by her failure to answer; he just nodded at the desk, where a paper plate held a sandwich and an apple accompanied by a tumbler. "Think food might help?"

"God, yes," she blurted.

He smiled—but if his expression held understanding and compassion, there was something reserved there, too. "Can you sit up, or is it lunch in bed?"

"I can sit," she assured him. She could even stand to get there, and though she still felt weak and wobbly, the haze had lifted. The drugs, out of her system at last. She applied herself to the turkey and Swiss on whole wheat, drinking the accompanying milk with enough gusto to leave a mustache.

"Looks like it's been a while," he observed. He seemed relaxed enough, but she got the impression he was ready for . . .

Something.

"I wouldn't know," she said, but looked with regret at the last bite of sandwich. Her unthinking response didn't seem to surprise him any more than the other oddities that had come along with her—oversized scrubs, oversized shoes, the blood splatter from the erstwhile doctor's battered nose. His stomach growled, and she looked at him in sudden realization. "I just ate your lunch."

"There's more where that came from."

She wasn't so sure. Nothing about this place gave her the impression of goods to spare.

"You missed the street class," he said. "But there's another one in an hour, if you want to sit in on it and get an idea of how we work around here. It's my tough love class, but the principles are the same—self-defense for the streets."

He thought she'd come for a class?

She vaguely remembered the room full of people she'd seen upon arrival here, all awkwardly assuming the same balanced pose. Street defense classes for street people? Okay, it made a certain amount of sense.

"It's free," he said, misinterpreting her hesitation. "As long as you don't have an address, that is."

31

"No," she murmured. "No address." And her thoughts moved more swiftly then, almost without bothering to consult her. Perfect cover, this—street person, new to the streets. Needing help. Blending in with the others. Let him think she'd come for his class. It'd give her time.

Give her the chance to figure out what was really going on. Who she was.

Who wanted to get their hands on her.

Only after she'd wolfed down Steve's lunch did she offer her name. "Mickey," she told him, halfway through the apple. "My name is Mickey. Mickey Finn."

For the first time, she startled him. "You're kidding," he said, and instantly wished he could take the words back. Those with reality issues had enough of people disbelieving them. Patronizing them. It didn't matter whether what they saw or heard was real to him—it was real to them.

But she didn't take it amiss. "Not kidding," she told him. "It's the only name I know."

"Come on out to the gym," he said. "Grab some soap from the freebies barrel—there's a shower in the locker room. I ought to have some clothes that will fit better than those, too." He always had such things on hand—donations or culled from the thrift store. And he couldn't help but eye the blood splattered on her oversized scrubs.

"You're just dying to ask, aren't you?" She said it with a smile at the very corners of her mouth, nibbling the apple right down to the seeds. She looked better with the food hitting her system; she seemed clearer.

It happened that way all the time. Moments of clarity, and then back into their own little worlds . . . "I'm worried," he said, having long ago learned that simple truthfulness was best. "If you've been off your meds long, there's a chance you could

32

have done something you didn't mean to do." And then he said what he always said. "If you need anything, I can recommend a good clinic."

Those bright, strong eyes shuttered, then cleared with sudden understanding. "Oh," she said. "I'm fine, really. I got these—" but she stopped, assessing him with quick skill that somehow seemed totally out of place, her gaze flicking from his casual gym wear to his oh-so-Greek features, and then around the office. Whatever she'd been about to say, she didn't. She shook her head, and explained simply, "The clothes came this way. They're scrubs; they were used. Doesn't seem like a big mystery to me." She plucked at the scrub shirt. "I couldn't be more grateful for a shower, though."

"With the offshore flow driving the temps up, you're not alone." He shifted to get up, to show her the way to the showers, but something on her face stopped him. A softness . . . no, more than that. She saw him as a person, not a vague figurehead. She *responded* to him as a person. He couldn't stop his mouth from saying, "What?"

"Just . . . thank you." She tossed the apple core toward the wastebasket, got it in one. "A shower, and then I need to—" But apparently she wasn't going to say that out loud. She finished, "Looks like I stumbled into the right place."

"I hope so," he said, not expecting the fervency of it—or the sudden doubt that he could do right by this woman . . . that she wasn't his average needy visitor. He wondered, with more than the usual curiosity, what those unspoken words had been.

But she just grinned at him, unfolding from the bed with the grace of a petite cat. Also not expected, given that she was nearly as tall as his five-nine, but there all the same.

He tabled his curiosity and led her to the freebies barrel and then along the back hallway—let's face it, a crummy back hallway no matter how he threw disinfectant around—and to the showers. He showed her the facilities, and headed back out to the gym. The kids would be trickling in soon, drawn to this safe place. Here, they could shoot a few hoops without being hassled or getting caught up in someone else's conflict. San Jose wasn't big on drive-by shootings, but in this area . . . the kids didn't take anything for granted. They noticed everything that happened, they kept an eye on the intrusions from other, even less savory neighborhoods, and since they'd been coming here, they'd learned to share what they saw. To be strong together.

Satisfaction. Not a feeling that could be faked, or artificially induced. Hard work, bearing fruit. Steve listened to them, quickly deducing the buzz of the day: several upscale cars had been cruising the streets, their occupants staring into dark corners and focusing on the features of every young Caucasian woman they passed. Looking for someone . . . not finding them. *Not cops,* the kids deduced. Someone more nefarious.

Curiosity and coincidence collided. *Except this is life, Spaneas, not a James Bond movie.*

Mickey Finn appeared just as class was about to start, straight hair drying into a sophisticated, face-framing cut, shorts and borrowed tank top revealing much in the way of wiry muscle. She might be hungry, but it hadn't been so long since she'd been in much better circumstances—since she'd been someone who took good care of herself. He watched long enough to see her settle cross-legged against the padded back wall, then turned his attention to class. All basic stuff, this class—about balance, about always being prepared—and a whole lot about how running away is always the best option. They practiced that, too—making opportunities to run, being alert enough to run before anything ever really happened. With some, the lesson was a lost cause—but others had become more thoughtful over time.

Near the end of the hour, several kids trickled away; sparring partners shifted around. Inevitably, Clinton—thirteen, gawky, too much in the way of teeth for the size of his mouth and simply born to be the Kid Who Gets Picked On—stood alone.

Not for long. Mickey had been so quiet that Steve forgot she was there—at least, until she stood and lined herself up with Clinton, glancing at Steve for permission. "Can I play?"

"You feeling well enough?"

"Fine," she said, though she lifted one shoulder in acknowledgment of the not-so-distant past and the faint it had contained. "Just for a few moments, okay? As long as my partner here takes it easy."

Class was almost over anyway. Steve looked at Clinton, assessing whether the boy found this flattering or embarrassing. With thirteen year-olds who spent a lot of time looking down at their amazingly big feet, it was sometimes hard to tell, but he thought the faintly visible flush on Clinton's dark skin was pleasure and not agonizing embarrassment.

Well, hell, he'd take Mickey Finn as a sparring partner any day. Legs more than long enough to reach the ground, plenty of shape lurking beneath that second-hand tank top. Just proved Clinton was no dummy. So he nodded, and he demonstrated the move he wanted the class to practice—a simple escape from a threatening frontal grab. "Remember," he told them. "Assertiveness counts; quickness counts. And size isn't everything. I have to look up to half of you, but I can take down any one of you." He gave a few of them a meaningful eye. "And have."

That got the ducked heads and rueful grins he'd been expecting, but he'd said the words with affection and the kids knew to take them the same way. Three years here and he knew them all. And so he knew that when Malik—one of the lifters, with good muscle and size for his fifteen years—headed for Clinton, his carefully neutral expression meant trouble.

"Ow!" A girl's voice slid straight up to ultrasonic upper registers in both annoyance and pain. Only Lucia had that particular skill. "You're not supposed to be hitting!"

"Be ready," her older sister told her righteously, parroting Steve's frequent words.

"*Hermanas,*" Steve said, and would have left them to work it out if he hadn't seen the honest tears brimming in Lucia's eyes—and the red mark just below one of those eyes.

"She did that thing you showed us last time," Lucia said. "That thumb thing."

"*Sarita,*" Steve groaned, and went to check the damage— hoping for the best from Malik.

But the rest of the class had sensed there was nothing of the best in Malik this day—no one was practicing. They'd dropped their ready stances and turned to the back corner of the gym. Even Lucia grew distracted as Steve checked her eye, transfer- ring her attention outward. "Dammit," Steve muttered, savoring the impulse to toss Malik out for a week. He turned to see the last thing he'd expected.

Mickey Finn was the one who faced Malik. Clinton stood uncertainly to the side, torn between the visible impulse to offer Mickey his manly protection and the obvious wisdom of staying as inconspicuous as possible. Steve checked his own impulse to rush in; Malik was obsessed with proving his own virile young manliness, but his goal would be to show up Clinton, not to hurt Mickey. And Mickey herself didn't look the least worried. Huh.

"Of *course* she's getting away," Malik said, lacing his words with scorn. "The way you holding her? You gotta get all up in her grill, a'ight?"

Clinton, wisely, said nothing. For one thing, his mother had been an English teacher and he couldn't match Malik's street- smart talk on his best day. For another, Malik didn't leave him the opportunity. He stepped forward to grab Mickey's arm, set- ting himself against her inevitable resistance—the instinctive shove and ineffective wiggling of any untrained victim.

Except Mickey didn't shove. While the other kids gathered around Steve, reacting with various disapproving noises, Mickey set her own feet in a perfectly balanced stance—and she *pulled.* Malik staggered forward in astonishment, and Mickey was the one who stepped into the movement, driving through with a fisted blow that came from the center of her body. Precise, driven, full of all the power left in that exhausted body—

By the time Steve realized she'd aimed that blow at the kid's throat—*a killing blow*—it was too late even to cry out a warning.

The sound of that impact generated a tangible knot of dread. Steve had known it would come one day, that this intersection of haven and violence, teens and street people, would produce injury. But he hadn't expected this clean efficiency . . . he hadn't expected it would come from a woman who'd seemed quite nearly sane.

And then he realized that Malik was still standing. Coughing, choking, his eyes wide with astonishment and his hands gone to his throat . . . but still standing. And that Mickey had returned to a poised ready stance so balanced it could bring tears to a trainer's eyes, her blow pulled with the precision of a surgeon— but with enough power remaining to give the young man a wake-up call.

Steve didn't for a moment think it was accidental.

And then the authority flowed out of Mickey's body and she staggered slightly, rising from the ready stance to look down at her hands with no less astonishment than Malik. The kid backed away from her with a wary eye, rubbing his throat. The others could have jeered at him then, but that wasn't the way of Steve's classes. The gym wasn't a dojo; wasn't structured over centuries of tradition and procedure. But Steve did demand respect—for himself and for the other participants. So while part of him watched Mickey waver, the rest of him caught Malik's attention. "You know the rules," he said. "You just messed with Clinton and Mickey both. Another time, I'd put you on notice. This time . . . I think you've taken enough of a hit."

"Don't even ask if I'm good," Malik muttered. His voice came out mildly hoarse.

"Son," Steve said, "there were two ways you could have come out of that one. I can see which way it went. You're good." He glanced at Mickey, found her looking over with hair hiding most of her face—everything but those eyes, and the pale white skin around them. Mickey . . . not so good.

Served him right, letting her mix it up in class only hours after she'd fainted inside the door. "Let it go, everyone," he said. "See you tomorrow, yeah? *Pame!*"

"Efharisto," they choroused back at him, completing their little ritual of the scant Greek he ever used these days. Chatter and laughter and subdued commentary rose as Malik stormed out and they trickled out behind him. By then Steve had reached Mickey's side, and it was his hand at her elbow that kept her on her feet.

"Naia," she murmured. She looked at her hands, ran fingers over the inside of an elbow that had seen far too many recent injections.

But he frowned at his own immediate assumption. Not just drug hits. IV needle. Bigger, and it had left a spreading bruise. Had she ODed? Made it to rehab? Been mixing drugs with her prescribed meds?

"I should get you to the clinic," he said.

"No!" She twisted away. He hadn't been ready for that wiry strength, no matter how he'd just seen it used on Malik. He stepped back, hands raised to placate her; in that moment he could find none of the smiling, charismatic woman who'd sat on the cot in his office and nibbled his lunch down. Just . . .

Wild fear. Confusion. A woman about to run.

"I need—" she said.

"I can't—" she said.

"I—" she said, and finally stopped for good.

"Just breathe," he told her. "It's okay."

"Naia—" She looked up at him in utter confusion, and the confusion made way for pure frustration, that quick gleam of perfectly composed and self-possessed awareness. "Dammit. I almost had . . . well, *some*thing. Blasted memory. They said the drugs—"

"Some of them do that," he agreed, and added gently, "You're still better off if you take them."

She gave him a startled look. "What are you talking about?"

Suddenly he felt like the one whose reality had to be skewed. He cleared his throat. "Schizophrenia medications."

She laughed. Right out loud, she laughed. Hard enough so she staggered a little, and this time she let him catch her. "Oof," she said. "I needed that. But no, I don't think so. I need help, all right, but . . ." She trailed off again, distracted by her inner landscape. Not good thoughts, those. Steve didn't have to wonder long. "I could have hurt that boy," she said. "I could have *killed* him."

She had that much right.

But he remembered what he'd seen. How precise she'd been. How controlled. And almost in spite of himself, he said, "I don't think so, Mickey. You're trained. You're *good*. You did exactly what you meant to do, how you meant to do it." And at that, he hesitated. "You're sure there's no one I can call—?"

He expected resistance, not the rueful twist of her mouth as she shook her head. "I just need a few days," she said. "Somewhere I can stay out of sight. Just until I can figure out—" she stopped, shook her head. It wasn't in response to anything he'd done, but he was used to that. Overlapping conversations with the same person. Abruptly, she said, "Can I stay here?"

"I don't—" he started, and stopped as she wavered.

"I'm sitting," she said abruptly. "Don't stop talking. I need this conversation to happen." And she sat. She barely gave him time to follow suit, bemused and wishing the air conditioning could handle the heat of the offshore flow just a degree or two more efficiently. "Look, I know this place isn't a shelter. And I know I could find a shelter if I went looking. But that's where they're—" She stopped short on those words, probably catching the paranoid sound of them. "I need a few days to—" she said, and decided against finishing that, too. "I know what you think I need. But I won't get in the way . . . I'll do whatever work you want me to, and . . ."

He hadn't said anything. He studiously hadn't said anything— although there was plenty to say. He couldn't establish a precedent . . . he couldn't say yes to her and no to everyone else. And the cot in the office was hardly private, hardly appropriate.

Besides, he wasn't sure he could keep his balance around this woman who, when not mired in quicksilver moments of confusion, struck him as one of the sanest people he'd ever met. He'd learned his lessons young—to love, but not to lose yourself. To help, but to know you could never help enough. He'd built those walls with care.

Mickey didn't so much blast through his walls as she simply appeared on the other side.

That's just what she did now, looking him in the eye. None of the evasiveness of so many off their meds, and none of the glittery intensity. Just pure, straight and honest connection. "Please," she said. "I just need to stay off the streets a few days."

When he opened his mouth, it was to offer a gentle refusal— for all the reasons that made so much sense. He simply couldn't give this woman the kind of help she truly needed. Cruel, to

40

pretend that he could.

Except she wasn't asking him to pretend anything. And when he sighed, when he looked away to grab some room to find his badly astray equilibrium, his gaze skipping over old floor mats and ragged wall posters to the big glass storefront windows covered with bars . . .

His gaze caught on a dark green sedan cruising down the street. Too slow to be going somewhere in particular; too fast to be preparing for the turn at the corner. Looking for someone, just as the kids had said. And here he was, with someone who wanted to stay off the streets. Curiosity and coincidence.

He'd already checked in with the clinics; they hadn't known her. At this, he ought call the cops. But the cops seldom paid much attention to the street community and its denizens, other than to pump them for information. One way or another, Mickey was probably on her own—and seemed to want to stay that way. Maybe for once he could actually *help*. Truly make a difference.

There was time enough to change his mind if he'd made a mistake. He turned back to the hope on Mickey's face and said, "Yes."

CHAPTER 4

Naia's classes were heavy with the literary and the arts; she was to emerge from Stanford as a cultured, intelligent young woman with no aspirations for career, and no particular foundation for one.

She really wished she could slip in a computer science class or two. Or better yet, resource management, with which she could do something to improve the way her country burned through its natural gifts. What good was it that the upper class had all the oil money they could imagine, when none of the outlying villages even had electricity?

So it was not with any particular enthusiasm that she gathered her notebooks for *Great Archeological Sites in Europe,* stuffing them into her briefcase as she reached for the bright scarf that would cover her hair in public.

It was with considerably less enthusiasm that, once she opened the door to her upscale apartment, she unexpectedly confronted her advisor, Badra.

Advisor. The woman was a chaperone, meant to keep her in line—meant to report back to her father. During her first days here, Naia had engaged in a fierce battle of wills with Badra. In the end—against threat of being recalled home—Naia agreed to maintain certain customs of her country's conservative social requirements, and to post her daily schedule. When she went to public events, Badra came with her.

But Badra *didn't* come to her apartment in the middle of the day.

And Badra never came with one of the San Francisco embassy's burly security men at her heels.

Naia tried to cover her instant plunge into fear and guilt—as though she'd never even met a woman named Anna who taught her about dead drops and casual lying and compartmentalizing her feelings. *"As-sallamu aleykum,"* she said, automatically greeting Badra with appropriate words. And then she dredged up resentment. "Whatever are you doing here? I've got class in half an hour, and barely enough time to get there."

"You should plan better," Badra responded, not the least put off. She didn't exactly push past Naia—she was too proper for that, too outwardly respectful. But somehow she made it into the apartment anyway, and Naia couldn't bring herself to stand in the way of the security officer as he followed. The door remained open. She felt an impulsive desire to dash through it.

But that wouldn't solve anything. And now she had a reason to stay in her father's good graces . . . she couldn't help him, she couldn't help her people, if she became so restricted she couldn't make contact with her CIA case officer.

Because now . . . I have a CIA case officer. Incomprehensible.

"I did plan," she said. "I planned to use this half hour to make it to class." She looked at the security officer—a man who blended well into this diverse society, and who didn't wear any head covering at all to attract attention to his nationality or religion. A small religious tattoo on his neck, nearly obscured by his collar, was the only sign of his devotion to a small, intense sect from northern Irhaddan.

"Then you will have to hurry. I'll be waiting here when you get back—don't tarry. Your father has become concerned about you. He insists that from now on, I accompany you outside this apartment. In the future, I'll attend classes with you. You may also expect to see Mr. Fadil Hisami or one of his associates at any given time."

Mr. Fadil Hisami gave her a respectful nod. She didn't see that same respect in his eyes.

Because now . . . I've been trained by a CIA case officer. . . .

They didn't know. They *couldn't* know. She hadn't done anything yet. Until recently, she hadn't even known that the CIA had operations within the United States—like most people, she assumed they were limited to working outside their own country. Only after making friends with Anna at San Francisco's society parties, after coffee shop dates and movies and shopping trips, had she learned about the Foreign Services Branch and how carefully they recruited those who visited their country. Only then had she learned her new friend was one of the case officers who operated this way.

She never would have guessed it of Anna. Anna was carefree; she was bubbly. She respected Naia's culture and yet helped her explore this new world. She giggled, she sang loudly to the car radio, and she doted on her cat and her high-end antiques business.

Naia supposed all that had made her the perfect woman to approach one such as Naia.

But she hadn't even *done* anything yet. They couldn't know! Not her father, not those who pretended to speak for her father.

So although ingrained habit demanded that she acknowledge her unexpected new restrictions, she found a way to tap into the new Naia, the self-assured and confident young woman who wanted only the best for her people and her family, and who could ignore the guilt surging in her throat. She said, "Then I shall see you when I return."

And all the way down the hall, all the way down in the elevator, all along the brisk walk into campus, Naia thought nothing of great European architecture. She thought only of how to reach Anna.

Huge brown-black eyes. Frightened eyes.

They haunted Mickey, pulling her away from her supper.

Earlier in the day, there in the gym, the teens had gone through their paces, giggling and clowning around and posturing, and Mickey had let her eyes go unfocused and her mind— still blessedly clear—go wandering for clues. *Eyes. Naia's eyes. Naia's trepidation. Her courage. Her . . . pottery?* Maybe that particular impression would make sense later.

Then there was the woman who had held Mickey prisoner— the woman who wanted Naia. Mickey thought about her, too, let her mind wander among possibilities, hoping actual memories would surface.

The silver tabby cat, crouched over a porcelain water bowl. The glimpse of a sitting room, a Black Walnut gateleg table with pristine lace runner and pewter Jarvie candlesticks.

And that's when she'd seen the gawky teenager standing without a partner, awkward and embarrassed, and she'd stood, still lost in her thoughts. She hadn't even paid particular attention when the larger boy stepped in. Not until he'd grabbed her—and then it was too late. Then she'd just . . .

Reacted.

Gone into adrenaline high, sapping every bit of the precious reserves from her nap and her meal. Left her reeling with all the implications—the awareness of how easily she could have killed the boy. *And who the hell knows how to kill someone without even thinking about it?*

That was the question.

God, was that the question.

"Pizza's getting cold," Steve observed, watching her in that way he had. Compassionate, but just a little as though he thought he already knew the answers.

Mickey could only *wish* he had her answers. No wonder he thought her ill. She looked down at the pizza—the meat lover's version—and realized she was completely stuffed. "I'm keeping track, you know. I'll work it off, or when I—"

When I figure out whether I'm a good guy or a bad guy, when I remember why I got into trouble, when I get out of trouble . . .

"I'll pay you back," she said firmly.

"I could use some help sorting the women's clothes. They don't all have sizes."

Mickey instantly stood. "That box in the showers? I can do—"

Steve laughed. A genuine laugh. Whatever he thought of her, he was comfortable with her. Not the least put off by the mental illness he'd decided she had. He relaxed on the office chair, leaving her the cot again, and seemed unconcerned about the slight froth of beer on his lip. She'd opted for milk, and together they'd made serious inroads on the pizza.

"Well," he said, replacing a half-eaten slice in the box on his desk, "whatever you've been through, I think you'll bounce back fast enough."

She patted her full stomach. "You mean, the skinny? I don't think it's . . ." No. She had no distinct memories behind those words. And still . . . she saw herself as wiry, but not underfed. She realized anew that she'd have to learn to trust those impressions. She wouldn't get anywhere if she second-guessed her every response.

Steve had apparently become used to her unfinished sentences; he didn't pay this one any mind. "Way too skinny," he said, but he smiled. Comfortable with her, comfortable with himself . . .

Only belatedly did she realize she was smiling. That she found herself liking him, in that way that came from within.

Stop it. You don't even know what kind of judgment you have.

Not to mention how attached she might be to someone else. Only one thing to do about that. . . . She glanced at the computer.

If she couldn't remember, then she'd just have to sleuth it out. Follow clues to herself . . . to her life.

And figure out who had handcuffed her to a makeshift hospital bed and drugged away her memory.

Done eating, Mickey insisted on picking up after the pizza and then picking up after the day—sweeping, restocking the freebies barrel, applying liberal amounts of disinfectant in the locker room and bathroom areas. Steve eventually settled into accounting work, muttering over the computer. She'd initially thought his clean desk was an effort to keep things secure, but as he worked—and as she explored more of the gym—she began to suspect he was simply an organized soul.

A defense against the chaos around him, perhaps.

She threw herself into the chores, dancing briefly with the broom and her own inner soundtrack. It cheered her—felt normal somehow, and entirely unrelated to her current predicament. She faltered at the impulse to scoop up a cat and raise him high to dance with her, but pushed it aside to tackle the gym mirrors with cleaner and rags. Finally she dragged a full bag of garbage out the back exit and into the day's fading heat, propping the door open while she dealt with the dumpster lid.

Just normal. That's me.

Uh-huh.

She was at her most exposed, stretched to fling and release the heavy garbage into the dumpster, when the car cruised by at the end of the alley. Only a few yards away, inching its way along the tiny cross-street.

She threw herself around the end of the dumpster, crouching with her back in the corner, her feet ready to run, and every hair standing on end. *What the hell?*

No second-guessing.

And on second thought, no reason to. She was in hiding, wanted by those who had drugged and imprisoned her. The men in that car . . . so obviously looking for someone. The only surprise now was that she'd responded so instinctively, so quickly. And she thought, really, that she might as well stop being surprised by such things in herself. Whoever she was, good or bad, she led the kind of life that predisposed her to be kidnapped and questioned. To keep herself fit and trained and aware.

Now if only Steve would head up to his second floor apartment and leave her free to noodle around on the computer . . . maybe she could even learn something about just who she was. If she'd been reported missing . . .

With a peek to assure herself the car had passed, Mickey returned to the gym, closing the door behind her with a reassuring finality.

Inside, she discovered new activity in the gym—another class, this one comprised of fit young men who focused on Steve's instruction and applied themselves to practice with much intent. *Kickboxing,* she thought, and then gave herself a pat on the back for not questioning how she knew.

She let herself back into Steve's domain and slipped into the desk chair—and found herself immediately caught up in the slide show screensaver. The first image showed a family photo— stout mom, sturdy father, and two little boys with beguiling dark eyes and black curls. The next, the boys in high school, in baseball uniforms, and a series of more recent photos. In these pictures, Steve was clearly identifiable. Younger, his hair not quite as tamed, his shoulders not quite so filled out . . . his expression somehow looking older than it should. His parents, formerly proud and beaming, had aged; their smiles no longer reached their eyes. And his brother—older, to judge by the photos, but not much—no longer looked at the camera at all. Tense, distracted, he looked aside—and from the way Steve's arm wrapped around his shoulders, Mickey thought he wouldn't be there at all without that quiet physical encouragement.

And then there were no photos of his brother at all.

"So that's your story," Mickey told the monitor. His brother had gotten sick. It wasn't a huge leap to suppose it had been mental illness, that which Steve now so easily saw in Mickey— and that he lived with every day, trying to help those who'd fallen out of the system and through the cracks of polite society. He'd lost his brother, it seemed, and now he spent his days with those who still remained. Understanding them, comfortable with them . . . perhaps a little lost right along with them.

"That's not me," she told him as he looked out at her, the most recent photo she'd seen yet. Balloons in the background made her think of a graduation party, or a birthday . . . maybe an anniversary. His badly aged parents sat with him, but the picture centered on Steve, one arm around each parent as though now he held them up, too.

Mickey had seen enough. She thumbed the space bar, kicking off the screensaver and firing up the browser. She hunted up the local paper, and then searched the recent archives. *Missing, lost, kidnapped* . . . nothing. She supposed it would have been too easy if she'd managed to find an image of herself staring back like a face on a milk carton.

They would have done it quietly, her inner voice whispered to her. The one that seemed to know what was going on, even if she didn't. *They would have avoided suspicion.* So many options . . . grabbing her on the way out of town, leaving notes and messages to her loved ones . . . if she had them.

Tucked at the front of the monitor she found a letter opener. It drew her fidgety fingers; she played with it, assessing heft and balance and running her fingers along the sleek silver edge.

Expensive. Maybe Steve, too, had lived a different life before coming to this place.

On a whim, Mickey searched on Naia. Why not Naya, or even Naiya? But no, her fingers said Naia and she left it at that, hitting the enter key to unexpected results: *National Association of Independent Artists. National Animal Interest Alliance. National Association of Intercollegiate Athletics.*

What if Naia wasn't a person at all? What if it was an industry, or an organization?

Mickey closed her eyes, and in her mind saw again those beautiful, exotic features. Saw again the fear. Nope. Naia . . . a person. A young woman. Mickey just needed a last name to get anywhere with this search.

Aurgh. She needed a cup of—

Tea. I like tea.

I have a cat. Somewhere, I have a home. I like tea. I know how to punch . . . and how to hide in small corners behind dumpsters.

Fatigue rapidly crept up on her, reminding her that she'd gone who knows how many days without food while drugged, and that her body still struggled to rid itself of its reactions to that drug. Much as she needed to find out who she was, much as she needed to know who'd grabbed her and why—much as she needed to protect Naia . . .

There. I can't be all bad if I'm so driven to protect this woman.

"Unless," she murmured out loud, "it's just because you want something from her." After all, her captives had fought to keep Mickey alive, too, after her bad reaction to the super knock-out drug.

And so she lost herself in the tangle of those thoughts a moment, fingering the letter opener until the monitor shifted back into the screensaver slide show and mesmerized her, images of Steve and his family jumping across their years together and then just a few pictures of Steve and a dog, Steve in front of a lake, Steve beside a mountain bike . . .

Steve alone.

The door to the office flung open with sudden violence, hard enough to slam against the wall and bounce back again. Mickey, startled from drifting thoughts, leaped to her feet, bringing her arm back, the letter opener suddenly familiar in her grip, its balance and weight assessed, the distance to the door assessed—

Only at the last instant, as the young man in the doorway stopped short in astonishment, did she angle her body. The letter opener slipped through her fingers and drove end over end to bury itself in the wall just beside the door, brushing a shirt sleeve on the way by.

"Shee-*it*," said the young man, his warm complexion paling.

Steve's alarmed voice came from down the hall. "Hey, Tajo, don't—"

"Too late," said Tajo, his voice a little hoarse. He cleared his throat, took a step back. "Sorry. Didn't know you had company, man." By then Steve had reached his shoulder—and could follow Tajo's gaze to the letter opener, now drooping in the wall.

After a long silence, he said, "Do I even want to know?"

And Mickey couldn't do anything but whisper, "No."

Steve thought his voice sounded admirably calm. "I told you to knock," he reminded Tajo, a young man already decorated with tats and yet struggling to grow that wispy soul patch. Tajo—street tough, well-schooled in kickboxing, cut with muscles—was still wide-eyed and pale. Steve put a hand on his shoulder, turned him around. "I'll get it," he said. "Go on back and lead the class in some timing drills."

"Yeah," Tajo said, not taking his eyes from Mickey. "Sure." Not until he was actually out the door did he tear his gaze away from her, heading down the hallway with unusual haste.

Mickey looked very small as she sat behind his desk, fingers twined together and somewhat clenched. She said nothing.

She probably had a pretty good idea that there wasn't much to say.

She probably had a pretty good idea that Steve was already second-guessing his decision to let her crash at the gym. He knew the number of the local precinct by heart; he knew the closest shelter and the closest clinic, and he had contact and location information for everything beyond right there on his computer.

What was she doing at his computer, anyway?

He reached out to pluck the letter opener from his wall, and hefted it. "Not exactly balanced for throwing."

"You know knife throwing?" she asked, somewhat weakly, but he saw the interest spark in her eyes.

"I know enough." He dropped the letter opener on the desk and picked up the newspaper that Tajo had come for in the first place—it held a small feature on one of the neighborhood kids who'd earned a scholarship. *I did tell him to knock, dammit.*

But who reacts by throwing a letter opener like the finest throwing knife? Who knows how?

"Earlier I saw you dancing with the broom," he said, perching one hip on the edge of the desk—knowing he'd taken an intimidating stance, and watching her for reaction. "What was that you were singing?"

"Cher," Mickey said, looking down at her clenched hands. "One of her songs."

He tipped the computer monitor far enough to see the browser she'd been using—to recognize the search engine page. "Hunting for something?"

She snorted, a little of her natural spirit coming through. "Yeah," she said. "Me."

And he shifted closer on the desk, watching her—saw her acknowledgment of his proximity, the faint draw of her forehead and the shift of those small, damned cute smile lines at the very

52

corners of her mouth. She said, "You're pushing."

"What if I am?" he said. "What if another of my kids comes in here like a macho idiot? What happens to him?"

"Dunno," she said. "You're the one who said I knew what I was doing. That I had control."

Convincing words. Almost as if she hadn't been caught unawares both times, in some fugue state that made her vulnerable to over-reaction.

That made everyone around her vulnerable, too.

He waited for her to look up at him, bright eyes open and honest and even beseeching in her search for understanding. But a muscle flickered at her jaw, giving away her game. "I might have bought that just now," he said, "if I thought *you* bought it."

She looked away, muttering. "Well, damn." A deep breath, and she said, "Nothing's changed. I just need a place, okay? Just a couple days. I can't . . . sort things out if I'm busy hopping park benches and underpasses."

"What makes you think you can sort things out anyway?" Steve shook his head. He wasn't that kind of enabler. He couldn't pretend the problem would just go away. Someone wanted to stay off their meds? Fine. But acknowledge the results. Deal with them honestly.

"I don't know if I can," she said, surprising him with an equal dose of that honesty. She stretched her fingers, freeing them from their entwining prison. "I just know I have a better chance." She looked wistful; he would have given anything—almost anything—to know what she was thinking in that moment.

He would have given that much again if he wouldn't keep forgetting to look at her as though she were one of his street clients, and instead looked at her as though—

He closed his eyes. Tightly. *Stupid, stupid, stupid.* He forced himself to say, "I don't know what's going on with you. But maybe it would be best for all of us if we called the—"

"*No*," she said, startling him with her intensity. She seemed to take herself by surprise, too. She inhaled audibly, let it go, and added in a much calmer voice, "You may be right. I just don't want to get tangled up in the system. Not yet."

The mighty system. He really couldn't blame her for that. The system shuffled people around . . . took away their choices.

She must have seen his assent on his face, for she relaxed. "You know," she said. "I'm not what you assume."

"What do I assume?"

She said matter-of-factly, "The mental illness."

She hadn't taken on that overly earnest look that generally presaged this particular conversation. But it didn't change what he'd seen of her over the course of the day. The confusion, the obvious disorientation, the apparent hallucinations. "Tell me, then."

She laughed. There was no humor in it—none of the lightness he'd seen in her that afternoon, or shared with her over pizza. "The story of me?" She shook her head, regretful—and where sometimes he felt she didn't have answers, this time he saw them going unsaid. "I can't do that."

Unexpected anger surged through him, tightening his throat. It caught him unaware, and it caught him just as unaware when his hand slammed down on the desk. *Dammit, how can I help if*—

She jumped, startled but not frightened. Then she just watched him.

I can't. That's the damned answer. The only answer. He understood the anger, then—the realization that he wanted this time to be different. He wanted a happy ending, and he wanted to be part of it.

The anger was because he knew better.

Neither of them spoke for a long moment, while Steve realized he'd really gotten too close, almost trapping her behind the desk—and that the loudest sound in the room was his own breathing.

She was the one who gave him space, watching him but not making any move, not reaching to reassure him or shrinking back in retreat. She did, he thought, look at him with empathetic understanding—and still a touch of that wistfulness, tinged with sadness as though she, too, realized they'd gotten a glimpse of something that neither of them could have.

When she finally looked away, her expression shifted, became something surprised. "I miss my cat," she said, quite nonsensically. There was wonder in her voice, as though this were somehow an important discovery.

Happy endings. Right.

Those were for someone else.

CHAPTER 5

Mickey should have been sleeping. Or at the least, plotting out just how she'd make this situation better—how she'd find Naia. How she'd find herself.

Instead . . .

The woman in her memory looked like Mickey.

She sat cross-legged on the cot and stared into the darkness, wishing her mind's eye would take a rest. Wishing it hadn't painted such vivid images across her dreams and into the small hours of the morning.

The woman looked like Mickey. Except she was dying.

Mickey couldn't say how she knew it. Seeing the woman against the dark rich green of the couch, propped by pillows, a cool cloth slipping off her forehead . . . she might have had the flu. She might have had a headache. She might have simply taken a few moments of private time from her children.

But Mickey knew better, just as she knew there were children. One of them responsible, trying to make it all better; one of them withdrawn and in denial, acting out at school and taking hits—literal hits from schoolchildren who knew how to flock around the weak one in the pack.

Trying to make it all better.

She felt that little girl's desperation—the refusal to believe she couldn't stop the inevitable. Another cool washcloth, another dinner made, another perfect grade. If she was good enough, if she tried hard enough . . .

And she felt the guilt of the woman's death. If she'd been good enough, if she'd tried hard enough . . .

And is that really me? Is that really some part of my life?

Or just hallucinations?

Stop that. Just because it was the middle of the night, without so much as the glow of the monitor to break the blanketing darkness of Steve's office. Just because it was so easy to doubt herself when the only person she even began to trust—she *did* trust—also doubted her.

Well, not quite true. He didn't doubt her at all. He just believed things of her that conflicted with what she needed to believe of herself.

She wished she could run her hand down short, sleek fur, feel the rumble of a deep purr. No point in that. So she turned her thoughts toward action. Not for the moment, but for the morrow. She'd had her freedom less than a day, and already it seemed that time was running out. Naia was still out there, still somehow tied to Mickey—somehow depending on her. Partners in crime, partners in business . . . Mickey didn't know. But she was younger, and she evoked in Mickey all those feelings—

Younger sister, acting out at school . . . surrounded by bullies, coming home with bruises and tears.

Mickey had done something about *that.* She was sure of it. *Slingshot.*

The image swam up from her thoughts with surprising assertiveness and would have sunk back down just as quickly if she hadn't grabbed at it—learning to recognize those things of herself that were *true.*

She'd best learn fast.

Tomorrow she had to leave this place. She hadn't wanted to face it, but in that, Steve was right. She couldn't chance another encounter, one in which she wouldn't pull her punches. And that car . . . those men. If they were looking for her as her instincts insisted, she couldn't bring them here. She wasn't the only troubled soul who considered this a safe place, and none of the others deserved her trouble raining down on them.

But she wouldn't go out there without more advantage than she had now. Steve . . .

Steve had known about throwing knives. He'd *known*. He'd handled that letter opener as though he wanted to try his own mettle on it, seeing if he, too, could compensate for its weaknesses, assessing its turn speed and distance to bury the point in the wall.

Tomorrow he had a woman's self-defense class. Tomorrow, Mickey would see if his upstairs apartment held the bladed weapons she thought it would. And then it was time to leave this place so its people would be safe, time to find herself, time to find—and protect—Naia.

It had been a luxury, thinking she might stay here until she could get some kind of a foothold in this maze that was apparently her life.

It had been a mistake.

Morning at the pottery co-op came early—kilns firing up, people checking on projects—and Naia was only one of several to climb the narrow stairs to the second-floor warehouse before most people were brewing their first cup of coffee.

None of the others had a chaperone, of course.

An unhappy chaperone, not understanding why Naia had to make this trip into San Jose at this time of day.

"This is my schedule," Naia told her, walking briskly up those stairs and drawing from the early days of her rebellion to get the convincing tone in her voice—to hide her concerns and uncertainty. "If you prefer to stay on your own schedule, that would suit me perfectly."

Badra obviously preferred just that. But she had little recourse other than to say, "That isn't an option."

"If it seemed you were imposing significant restrictions on me, it wouldn't present the image of Irhaddan that my father is trying to portray," Naia reminded her, turning around the narrow landing to take the final flight of stairs. Badra wasn't a young woman and she wasn't physically fit, and Naia in no way accommodated her. So it was natural that she reached the pottery co-op before Badra . . . not surprising that her firm stride took her straight to the shelves with their assigned project space, or that she'd managed to palm her short, concise note—*need help/advice—blown?*—between her fingers, slipping it into the dead-drop behind her own current project even as Badra entered the huge, open area. Naia kept her composure, pushing the hollowed brick back into place.

Because Anna's people had prepared it, had smoothed it top and bottom and inserted a slick Teflon base, the brick slid easily. Silently. And when Naia turned around to Badra, she had a hand-formed vase in her careful grip, examining its newly fired glaze with a critical eye.

Badra gave it a dubious look. "It's lopsided."

Naia considered telling her it had been a firing accident, but, flush with her success with the dead-drop, told the truth instead. "I made it that way."

"Flawed? On purpose?"

"No," Naia said, quite distinctly. "Individual."

Badra was silent a moment. Then she said, "The color is pretty."

As close to victory as Naia would ever get. "Thank you." She returned the vase to her project space and hovered over the class schedule and kiln sign-up sheet, then spent a few moments admiring the other projects in process.

No sign of Anna's presence. Her quirky vase—a daisy vase with a dozen stem ports and giant, splashy daisies painted in unfired glaze—hadn't moved since Naia's last visit to the co-op. It was so *Anna,* that vase. Even dressed for high society, wrapped in designer gowns with her hair in an up-do and her fingers elegantly be-ringed with her antique jewelry, Anna managed to convey the quirky, impulsive side of her nature. It was something in her smile, Naia had thought from the start. It had been that smile that drew Naia to her friend in the first place. With all the pasted, faked, cultured expressions surrounding her in that party, Anna's smile had stood out as real—faintly flawed, not quite symmetrical, and genuine.

Ironic that she, of all people, would eventually recruit Naia to spy on her countrymen.

Countrymen who are hurting my country, she reminded herself. She signed up for a work time in the next afternoon so she could check the dead-drop. She'd have to come up with a new project concept by then.

Though if Anna hadn't picked up her note, faking enthusiasm for a new project would be the least of her worries.

Mickey should have known it. Actually, she should have known two things.

One, that Steve's lofty apartment would be every bit as neat and organized as the rest of this place. And two—Mickey allowed herself to dance a brief little jig—that he'd pursued his interest in weapons with the same dedicated follow-through. *Jackpot. A total glut of weaponry.*

He liked projectile weapons, that was clear enough. Anything but guns. Two competition recurve bows sat in a metal stand with straight-fletch, practice-point arrows. A pistol crossbow in a glass-front corner cabinet along with several braces of throwing knives. To judge from the heavily gouged wood target planks leaning against one painted cinder block wall, Steve really enjoyed the satisfaction of the blade striking home, that feel of metal slipping through fingers, the *knowing* when the throw was righteous, the sound of it. . . .

Mickey looked down at her hand. It twitched, fingers already placed for the throw. *I guess he's not the only one.*

And then she saw the slingshot. A simple thing, really—a folding steel frame with wrist brace and surgical tubing, a box of ammo beside it. *Younger sister, acting out at school . . . surrounded by bullies, coming home with bruises and tears . . .*

Slingshots were cheap. They were unexpected. And it hadn't taken much practice. Rotten yewberries, raisins, cat droppings . . . even those, at short range, went where Mickey sent them; if they didn't sting, they stunk. And still she'd been able to stay out of sight, to keep her sister's protection an anonymous thing. An unexpected thing. Until the bullies got the message— *mess with this girl, and you never know where, you never know when . . . and you never know just how disgusting it's gonna get.*

Memories. True, hard memories. *Her* memories. No names attached, no locations. Just that feeling of satisfaction . . . the realization of just how good she was at the game.

Mickey opened the corner cabinet and gathered up her chosen arsenal. A brace of four small knives, a shoulder harness that looked unused and might even adjust down to fit her, and the slingshot. Both easy to conceal . . . both utterly familiar to her hand.

With any luck, it would take a while before he realized they were gone.

Mickey gave the target wall a wistful glance. Not just the knife planks, but the wide variety of gallery targets. Playing card targets, bottles and cans targets, command training targets . . . and of course a variety of bulls-eyes. No silhouettes, not human or animal. And the whole doggone wall was lined with home-made archery backdrops—old carpet being a favorite—as well as gypsum board leaning against brick.

This was one bachelor pad Mickey found she could appreciate.

The rest of it . . . also purely Steve, from the faint spicy smell of aftershave to a collection of family portraits by the entry area. Three of the vast brick walls were painted white; the third, over by a queen-sized bed, was natural brick. The bed itself wasn't closed off by anything other than its position in the corner, and she thought the walled extrusion between the bed and the kitchen was probably the bathroom. Jutting out from the wall and over the bed, a loft pushed into the room, shadowing that whole area. Up above she could see shelves and part of a recliner, but the rest of the loft was a mystery.

She realized, then, stepping back to take in the big picture with a detail-oriented approach that seemed as much training as impulse, that he'd built this space to his own specs. It had probably been a dance studio, scuffed wooden floors still there, still full of light from the two giant banks of windows along the building's front wall. And now it was full of Steve, from his hobbies to his penchant for clear space and clean lines.

And she was stealing from him, and then she was going to run from him.

Even if she was doing it *for* him.

For all of them, actually. The women in the self-defense class below her, street people who would trickle in that afternoon, those in the weight room throughout the day, the kids who came in after school . . .

They didn't need to deal with her—not her mysteries, her vagueries, or her unpredictable reactions.

They sure didn't need to deal with people who were looking for her.

Standing there in the middle of Steve's very personal domain—stolen goodies in hand, the leftover pizza scavenged from the fridge and a grocery bag full of fruit and protein bars waiting by the door—Mickey had her first serious doubts. Were the memories real—any of them? Right down to those first hazy moments of being handcuffed to a bed? What if she'd just twisted memories of restraint in a real hospital? What if some clinic was frantic, looking for her?

Very deliberately, she walked to the nook that served as Steve's personal exercise corner. Television, elliptical trainer, weights. And, of course, the full-length mirror all weight lifters seemed to need; it reflected her in all her glory. *There. That's me.* Mickey Finn, a name stolen from the barely remembered conversation of someone who'd kidnapped her for interrogation. Two borrowed layers of tank tops, one tight to make up for the missing bra and the other loose to hide the fact the first one didn't quite do the job. Old running shorts—no panty lines, because . . . no panties. She had color in her cheeks, unlike her first view in the "hospital" bathroom. Now her strength showed through . . . and on her face, determination. "Yeah," she said. "Me, meet me. Could be crazy. Could be just what Steve thinks. Could be I should just hike straight to the closest cop shop and—"

No. In the mirror, she frowned back at herself; her eyes seemed unnaturally bright. *If I don't trust myself, I have nothing. If I don't follow my gut instincts, I have nothing.*

This might be crazy, but at least it was something. Goals. Somewhere to start, while she looked for the rest of it.

And hoped she could live with what she found.

CHAPTER 6

Steve practiced the words in his head. *Mickey,* his internal voice said, *I know I said you could stay here. But I know more now, and don't think it's safe.* Not safe for anyone else here, that was.

Wuhggh! He landed on his back on the gym mat, blinking painfully up at the wiry black woman who'd put him there.

She put her hands on her hips and gave him a critical eye. "Mr. Steve, honey, you ain't payin' the least attention to this class this morning."

"Head in the clouds," came the murmured agreement from the background.

"Bet it's that woman."

His ears still rang, but Steve knew that particular comment could only come from the young single mother who'd been trying to catch his attention since she joined the class. Gaynell.

"How—" he started.

Dawnisha, the student who'd taken him down, now helped pull him to his feet—as wiry in her strength as Mickey. "What, you think we spend all our time sittin' in front of soaps when we're not here? Those kids talk, Mr. Steve. You got some woman stayin' here, and she knows how to take care of herself. That's what we hear."

Nods and affirming noises followed this pronouncement. Steve grabbed a moment by brushing himself off, straightening his red *Steve's Gym* T-shirt, pushing hair out of his eyes.

Gaynell came to stand next to Dawnisha. "I think she's got

something to do with those cars cruisin' this neighborhood yesterday, what do you think?"

Suddenly Steve was surrounded. Women in brightly colored gym clothes and scarves, too much spandex where there shouldn't be any at all.

"I hear she didn't look good."

"I hear she's fine."

"I hear she don't look like she belongs on the street, no matter how many old clothes you put on her."

"I hear she fainted."

"Those men don't belong here, neither. Not in those smooth rides."

"My Tajo says you oughta watch it with that one. She trouble."

Steve briefly covered his face with his hands. This was a kind of self-defense he'd never mastered. "Air," he groaned dramatically. "I need air."

"There, there," Dawnisha said. She was the oldest, with four children and a night shift job at the nearest 24-hour walk-in clinic. "You just in over your head, that's all."

Steve widened his fingers just enough to glare at her. When she laughed, he dropped his hands altogether. "Seriously," he said. "I think she's in trouble."

Someone couldn't resist a mutter. "I think she *is* trouble."

He wished he could have ignored that. "That's the problem." He looked at them all, found them interested . . . found them concerned. Faces of color, mostly. His own olive complexion wasn't the lightest here, but it was close. "It's both. She—" He stopped, beset by the memory of her expression as the letter opener sagged in the wall, by her earlier realization of how close she'd come to hurting Malik. By her struggle to deal with her situation—never answering his questions less than honestly, even if that meant telling him she couldn't answer them at all. Never veering away from direct eye contact. Not letting her pride get in the way of asking for help.

"There, you see?" Dawnisha said. "He's a goner."

"I think I have to ask her to leave," he blurted.

The general clamor to greet this eloquent declaration gave him just enough time to imagine Mickey's reaction to such a request—disappointment, maybe fear, but acceptance. No begging or pleading, not after she'd already made her request to stay. She'd just look at him with those bright, direct eyes of hers, and—

Since when did he think he knew her that well?

"He's right," Gaynell said. "She's in some kind of big trouble, and that makes her a problem for *us*. Me, I got enough problems already. This place is the one place we can count on. We send our kids here. Them homeless people . . . they need this place, too. She get in the way of all that, we don't watch out for ourselves."

Dawnisha turned on her a look of complete understanding— not of the sympathetic sort. "And where would *we* be, if that's the way this place was run? Where would our kids be, and the young men Steve is keeping off the streets? They work to pay for their classes—that teaches them something too. And helps pay our bills besides." She raked Gaynell with a scowl. "You just not wantin' any competition."

"Bitch!" Gaynell gasped, as the other women nodded emphatic and bristly agreement with Dawnisha's words.

"Whoa, ladies!" Steve's panic wasn't the least faked. He could—and had—handled himself out there on the streets. A few hard knocks in pursuit of his brother had set him on his own path of learning, and eventually led him here. The gym, his work, his life—all built on hard experience.

But he wanted nothing to do with group of angry women. Not once the *bitch* word started flying.

"Chill, woman," Dawnisha told Gaynell, putting her down

with a look that reminded Steve that she, too, had come out of hard days on the street. That and her total lack of concern as she turned her back on the woman and put hands on hips to give Steve a look he'd thought reserved for local teenagers. "You just frightened."

"Hey," he said, dignity wounded.

"Honey, you ain't scared for us, you just running scared for your own self. There's somethin' about this girl reaches you. Think it don't show on your face? You chase her off for our sakes, and you don't got to take any chances."

Warmth flooded his face—embarrassment that these women knew him this well, shame that some part of him thought she might be right. "This gym has to stay a safe place."

Dawnisha crossed her arms over her thin chest with some finality. "Then you'll just have to find a way," she said. "You keep it safe. You let this girl find herself here."

At that they let it drop, and he drew them off into play-acting encounters on the street—the wallet throw away. Problem with these ladies wasn't that they'd panic—problem was that some of them were so tough, they didn't hit the *run away* button when needed. So he passed out "wallets" of duct-taped cardboard and they practiced accosting one another, then throwing their wallets for their "muggers" to chase after while they ran away. Steve egged them on into the drama of it, play-acting in high shrieking voices, lots of arm-waving and personal woe. Might as well have fun with the wicked world.

When class was over, they gathered up the wallets and handed them to Dawnisha, who dumped them on the counter behind the freebies barrel. There Steve had a mini-fridge, and he was stuck in the middle of a long pull on a bottle of water as Dawnisha walked by. Just as well. When she admonished him, "You think on it," he wouldn't have had anything to say anyway.

Because he *was* thinking on it. Had *been* thinking on it. Had more than enough time to accept the truth of her words.

Mickey scared the crap out of him.

In the middle of her confusion and fear, she'd gone dancing with a broom. She met his gaze without reservation—she sucked him right into her, right through the walls he'd carefully and deliberately built. If she stayed here, it would only continue to happen.

And yet he knew what she was. What he'd go through if he let her in.

You just frightened, Dawnisha had told him.

Terrified, more like it.

And of course they'd all been right. This place of safety . . . it had never discriminated. If Mickey lashed out when threatened, then he'd make sure she wasn't threatened. If there were indeed men cruising the streets in search of her, he'd find out what they wanted—find out if they were on her side, maybe even looking to take her home. He doubted it—he trusted the kids, and his own gut reaction when he'd seen that slowly gliding vehicle—but if they weren't on her side, then she could hide inside the gym until they gave up.

It was what he did.

Frightened or not.

So he took a deep breath, stuck the water back in the fridge, and went back to see if Mickey was awake. And then he stood in the office door, sledgehammered by what he found.

Awake, yes.

Awake, tidied up, and gone.

He didn't have to search the back rooms to know that gone was *gone.* She'd left the sheets neatly piled on the cot to be washed. She'd taken the flannel shirt she'd scrounged the evening before, even though it was another hot day.

And beyond that, he just *knew.* She'd seen the look on his

68

face when he'd found the letter opener in the wall. She'd seen his doubt.

And she'd gone.

CHAPTER 7

Options.

Not many of those.

Mickey pondered them nonetheless.

There was the library. First she'd have to get there, of course, but once inside . . . air conditioning, and a week's worth of papers. She could skim for whatever hadn't made it onto the web version. Anyone missing a young woman about yay tall?

But she'd rather get cleaned up first—get herself squared away. And there were other options to ponder. Turning herself into the authorities, for one. If they didn't know who she was, they could probably find out.

Yeah, and what if you've got worse crimes on your rap sheet than knowing all the Barry Manilow hits?

Which she did, apparently. They'd certainly come to her with ease, humming through her brain as she'd taken back streets and alleys away from Steve's gym toward the center of town, munching the remains of the pizza.

She winced at that. *Sorry, Steve. I guess that's what they really call eat and run.*

At least she'd found a trashcan for the pizza box.

So still no authorities—no more now than when she'd stopped Steve from calling them. Not until she had no choice—until she knew for sure whether she was the cause of Naia's problem, or her only hope. She had to keep herself footloose and ready to move in case she remembered something.

She shook off the doubt, and turned her thoughts toward more constructive paths. No cops, no clinic . . . not yet with the library. Maybe she just needed to take some precious time to scope out some safe places here on the street. To get herself some working funds. Just the rest of the day, that's all. And then . . .

A final option occurred to her, one that slotted neatly after plan number one—scope out a new safe place—and might possibly lead to answers for plan number three.

Find the building. The place that had been her prison, and held the only for-sure clues to her situation. Possibly still held the people who'd imprisoned her.

And this time she wasn't unarmed. Wasn't sick, wasn't weak, wasn't confused. This time she had some idea of her abilities.

Yeah, when up against a kid and an unresisting wall.

Still.

After a moment she realized that the very idea of hunting the place should have surprised her—should have filled her with fear and doubt.

The very idea didn't.

She suspected that imaginary rap sheet might have something to it after all. But as she rose from the cement block in the back corner of a the parking lot that had been her thinking spot, heading for plan number one—scope out a new safe place—she found herself humming *Copacabana* with a dramatically cheerful air.

"You don't belong here!"

That voice was rough and insistent, and Mickey reversed course out of the cardboard box she'd been inspecting. She'd found herself beneath the overpass, drawn by a hazy memory of stumbling over the pedestrian path above the nearby river.

The man she currently faced could have been another of

their victims. Confused, angry, his demeanor set to "belliger-ent."

"Sorry," she said. "Is this your box?"

"No," he said, and brushed away a bug that wasn't there. "But it's not yours!" Bad hair, bad teeth, bad breath, bad manners.

"You're right," she said. "But I was thinking of hanging out over there." She nodded at an area near the riverbank. "Nice culvert there, doesn't look like it's being used."

He snorted. " 'Cause it floods in the wet."

"It's the dry," she told him. "And I'll only be there a few days." At most. If that. She just wanted a bolt hole . . .

His laugh was true amusement, something of his original personality peeking out. "That's what they all say, darlin'. That's what they all say."

Mickey earned the good will of her neighbors by sharing the bounty from her raid on Steve's fruit, cheerfully explaining her source.

"Oh, *Steve*," said a worn woman whom Mickey suspected was less than ten years older than her own thirty-two but looked about sixty. Meth had ravaged her features and her teeth. "He's something, Steve is. His brother used to be one of us, you know. Mosquito really used to hang with him."

"I had the feeling." But Mickey didn't ask for details, because it felt strangely like prying . . . and because she thought she probably knew the important parts already. Except . . . "He's dead, right?"

"You done took this food from a dead man?" Her first contact, the man called Mosquito, spoke around a giant bite of pear.

For an unpleasant moment she thought he would spit the masticated fruit at her feet. "No, no, no," she said quickly.

"Steve's *brother*. He's dead, isn't he?"

"Long time," said the meth woman. "Looong time. Steve used to haunt our places. Mooning around with those calf eyes of his, trying to drag Zander back home. Finally gave up. Some of us belong out here."

"It's our own choice," a man muttered from behind the battered, flattened cardboard box he'd brought with him, always keeping it as a shield between Mickey and himself—though one hand had appeared to receive the half-apple she'd pressed into it.

"Zander got himself stabbed." The meth woman waved in a vague, unidentifiable direction. "Went out to Mugsville. There's always someone at bat there." She laughed, pleased with her chance to use what was obviously a tried and true line.

"Damn *bugs*," Mosquito snapped, and stomped away, waving his hands at his face.

"He got a bug thing," meth woman said, as if it needed explanation. "Not so bad, otherwise."

"Mugsville?" Mickey asked, though she had a good idea.

"Well, hell, honey, you know." The woman tucked her hands into her belt, which happened to be a couple of plastic grocery bags twisted and tied around her waist. "Muggers. They don't care how little we got, they want it. And it's kind of uptown, so we don't belong there anyway. I think Zander was hunting out his folks—they liked the little theaters. But there's this line—the rich folk stay on their side, we stay on ours. Problem is . . . we know that line a lot better than some of them do. There's always fresh meat for them as wants it."

Mickey affected a shudder. "I don't want anything to do with it, then. Where did you say? By the little theaters?"

"Not too far from that fancy museum of theirs." Meth woman gave her brief directions, her expression showing increasing anxiety. Mickey thought it was the conversation, but no. "You got any money?" The woman offered up a smile that was so fake as to be scary. Not to mention it showed her heavily damaged teeth to their full advantage. "Just a few bucks, that's all I need."

"Just the food . . . and that's gone." The truth, but Mickey wouldn't give the woman money if she'd had a fistful. A nice burger, on the other hand . . .

Thing was, she needed the money herself. She needed enough so she could do whatever she had to, not worrying about where she would stay, what she would eat, what she would wear. . . .

A forming thought tickled at her mind. It even scared her, because it came so easily, renewing concerns about who and what she was. But the thought followed her right back to her culvert, where she stashed her remaining things—one grocery bag, handle stretched and deformed, now containing only the old clothes, a toothbrush, and a travel tube of paste, the latter both from the freebies barrel and thank goodness for them. Then she pulled the flannel shirt and worn sweat pants on over what she already wore—God, she wanted some underwear— and the thought followed her back out again.

She had the knives; she had the slingshot and plenty of ammo—all for mugger mugging, the latest city sport. But who was to say she had to stop at filling her immediate needs? Who was to say she couldn't even the score a little, and then spread the wealth?

Start by getting there. Hoofing it in flip-flops from the gym, little raw spots worn between her big toe and the next. Not exactly stealth footwear . . . but she never intended to get close.

He'd been foolish to think he could find her.

Just because he'd always been able to find his brother . . . always knew where to look, according to the weather. Not because inclement weather drove Zander to find shelter, or bright weather lured him out to the parks, but because to Zander, the weather assigned his position in the city.

Which is how Steve, having checked all the other obvious places, found himself gravitating toward the border areas. Those places his parents and his brother used to intersect on clear summer nights when the occasional offshore flow warmed San Jose and kept the city awake late into the night. Just like tonight.

His parents had had some close calls in this area.

His brother had died here.

Being here wasn't something Steve took for granted. He carried ID and a little cash, but no credit cards. He didn't linger; he walked the pavement with authority. Without Zander, he really shouldn't be here at all. Not at this time of night. Not when he'd taken what remained of daylight to search the shelters and clinics and hang-outs between his two private lessons of the afternoon.

The streetlights ahead were blackened, leaving a swath of darkness across the sidewalks and street, an area even the cars rushed through. Time to turn around. If Mickey had landed anywhere near here, she was either hunkered tightly in, or already on her way to an ER somewhere. His best hope . . . that he'd already passed by her hidey-hole, and she'd stayed tucked away. He'd check around again tomorrow—by then, the locals would know her.

But while he was thinking of turning around and before he actually did it, he saw something up ahead in those dark spots. A man on the sidewalk, moving along with casual confidence, hands jammed into the pockets of a light jacket in a way that made Steve think at least one of them was wrapped around a weapon. No surprise, not here and now. And at that Steve would have turned to walk back toward brighter, more welcoming streets, except for the sudden cry the man gave. He jumped in surprise, he batted at his rump, and he followed the moment with a string of boringly overused curses. He turned to glare at the street, but didn't appear to know exactly where to target his wrath.

And then he did it all over again, except this time those curses had real feeling. Steve's surprised amusement tripped over to concern as he heard another voice—only faintly, at this distance, but enough to know it was a woman. No doubt someone with impaired judgment, engaging this man's anger—however she was doing it.

Except as the man took a step toward the street, he clutched his leg and howled in earnest, hopping briefly in a one-legged dance around one of those darkened lampposts. When he finally straightened, his posture turned furtive. He'd had enough. Steve stood transfixed as the man took one lurching step of flight, then flinched wildly back; a crack of noise sounded off the brick building beside him. Bullet ricochets? But there had been no gunfire.

At this point, the man wisely froze. In the silence that remained, the woman's voice called out an order—clearly an order, even if Steve was too far away to hear the words. Steve couldn't stop his jaw from dropping ever so slightly as the man, his movements jerky and resistant, reached into his jacket and dropped something on the ground; it clattered. Knife or gun, no doubt.

Another verbal prodding and the man augured into his pockets, dropping the contents with a gestured flourish that was easy to interpret: *there, happy now, bitch?*

And apparently she was, for she said something dismissive and he didn't waste any time. He ran down the street, limping distinctly, and if he considered turning back on her, the range of her mystery weapon thoroughly deterred him.

She waited until he was a full block away, and then Steve saw her run out from an alley on the other side of the street, staying fast and low, and gathering up her booty with swift efficiency.

What the hell had he just seen?

"Yo, mutha." Amused and confident, the low voice behind Steve made him freeze with understanding.

He'd come to this part of town and he'd forgotten to watch his surroundings; he hadn't kept moving. He had, in fact, just stood there like an idiot, completely entranced with the darkened scene before him. *First mistake.*

And then he realized his second mistake.

Taken unaware, he'd forgotten everything he knew about remaining submissive, about giving the man what he wanted— about throwing the wallet to the ground and taking off, pride in tatters but body whole. Instead, he'd dropped into a balanced stance, an immediately recognizable postural shout of resistance.

He had only that instant to realize it before everything about his world exploded, literal bursts of light inside his head and then just as suddenly the cracked sidewalk slammed up against his face. Hands patted his pockets, digging in after the small fold of bills, and the words, "Bad move, asshole. You swipe at me, you—sheeit!"

The thwack of sound made no sense, even as Steve struggled to pull his thoughts back together. Something had smacked his mugger, but—

Thwack! Harder, this time. The man left Steve's pockets alone and kicked him instead. Kicked him hard and did it again, both blows somehow bouncing off the same spot on his hip. He tried to curl up into a protective ball, and realized to his annoyance that he only clawed ineffectively at the concrete, one arm going so far as to flop. *Mind and body, not speaking.*

The woman's voice spoke. "Leave him alone, you fool."

"You crazy bitch!" The man snarled with menace. "You better *run.*"

Thwack! Even harder, and it got a yelp of pain; the mugger stumbled over Steve as he recovered from the blow, not the least bit careful where he placed his feet. Steve swiped at his ankle, a clumsy move. The man kicked his hand away and gave him another in the ribs just for good measure.

"*Who'd* better run?" That voice was low and full of menace. "You think you can bring that gun up before I can take your eye out? Or your nose? Are you especially fond of your nose?"

"You're damned crazy—!"

"Then there's no telling what I might do, is there?" *Familiar, and yet . . . still not.* "And you know what? While you're at it, you just empty your pockets on the sidewalk. Drop the gun first. Then I want to see something come out of every pocket. You got dope? You keep it. Everything else is mine. All your take." *Thwack!* and this time it sounded different, a softer impact—a louder protest. "You want I should call my target first next time? I can damned well put a stone up your left nostril if that's what I want." A drop of something fell on Steve's hand.

Blood.

The crazy woman meant business, bless her heart. He twitched that hand; withdrew it a little. *Might be something to that brain-body connection after all.* But he let her carry the show. Especially as something heavy fell on him, gouging into sore ribs. He couldn't help but grunt, and then again when leather and chain—*wallet*—smacked down on him, followed by coins and . . .

She'd done it. The man was giving up the goods, dumping them down on Steve in one last act of defiance. Muttering along with it. "You ain't safe here after tonight. Not anywhere in this town."

Her voice was deceptively low. "Gonna tell your friends a soft little white chick took you down? Gonna tell them it was a crazy little white chick, shirt on her head? Gonna tell them what I look like under all this, or you just gonna guess?"

Steve realized he was, somehow, laughing. Silently, eyes closed, head ringing, body aching . . . silent, helpless laughter. The mugger realized it, too, and dealt him a swift kick. Steve grunted at the impact, and barely heard the woman say, "Run, now. Run away. Go tell your friends. See what happens if you do find me."

With one final spit of a curse, the mugger did just that. Steve got only a glimpse of him, enough to know he was young, still coming up on the streets. Very much the age of his boys at the gym.

"Hey," said the crazy woman, and she crouched down next to him, wrapping her fingers around his upper arm. "You got anything left? We really can't stay here." And then she gasped. "*Steve.* What are you doing here?" Just a hint of a pause before more words tumbled out, the voice no longer low, no longer menacing. "You're looking for me, aren't you? I can't believe it. C'mon, get up—that kid's gonna wipe the blood off his face and start looking for ways to get tough at me."

The tug on his arm grew more insistent, but not enough to override his shock of recognition. "*Mickey?*" He did get up, then, at least halfway—enough to look at her. That, too, was a shock. She had no shape; her mid-section had turned lumpy and bulgy beneath the single tank top above her shorts, and on her head—

Yes. It was a tank top, the straps tied in a bow at the top of her head and two eye-holes cut out for those bright eyes, a gaze even this poor light fought to diminish.

Coins slid off his shirt to hit the ground in a brief tympany; she ignored them to scoop up the gun, stuffing it under her shirt. She scooped up the wallet, the scattered cash, and left everything else where it was.

He couldn't hide his disbelief. "You . . . you're mugging muggers?"

"Why, yes," she said, gave it a moment's thought, and added a brusque nod. "Why, yes, I am. And an entertaining and lucrative evening it's been." The goods disappeared into the nebulous stuffing under her shirt. "But it's not over yet, and it's going to end with a bang if we don't get out of here. So pull your scrambled egg brains together and let's *go*."

This made a certain amount of sense, and he lurched to his feet, swaying into her hard enough to make her stagger away; she caught herself and came back to sweep his arm across her shoulders, steadying him. "*Are* you crazy?" he asked, finding his tongue remarkably loosened by circumstances and probably concussion.

Her response was dry, and she didn't hesitate in steering them a course across the street and toward the overpass. "That's what they say."

He'd have to think about that one. It didn't seem like an answer at all, not when he'd finally come to blurt the question outright.

Of course, he probably wouldn't remember it anyway.

Mickey was more than relieved to learn just how much she could count on her own wiry strength. Enough to drag Steve back to the underpass, although it would be fair to say he needed little more than the stabilizing effect of his arm over her shoulder.

It would also be fair to say she was as much relieved that he wasn't the Schwartzenegger-type of gym owner. His compact body-by-Michelangelo suited her just fine . . . and didn't knock her down when he stumbled.

"You know," she said, easing him down beside her drain pipe, finally able to wipe the sweat from her forehead with something other than a furtive rub against an upraised shoulder, "I left for a reason. I left so no one at the gym would get hurt. That included you, for the record." She pulled her second tank top— the one with the eye holes, and which she'd removed after they'd fled a block away from her final encounter of the night—out from beneath her shirt where she'd stuffed it and untied the straps so she could shrug it back on, working it beneath the first one.

It really wouldn't do to walk around with the eye-hole shirt as the second layer, not when she'd just worn it to take down a handful of muggers.

Steve muttered, "You didn't ask *me*."

"I didn't have to. I happen to think your concerns were valid." She pulled the flannel shirt from where it had been tied beneath her clothes. Not only had it completely obscured the nature of her breasts, it had served as a fine pouch for her night's work.

Work she had, in fact, found tremendously enjoyable. Both the slinking in the shadows, targeting muggers in action . . . and relieving them of their own belongings afterward, when they were—for the moment—all cocky and pleased. In a perfect world, she'd have interrupted the muggings as she did with Steve, but there were too many variables to that plan. Too many opportunities for things to go wrong, and for the victim to be hurt or killed instead of just robbed. Her way, she'd stayed entirely unseen—at least until she'd pulled that young punk off Steve.

She'd turn her credit card booty in to the cops. The cash . . .

That was another story. She had plenty of use for the cash. *Just call me Robbin' in the 'Hood* . . . Or not, because having one assumed name seemed like enough. But Robin Hood in spirit she'd be—and at least half the cash would go for food and supplies for those who lived here. The underpass people.

She might not know who she was; she might not understand

the urgency behind her need to find Naia. But she had a purpose again, and she found that it filled an anxious, empty spot within her.

"You should have *asked*," he said, charmingly stubborn even in a vaguely hazy way. He pressed fingers to the side of his head and inspected them as if he could even see them in the darkness.

"Yes, there's blood," Mickey told him. "What did you think you were doing, going macho on that scrub? If I had more time I'd poke around your ribs, make sure nothing was broken."

"And how would you know?" He cast her an irritable glance, which she took as a good sign.

"By how loudly you yelled," she told him with cheerful satisfaction. She'd dumped the shirt full of goods onto the ground, and stripped the sweats she'd tied around her hips. She'd been a totally shapeless lump in the darkness, but now that it was cooling off, she put them on the normal way, stepping out of the flip-flops.

"I wouldn't yell at all," Steve told her, with enough dignity to assure Mickey that he was getting his balance back. "It wouldn't be *macho*."

"Uh-huh." She sorted the weapons aside—those would go to the cops, too. A nice neat bundle in a chic plastic shopping bag, deposited on their doorstep.

Steve felt at his own ribs. "Ow, dammit. I'm never going to live this down at the gym. And what the—what were you doing out there? With a . . ." he frowned, barely visible in the darkness, and shook his head. "I *do* remember it. With a *tank top* on your head?"

"Hey, it had eye holes." Mickey crouched, held up a nice wad of cash. "What do you think I was doing? I need underwear."

She should have had pity on him. She should have explained it with short words and concise sentences. But she thought he should have respected her decision to leave, and she didn't feel like making life easy for him.

At least, not as long as she knew he hadn't taken *too* much damage from his encounter with the punk.

"Hey," he said, having pondered the situation in silence while she finished her sorting and jammed the cash into the front pocket of the flannel shirt. She'd count it later, when she had light, and put aside as much as she could for Big Box combat shopping. "Hey," he said again, more to himself than to her. "I know this place."

"You should," she told him, finally straightening out of her crouch to shake some feeling back into her feet. "They sure know you. They knew your brother, too." But her mouth was mainly on automatic; her thoughts had gone on to plan the next twenty-four hours. Dump the weapons and wallets at the nearest precinct. A night in a hotel, even a fleabag hotel. Shopping the next morning. And then on to find the building where she'd been drugged and imprisoned, hunting clues. Hunting Naia.

"Listen," he said, and seemed to realize she was ready to move; he got to his feet. Slowly. "If I asked you again, what's going on . . . would you answer this time?"

"No," she said, without thinking. And then, "Maybe." And then, "It depends."

He stood there with his mouth halfway around a word, no apparent idea how to respond to that.

"Come with me," she said abruptly, slipping the shopping bag handles over her wrist so she could use that hand to grab his.

He might not understand, but he didn't resist. She took him along the underpass, then cut uphill once the slope gentled out. He had trouble with it, not quite as pulled back together as he made out, but he was still with her when they stopped beneath the first available street lamp. She could have wished for a park bench, but she'd settle for the light traffic and the lack of interest from the rest of the world. "If we're going to talk about this," she told him, setting down the shopping bag full of weapons and wallets, "I want to be able to see your face. Besides, I've got places to be. So ask me again."

"You've changed," he said.

"Decided to trust myself," she said shortly, and waited.

"Tell me, then," he said, repeating the words he'd first used in his office—the ones she'd first refused. Except this time he was the vulnerable one, pale beneath that Mediterranean complexion, blood down the side of his neck and staining his shirt and black in the lamp light.

And for someone who still had no true idea of what or who she was, Mickey wasn't nearly as frightened as she should be. "You still think I'm off meds? That I need to be popped back into a psych ward and reconnected to reality?"

He shook his head, looking weary. "You don't act like any psych ward drop-out I've ever dealt with. Then again, you don't act like *anyone* I've ever dealt with."

She grinned, amusement at his honesty and something darker at the truth behind it. She put a hand on the lamp post, did a slow circle around it, and stopped when she reached him again, letting him wait for her own truth. He wasn't taking any chances; he leaned against the post to block her way, wincing at the stretch of what surely must be wickedly bad bruises. She said, "What's going on is that I don't remember. I woke up one morning handcuffed to a bed, and I don't know why. I was drugged, the doctor said—there was a doctor. I broke his nose and I took his scrubs. Remember them?"

"The blood . . ."

"His. And he deserved it. He used some kind of knock-out drug on me, something experimental, and it blew away my memory. He said he didn't know if it would come back."

"Knock-out drug," he repeated, and then sent her a narrow-eyed gaze. "Mickey Finn."

"Yeah. I'd claim I was being terribly clever except when I first woke up and heard them talking, I really did think my name was Mickey."

"So you woke up with no memory, escaped from the people who drugged you, and made it into my gym before fainting."

She frowned. "I think I stole an apple on the way. Maybe. And I know they asked me a lot of questions about a young woman. I think she's in trouble . . . I need to find her. But yeah, that's the short version."

He just stared at her. For a long moment, and then another. Then he shook his head and said, "That's the craziest thing I've ever heard."

"Isn't it?"

"Why wouldn't you tell me—?"

She snorted. "You can answer that, if you think about it. A partial answer, anyway."

He could, too. He looked away, absurdly thick dark lashes obscuring his eyes. "You figured I'd *really* think you were crazy."

"Bingo. Not to mention I really wanted to keep you out of this. But once I saw those guys cruising past—"

"You saw them, too?" That fast, his gaze flashed back to hers, interest overriding the guilt.

"Out back, when I was putting out the garbage. Figured they were after me. And me . . . I've got things to do. Your gym just seemed too small—and everyone there has their own problems. They don't need letter openers flying around."

"Tajo shouldn't have—"

"No," she interrupted. "He shouldn't have. But enough was enough, don't you think? Besides, you don't need to be involved in this. I might not be your brother's kind of crazy, but there's nothing sane about what's going on with me."

He scowled at her. Deeply. It shifted to a slow and dawning comprehension. "Damn," he said. "So this is what it feels like."

"How's that?" She eyed the shopping bag, unsettled . . . ready to move on. This had been a good spot for a conversation . . . not a good spot to hang indefinitely.

"Being told what's good for me. Someone making decisions for me."

"Oh," she said. "That. Yes, that's what it feels like. But if you think pointing it out will change anything—"

"Let's just go back to the gym," he told her. "Talk about this in the morning."

"Nothing will be different in the morning. Besides, I have other plans."

"Not more Tank Top Woman."

"No. And not just because that's a terrible name for a super hero." She considered the thought for a moment. "Though I reserve the right to a return engagement, if I get the urge. It's a multi-purpose charity funding activity. Keeps me on my toes, takes from those who deserve to lose . . . discourages them from doing their thing in the first place."

He frowned, his eyes going distant. "How did you—what did you use?"

"Oh." She wrinkled her nose in chagrin. "Something of yours, actually." She decided against pulling out the slingshot to show him—she didn't want to argue over it if he wanted it back. So she barged on with a little misdirection. "Look, I'm heading toward the nearest cop station. You know where it is? Because I'll walk you there, and I'm sure they'll get you home."

"I thought you didn't want anything to do with them."

"Well, I don't. I mean, who the heck knows who I am, right? I could be on the most wanted list for all I know, and considering what I've learned of me it seems all too likely. But you're the one who needs to get home."

It didn't take a blinking neon sign to see the stubborn crop up in his face again. It showed in his chin, in the hardened line of his jaw. He knew better than to argue, but he thought he'd change her mind between here and the station house.

Well, let him. Mickey had gotten reacquainted enough with her own mind to know he didn't stand a chance.

CHAPTER 8

"Hey," Steve said, and put a hand to the stitch in his side until he realized he'd hit a bruise and made it all worse. The local Community Policing Center—*precinct lite,* Zander had liked to call them—was just down the block. Perfect for a weapons drop-off. "How about a breather? There's no real hurry here, is there?"

She eyed him, no longer the blobby amorphous super hero but back to slender curves that would fill out with a few more pounds, her hair still mussed by the tank top but starting to fall back into the lines of its society cut. She still had that new look on her face, the one he was beginning to recognize as confidence. When she'd arrived at the gym, she'd needed him—she'd needed help. Now he wasn't sure she needed anyone.

She said, "Only hurry is to get you there before you fall over."

"Excuse me," he said, unable to stop that defensive ruffling. "But I'm fine."

"Uh-huh," she said. "I know. Self-defense instructor." She poked his side and he grunted, doubling until he caught himself. "You shouldn't have come after me."

Finally. Someone who *didn't* want his help. Not any longer, anyway.

He thought it should be easy to turn around and walk away.

It should *be easy.*

And yet he didn't.

Maybe he'd figure it out later. For now, he straightened himself up and tried to ignore the flicker of . . . *something* that made it easier than expected. Hope?

Not likely. Belatedly, he said, "No poking. Let's go."

She lifted her hands to look down at herself, a distinct *hey, I'm ready to go* gesture. And they went, an inconspicuous pairing of a homeless amnesiac with no discernible panty line and a buff Greek gym rat who'd had the stuffing beaten out of him.

When they reached the cop mini-shop—hardly more than a red tape outlet in a storefront—Steve straightened his shoulders enough to remove the last vestiges of fetal hunch and put a little casual saunter into his step. Mickey said, "I'll catch up with you when this is all over, tell you whatever I find out. I owe you that much. Plus a pizza."

He felt her puzzlement when he didn't respond, and was impressed with how she somehow faded out of sight as he took the bag of weapons and walked them up to the storefront. Flyers filled the glass-fronted case beside the door, official-looking notices of classes and community resources, and he would have ignored it all and casually deposited the bag if he hadn't been caught by the small patch of flyers off to the side, shadowed but still legible. Lost pets, lost people . . .

Lost Mickey.

Jane A. Dreidler, and a photo of amazingly bad quality with Mickey—Jane?—looking dazed. No real details, just a phone number and a plea that the missing woman had been ill.

In that moment, his hope plummeted.

But he couldn't quite lose it all. Not that suddenly. And if he hung around here any longer, he was going to grab the attention of the uniformed woman behind the high counter. For the moment she was bent over paperwork, but it wouldn't last.

He set the bag against the door and took himself back out to the sidewalk.

She was gone.

"I know you're here somewhere," he said through his teeth.

"And I'm going to march back in there and tell them about Tank Top Woman if you don't—"

Somehow, she was behind him. "You were supposed to go *in.*" She glanced over her shoulder at the center and took him by the arm, walking him away from the well-lit plate-glass storefront and the cop within. "You were supposed to get *help.*"

"Jane A. Dreidler," he said.

Her expression didn't change, but her fingers tightened on his arm. "Where did you hear that name?'

"I read it. Where are we going?"

"To someplace with a bed. Read it where?"

He gestured back at the center. "Right there. They're looking for you."

"Already knew that much," she said, tugging him off the sidewalk to jaywalk over to the next block. "As it happens, now *I'm* looking for *them.* Don't tell me they put up one of those posters?"

"Milk carton could be next." He took a bad step on at the curb and would have fallen had she not kept her hold on his arm. "They said you're sick."

"You should have gone in." The turn of her head hid her face, but couldn't hide the sound of her scowl.

"I thought you'd want to know." He caught his balance and his breath and added, "Jane."

She snorted. "That's what they called me, and it's a name I know, but . . . it's not me."

"You sound pretty sure." He suddenly realized they were heading for the local roach motel, and put the brakes on. Or tried to. She wasn't having any of it, and she seemed to know how to shift his weight just *so* until he found himself moving right along. The ease with which she did it made him realize all over again that there was more to her than it seemed . . . and that he'd really taken a hit this evening. Lucky to still be on his feet.

Foolish to have gotten into that kind of trouble in the first place.

It was how his brother had died.

"I *am* sure," she said, undiverted by his hesitations. "Memories, I don't have. But reactions . . . those are there."

He pulled back again as they reached the Star Motel—*rates by the week, by the hour*—and this time she let him go. Of course he staggered; of course she righted him. And she said, "This is it. You lost your chance for your own nice soft bed when you walked away from the mini cop shop. Now I'm not giving you the choice—you're not staying out here all night, and don't even try to convince me you'll make it back to the cop shop." She opened the dingy door and gave him what was probably a gentle shove; he made it inside just in time to grab himself upright at the nearby stair railing, and then gave up and sat on the stairs.

Mickey made quick negotiations for a room, paid in mugger cash, and returned to Steve with a key flashing in her hand. "Here we go," she said.

Right. *Here we go.* Steve had no idea just where they were headed . . . but he was beginning to think that if anyone could get there, it would be Mickey.

With or without anyone's help.

Mickey rinsed out the dingy washcloth and squeezed it until runnels of pink water made their way down the sink. "Ought to be in the ER," she said to him through the open bathroom door. In truth, *open* was the only way it came, as the warped door refused to move from its permanently ajar position. "Or an all-night clinic."

"You knew this place was here?" he asked.

"I seem to have." She returned to sit at the side of the bed—a twin bed, not at all happy to hold the weight of two. He sat propped against the headboard, one arm protecting his ribs and a hand exploring the side of his head. She gently slapped it away, separating the wet waves behind his ear to get another look at the cut there. "It's hard to tell what I know. Sometimes I don't realize it until afterward. And sometimes I get these . . ." she trailed off, no longer seeing his hair or his blood, but the now-familiar image of Naia, accompanied by that now-familiar wave of urgency. *Do you have something I want? Are you* someone *I want? Am I using you? Do I care about you?*

A little of both, she thought. There was more to that urgency than calculated goal. There was caring . . . there was familiarity and responsibility.

And as memories went, it was the clearest thing she had. The *only* thing she had. If she couldn't find Naia, she'd find the people who had drugged her—who had put her in this state, fumbling around San Jose in confusion, not sure if she was the hunted or the hunter.

Steve's voice grabbed her out of that potentially endless reverie. "You okay?"

She refocused on him. He was close—closer than she'd expected. He'd leaned forward, she realized—but he was sore and tired and it showed in his eyes, and he didn't stay there long. Not once he saw he had her attention.

Poor guy. He'd only wanted to help. It was what he did, obviously enough. Helped those who struggled against what fate had dealt them . . . helped those like his brother who didn't have any true hope. So of course he'd gathered her up when she'd come staggering into his gym. Of course he'd found it no surprise that she'd fainted at his feet. She sighed, and dabbed the dried blood on his neck. Stubborn thing, dried blood. It found every crack and crevice of skin.

Dried blood, a dead woman on the floor and partially covered with a lemon yellow raincoat. Expensive London Fog raincoat, not hers . . . because it wasn't big enough to hide the blood, or the shoulder-length grey hair fanning across the plushly carpeted floor.

What the hell? What was that? New, these stains of violent death in her memory. New, and yet . . . the true start of it all.

"Mickey?"

There she was, frozen in mid-dab. "I'm sorry," she said, and then caught his gaze to say it again. "I'm really sorry. You had no idea what you were getting into when I showed up. It really wasn't fair."

He tipped his head back against the water-stained wall. "None of it's fair," he said, and she knew he meant more than her arrival, more than what had gone down on the street tonight. "Just for once, give me the chance to really make a difference." His lips barely moved; his eyes twitched slightly behind closed lids.

She'd meant to get some sleep. Instead she'd be checking him every couple of hours just to see if he could wake up after that concussion. "You don't even know what you're saying," she murmured, and withdrew the washcloth, giving up to rub at the stubborn spot with one wet thumb.

"Do too," he said, but he didn't move.

Mickey watched him another long while, cataloging the pasty nature of his skin, the purpling of the bruises—knowing there were more beneath his *Steve's Gym* shirt. She found herself waylaid by the dark sweep of lashes shadowing the thin skin beneath his eyes, and in remembering the eyes themselves . . . first so determined to help, and then most recently—whether he knew it or not—so determined to hope.

"We'll see how you feel about it tomorrow," she told him, and curled up in the small portion of bed available, pulling up the thin sheet to cover them both.

★ ★ ★ ★ ★

He remembered that she had a soothing touch. He remembered her quietly sardonic voice in his ear. He even remembered being woken up several times that night, being asked who he was and what year it was and who was president.

He didn't remember expecting to wake up alone.

CHAPTER 9

Badra didn't try to hide her disapproval of Naia's planned schedule. "Two days in a row? For this clay, you neglect your studies?"

Naia almost succumbed to the knee-jerk impulse to explain herself. In Irhaddan, it was expected. Here, she had no need to remind Badra that she hadn't neglected anything; that she was well abreast of her studies and that she had no classes this morning in any event. Or that her interest in pottery was just the kind of thing of which her father would approve. It allowed her to mingle with the Americans, allowed her to be seen. Allowed her father's benevolence to be seen. And at the same time, it was properly conservative.

In the end, she couldn't quite hold her tongue. She said, "I tried to sign up for parasailing classes, but they were full."

Badra's stricken horror was all Naia could have hoped for—except, of course, that she quickly realized she'd been had, and turned the expression into a ladylike snort.

Who would have guessed I would be so good at this? For by letting Badra come to her own conclusions—letting her rule out the outrageous—Naia had only nudged her further away from any suspicions that she would do outrageous things in the first place.

Such as spying on her own country.

No. Not my country. Just those people in it who are causing damage.

And still, as she ascended the narrow, twisty steps to the second floor pottery co-op, she hoped to find a response from Anna. Anna, on whom her safety suddenly seemed to depend. *Insha'Allah.*

The first time she'd met Anna, Naia had been at a famine relief benefit auction, her mind on the Lit 110 test she'd had the following day and her face trying out an unfamiliar public smile. She wasn't accustomed to being seen at such things. In fact, she was more accustomed to being distinctly hidden.

What had her father thought would happen when he dumped her into this democratic, liberated culture? Had he not understood that she could love her land and her own culture, and yet absorb the good from this one? He surely hadn't expected her to run into a woman like Anna. Not so very much older than Naia, who at twenty-two had started her university schooling late. And there she'd been, amazing in turquoise and chocolate swirls on silk chiffon, a dress that wrapped her waist and hugged her breasts and fell away from her hips, a dress Naia had instantly wished she had the nerve to wear. On Anna the dress was streamlined; on Naia it would reveal curves she'd only recently realized she wanted to reveal at all.

It took a moment for Naia to realize that what truly made the dress amazing wasn't Anna's figure or the art nouveau necklace and earrings that set it off so perfectly or even Anna's hair, an elegant up-do with enough loose strands at her nape to show her independent personality.

No, it was her smile. The confidence of it, and its genuine nature—no matter which dignitary she spoke to in the crowded benefit reception, extolling the virtues of antique jewelry she'd donated to the cause. And, as far as Naia could tell, occasionally singing along with the live band in the background, even when she was right in the middle of a conversation.

Nothing seemed to faze her.

In that moment, Naia wanted to be her. To be an Anna, completely confident in herself no matter the circumstances. Maybe Anna had seen it in her, that wistfulness. She'd been kind from the start. And she'd eventually shown Naia how to fit in, and how to find her own way.

She'd never been pushy. Not even once Naia realized exactly where their friendship was leading. She gave Naia the room to decide what was important, and how she could best act on it. And then she'd given Naia the outlet to do just that. When she'd casually mentioned that some informants received gifts and money for their work, she'd known better than to suggest such a thing to Naia. "Here's the deal," she'd said, straightforward as always. "The agency is used to paying for what people bring in. So let's funnel that money off to your favorite Irhaddan charity—didn't you mention something about an orphanage?"

And that's what they'd arranged. They'd trickled off their social outings, meeting only at the same receptions and functions to which they'd each always gone—Anna because she traveled in exclusive circles, providing rare and startlingly valuable antiques to the discerning collector, and Naia because she was expected to be seen. They'd arranged to spend time at this co-op, though rarely at the same time. And Anna had given her the dead drop, the one they'd only begun to use.

Naia wasn't naive enough to think the timing of the dead drop introduction—right before she left for a long visit between spring and summer classes—was coincidence. Especially not after she arrived home and realized the differences in herself—her confidence, her attentiveness to nuance and detail . . . a new curiosity that drove her into situations she formerly would have avoided. Drove her right into a bit of startling secrecy that she'd wanted to tell her father above all . . .

And knew she couldn't. He wouldn't believe her; he wouldn't

take her word over that of a trusted colleague. He'd say the United States had confused and corrupted her and denied her the opportunity to return.

And she'd known that waiting in San Jose, she had a friendly ear, someone to whom she could tell everything. A means by which to do it.

No, nothing about Anna was coincidence. Probably not even the way they'd met that first time. And when Anna saw to a detail, it stayed seen to. It did as expected.

Which is why when Naia reached the dead drop and quickly thrust her hand into the hidden space, she was absolutely taken aback to encounter her own note.

Her own cry for help.

Unanswered.

Mickey left Steve sleeping after a restless night of interruptions. Steve was a mess, the bruises stark in the morning light, but his sleep was natural enough; the concussion slight. She paid the desk clerk to leave him alone and headed off to pick up some essentials—precious underwear, a few stretchy sports tops, pocket-filled shorts, sneakers.

Not so easy to shake the guilt over Steve's battered state, or over leaving him alone in the ratty hotel. *I didn't ask you to follow me,* she told him in her mind, heading back out on the street. But he had—he was that kind of guy, she got that—and he'd been beaten up for his trouble. Pretty much exactly why she'd left in the first place—so no one else would get hurt because of her presence.

I'm sorry, she told him. And then she pulled her newly purchased sunglasses from the top of her head and settled them on her nose, and she headed back for Steve's neighborhood. Not to visit, not to linger—not even to be seen. But to backtrack her steps as best she could.

To find the people who'd done this to her.

Because when it came right down to it, Naia was all she had.

Finding Naia was all she had.

Keeping Naia safe . . .

All she had.

She thought they might still be looking for her . . . but she didn't expect the tail she picked up not far from Steve's gym, carefully backtracking her way out of the neighborhood.

She couldn't have said just how she knew, or why the thought even came to her. One moment she puzzled over a corner street sign, trying to decide if she'd come that way, and the next she strode briskly off in the one direction she hadn't even been considering. By then she realized what had triggered her concern, that she'd had a glimpse of the same nondescript hat one too many times—sometimes a block behind her, sometimes much less. By then she'd entered an ice cream shop, slipped straight out the back, and circled around to come up behind her own trail.

She didn't find anyone. Whoever it was had realized they'd been made . . . and hadn't wanted a confrontation. Hadn't wanted to go public in any way.

She spent the next hour pulling flushing techniques. Alleys, double-backs, lingering at storefronts to watch the reflections. And, finding nothing, she ducked into a bodega to grab a cheap straw sunhat and to turn her tote bag into a something resembling a backpack; she put the old flip-flops back on her feet and stuffed the sneakers away. When she came out, she put more than a little twitch of *hooker* in her hips, and then she ran through all the flushing techniques all over again.

She'd lost them . . . or they'd decided to try again later.

But she'd also lost time, and she'd lost energy. She found her nerves stretched thin and her body losing its edge to hunger and lack of sleep. Nor had she truly returned to herself after her stint at the make-believe hospital.

At least, she hoped she hadn't. It would be a bitch to be this tired all the time.

Urgency drove her onward . . . common sense stopped her and pulled her into a sub shop. She bought a footer and put half of it away for later, and when she returned to the street she knew her tracking exercise was a temporary thing. She put herself to tracing her steps and got as far as the footbridge over the Guadalupe River before admitting she'd had it.

That, too, seemed like a response to training, just as her footwork had to be. Such an objective evaluation—the awareness that she could go on if someone's life directly depended on it, but that the circumstances didn't currently warrant the risk.

She gave the city on the other side of the footbridge a rueful look, and she turned back. She bought bottled water from a corner vendor and sat down at a bus stop bench to eat the rest of her sub. "Tomorrow," she promised the spread of buildings.

For she already had plans for the evening.

She found a new fleabag hotel—no shortage of them in this part of town—and dumped her few belongings there, switching back into sporty mode with sneakers and yoga pants. She gave herself thirty minutes of rest, and headed for the nearest PW grocery store. There she stacked a cart full of peanut butter and tuna and crispy crackerbread that wouldn't get stale; she jammed the bottom rack with tissue and toilet paper, and crammed toothbrushes and paste into the remaining crevices.

The muggers paid for it all.

She headed out of the store with a step lighter than any amnesiac being hunted by really angry mystery enemies should ever have. She'd gotten a good cart, too—it let her shove it on down the sidewalk and jump up to coast along, and when she hit a downhill stretch she just went along for the ride, trailing one foot behind as a stabilizing rudder. Music bubbled right on out of her throat, something that went along with her long sweeping movement. Manilow. Sweepingly, dramatically . . . one of the ballads. ". . . Ohhhh Maaaan—" She had a fumble, a lost note as she navigated a curve, but picked it right back up again. Another oldie, she realized, and decided to update herself, fumbling for another tune. Celine Dion, that would do it. Celine was *now*. Right to the power chorus—"I'm youuur la—"

She stopped the cart. Celine Dion might be now, but her fickle memory was happy to inform her that the song came from the eighties. "Fine," she muttered to herself. "I like the oldies." And she pushed off, launching back into the Manilow song.

No one along the way seemed to care one way or the other, and that suited her just fine. She drove her little shopping cart right down to the underpass, taking the long way around to avoid the steep bank, and by the time she approached the underpass itself—breathless, but still singing—she had a wary welcome committee.

"Thought you was gone," Meth Woman said with a sniff. "Saw you leave last night. Wasn't that—"

"Zander's brother," Mosquito interjected, swiping at something invisible on his arm. "She's sweet on him. I saw it."

"Maybe it was." Mickey waved a box of tissues, enticing them and changing the subject in one fell swoop. "I hope you like peanut butter. It keeps. And tuna—"

"Oh!" Meth Woman snatched the can out of Mickey's hand. "Gourmet choice!"

"Nothing but the best," Mickey said, and after that the cart emptied apace. She was bending to get the final tissue box when a gruff voice spoke beside the cart.

"Yesterday you were one of us, and today you bring us this

stuff? You got new clothes?" There was warning to the words.

Mickey stood to face the man who'd appointed himself to look a gift horse in the mouth. She said, "You just keep my business mine, and any trouble following me around will stay clear of here."

"You think bringing this stuff makes up for that risk?"

She straightened, offering him the tissues. "I think bringing this stuff was something I could do, so I did."

He offered her only a skeptical look.

"Plus, I found it to be sweetly ironic revenge on the fellows who used to have this money."

His eyes widened slightly as he absorbed the implications. "You?"

"Word getting around already? Good." Although that would only make it harder later.

"You wore a shirt on your head with eye holes in it?" He snorted in amused disbelief.

"*Hey,*" Mickey said, stung. "And what about a little black cowl with bat ears *isn't* silly?"

He seemed to consider this. Then he took the tissues. "I saw you at the gym." At her surprise, he added, "Not my turf, but Steve don't care. I'm thinking Mosquito's right—you're sweet on that boy. You're smart, you won't bring him your trouble, either."

She opened her mouth to protest. Plenty of protest, most of it having to do with how she'd left the gym specifically to take her trouble away and he'd only followed. But the man turned his back on her and ambled away, and she realized he had few enough victories in his life . . . she'd give him this one. "Cart's for the taking!" she announced to the underpass as a whole. And with any luck, Robbin' in the 'Hood would be back in a day or two to distribute more mugger money.

Lots to do between now and then.

And most of it involved people who wanted to get their hands on her.

CHAPTER 10

The bus pulled away with a grumble of gears and lingering diesel smoke, leaving Steve to walk a block to the gym in the late afternoon heat. He liked to think of it as walking, at least. Other people obviously considered his movement more of a borderline lurch, and they gave him plenty of room.

He wondered if his brother had felt like this. Watched. Judged. *Of course he did.*

With effort, Steve straightened his shoulders, lightened his walk. But by the time he reached the gym, fumbling for his keys, he'd already attracted attention. *Dawnisha.* She ground a cigarette out on the sidewalk and picked up a full garbage bag, and he realized that she'd been waiting there. Then he looked at the bag again and realized—*Tuesday.* The day Dawnisha brought over Sunday's take from the hotel where she worked. Soaps opened and barely used, toothpaste left behind, lost and found items never picked up. Officially, the hotel didn't know that these things didn't end up in the garbage. Unofficially, the other maids pitched in to make sure the Tuesday bag was bulging.

"Don't you look fine," she said to him.

Steve offered a vague, evasive gesture and opened the door. He hadn't realized how hot he'd been until the cool interior air washed over him; he might have stood in that doorway for the next year, eyes closed and head tipped back, if Dawnisha hadn't nudged him. And at that he let out an involuntary yelp, jerking aside as she marched in and dropped the bag beside the freebies barrel. She turned around, crossed her arms, and looked him up and down. "Uh-huh," she said. "Locked it up with someone, didn't you?"

"In the loosest possible terms," he muttered.

"And came back without that Mickey."

Couldn't argue that.

"Doing anything about it?" The challenge was right there in her eyes. He'd spent years telling the people in this neighborhood to take charge of their own fate, to reach for what they wanted. Clearly enough, she thought it was his turn to walk the talk.

"Shower," he said. "Long one. All the Ben Gay in the world."

"That'll bring the ladies running," she noted. She flicked her fingers at the training room. "World won't end if you close this place for the whole day. You've gone and missed most of it already."

"It might." But he didn't meet her gaze.

"Be just as well," she said. "Been 5-0 hanging around here all day, I hear."

"Cops?" That surprised him. Nothing he'd seen so far indicated that the cops were in on Mickey's little adventure.

She shook her head, brisk and disapproving. "Someone's muscle, trying too hard to look like they aren't watching the place."

Steve rubbed a careful hand across the back of his neck— very careful. "Maybe I should stay here, then. Give them something to look at." Keep them from looking in Mickey's new direction.

"*Scared,*" she said, picking up on their previous conversation and letting scorn put an edge to it.

He didn't respond, and she dismissed him with a wave, leaving the gym with an I-own-the-world walk. But of course she was right. Scared. Of what would happen if he found Mickey again; of what would happen if he didn't.

Just because she didn't want help didn't mean she didn't need it.

And Steve . . .

Didn't even really understand what was at stake. He just knew it had quickly become far too important to him that she come out on top—alive and kicking and singing some old pop tune while she was at it.

Except she had a right to make her own decisions . . . to make her own way.

Maybe that shower would help. Maybe it would clear his mind, make everything clear. What to do next, how to get her to that happy ending.

But he didn't think he was headed for easy answers.

Mickey stood in the cool evening shadow of a dun brick building, but her shivers didn't come from the shade at all. *Here. This is the place.*

Where she'd woken, a mystery to herself. In handcuffs. Facing down the cold expression of a woman who was used to getting what she wanted.

At the time Mickey had been frightened . . . confused . . . more than a little sick.

Now she was suddenly just mad.

It didn't matter who she was . . . what she might have done. How *dare* they play around with experimental drugs? How dare they leave her fumbling to figure out who she was, who she could trust, and who she needed to find? And dammit, what if no one was feeding that cat?

. . . silver tabby, pretending not to see the twitching, dangling toy just out of reach, braided rug beneath tucked paws . . .

The building across the street loomed sleek and new . . . and yet somehow also looked abandoned. The small, neat name and logo combination on the corner of the structure created an air of snooty arrogance. *If you don't already know who we are, we don't care if you notice us or not.*

CapAd.Com. A dot-com building, busted right down to emptiness.

Mickey circled the building, always staying across the street, sometimes ducking into those buildings—a bank, a bakery— sometimes circling the block before lingering to watch CapAd .Com.

No one went in; no one came out. Eventually, she discovered that all the doors were locked. Eventually, as night fell, as the business area shut down, she discovered that no one turned on any lights.

Gone? Or just really, really good at hiding?

Hard to find rocks of any substance in this manicured neighborhood. Mickey settled for a heavy pot of pansies, acquired from outside the bank. Heavy, no doubt, to discourage people from picking it up and hefting it through someone's glass front door.

Which is exactly what she did.

The resulting crash—glass raining down, pot smashed inside the door, pansies scattered everywhere—was eminently satisfying, but it brought no one running. It brought no one walking, or sauntering, or otherwise into evidence at all.

So whatever else she was, Mickey was also now a vandal. "Sorry, pansies," she muttered at them, watching from behind the big blue mail drop on the corner. And to herself, "Sorry, Janie A. Looks like there aren't any answers waiting here." No people . . . no one to interrogate.

But she couldn't help herself; when no one responded to the broken door—no police, no curious onlookers—she slipped across the street and through the jagged hole she'd created. Glass crunched beneath her feet, grinding into the carpet.

Familiar pattern, that carpet.

She found the stairs; she wished for a flashlight. But by the time she'd climbed those three unlit floors and emerged into the hallway, her eyes were so accustomed to the darkness that the city light through the bank of windows seemed a luxury.

And standing there at the end of the hallway, unable to suppress another bout of shivering, she thought the dim light was probably also a mercy. It softened the details . . . blurred them. There was the bathroom, where she'd taken down the doctor. There . . . that room halfway down the hall, with the door ajar . . .

That had been her room. Her prison.

She made her way there, sneakers silent on the carpet, and pushed the door open.

They hadn't cared enough to clean up after themselves. The bed was just as she remembered it, and the medical trash still created vague visual lumps on the typing table turned bedside table. She supposed there had been no real point in cleaning up beyond this; anyone who stumbled across the room wouldn't have the faintest idea what had happened here, and anyone who knew it was significant also already knew it was here. These people knew how to get while the getting was good.

She surprised herself with her own reaction to the room—the flush of prickly heat across her face, the faint feeling of disassociation with her body. As if she'd float right on out of it while her body slumped to the ground. *Get a grip, Mickey Finn.*

She forced herself to enter the room . . . to walk around it. To look at the spot where the woman had sat, smiling coldly, offering threats as though they were perfectly reasonable options. She found herself humming, quavery at first, but soon enough it grew to real words, real notes, determined but low. A certain rainbow song, sung by a certain green frog puppet.

The darkness soaked up the words, leaving a profound silence as she trailed off, running the backs of her fingers down the bed. She wondered if they'd even left the handcuffs in the bathroom. She murmured optimistic lyrics into the room, not much more in tune than the original Muppet version.

Optimistic or not . . . there was nothing here to offer her hints about her situation. The other rooms offered no more, not even the clothes she'd arrived in. No conveniently discarded purse, no file on the woman named Naia, no stray driver's license. She supposed she could search the whole building, but she thought this floor held the best potential—why would they have spread themselves out? And it wouldn't leave her stuck here all night, vulnerable to discovery and imprisonment from either the cops or her mystery enemies.

But when she turned for the stairs, she found she couldn't quite bring herself to walk away. Humming about rainbows didn't help; the notes went wobbly and then stuck in her throat as she turned her back to the wall and slowly slid down until her bottom hit the carpet. There she stuck, her knees bent, her hands wrapped around her shins.

How the hell had she ended up here? Who the hell had she been before she'd gotten here? She let her head tip back against the wall and then let her mind wander. By now she knew better than to actively hunt answers and memories. She could make room for them, but if she went chasing after glimpses they could run farther and faster into the deepest corners of her mind than she could ever follow them.

Images surfaced, and smells. Emotions, unbidden and uncontrollable, gripping her, wringing her until her breath caught. Frightened faces, splattered blood, anger so thick it might smother her—

But no answers. Only more questions.

She pulled herself from the reverie, refocusing on the dim carpet patterns in diffuse city light, becoming aware of just how tightly she'd wrapped her fingers around her shins. Ow-worthy, that was. She forced them to relax, pushing up to her feet and shaking out her hands. "Some day we'll find it . . ." she whispered to that empty hallway, and turned to the stairs.

The whole city might have been asleep to judge by the empty streets to which Mickey emerged, but she knew better. She might not have a watch, but she discovered she trusted her sense of time. Late evening, that was all. Plenty of time to return to her little closet of a hotel room for a full night's sleep. And tomorrow . . .

She wasn't sure about tomorrow. She'd hoped to learn something here, and she'd only come away with more questions—and though she could now dress herself nicely enough to hit the public library without gathering attention, she didn't think she'd find anything in their newspaper archives that she hadn't found online. But she preferred hardcopy, so—

"See there?" she told herself, voice low in the darkness as she crossed the street and pondered taking the cross street against the light. "You did learn something." *I prefer hardcopy.*

One had to start *somewhere.*

But she wasn't so distracted by her situation and her options that she didn't notice a shadow detach itself from a building and head her way. "Dammit," she said out loud—quite loudly at that. "And I don't even have my superhero costume."

That made the shadow hesitate. It gave her time to spot the second shadow, a husky woman, as she approached from the other side. And Mickey didn't play any games. "I see you both," she said, "And I'm armed. So let's just chat from a distance." She had the knives, the harness wrapped awkwardly around her waist and under her shirt. She had the sling shot, and she took it from her back pocket, unfolding it—keeping it close to her body. Hidden, in this darkness.

"We'd prefer to talk in privacy," the man said.

"And I'd prefer to talk in strong daylight in the middle of a crowd, but I don't think either of us is getting what we want." Mickey considered that a moment. "Okay, you're actually pretty close to yours. So you start. Can I help you with something that doesn't involve pain or injury for me? Because if not, we're already done talking."

"We want to bring you in," the woman said. She'd managed to inch closer in the darkness.

Mickey casually loaded up the slingshot, loosing a desultory ball bearing without moving the slingshot away from her body—a side shot, just to let the woman know she'd been seen. To keep her wondering about the silent weapon that had bounced steel off the parking meter beside her. "I don't want to come. Next topic of conversation?"

"Look," the man said, holding up a hand to cut off the stronger response of his partner. "You've been compromised, but nobody's judging you. The problem is, you didn't come back in once you got away. You've got to see how that creates concerns. We know they're looking for you, so it just doesn't make any sense—"

"—Why the hell you didn't come in," the woman snapped. "We've kept this within the agency so far, but Irhaddan hasn't been so quiet that we can expect that to hold. Is that what you want? The FBI to get in on this? Homeland Security?"

Whoa.

Apparently this wasn't just about her. It wasn't just about her Mystery Naia. And her recent captors and their mad scientist doctors weren't the only ones she had to worry about. *Irhaddan?* "What I want," she said into their silence, "is to be left alone."

The woman made a rude noise. The man had somehow contrived to move closer. Mickey wasn't about to move back;

she had the slingshot loaded. If they wanted to hurt her, they'd have their weapons out, but they didn't. Not yet. Though she thought, in the darkness, that the woman's hand hovered near her waistband. The man gave his partner another hard look and turned his good cop act on Mickey. "You've got to know that won't happen. Things aren't going to get better . . . they're going to get worse. I know you—you probably think you can handle this, whatever it is. But you can't."

Mickey said, "I didn't ask you to come any closer. And I won't warn you again." That stopped him, enough for her to switch right back into casual voice and ask, "How'd you find me?" *And who are you?* What *agency?*

But she wasn't about to ask that one.

Still, the woman made her rude noise again. "As if we haven't had them tagged since they got here. It's been rather amusing, watching their frantic attempts to track you down. How they missed you at that gym—"

"Until now, you haven't had any better luck," Mickey pointed out. "And you didn't answer my question."

The man did, clearly willing to be more direct than the woman. "We've been watching this place. Not for you . . . you're just a bonus. Why did you come back here? We thought you were taken against your will, but this casts some doubt on that scenario."

"Oh, I was taken against my will, all right." She had no qualms about revealing that much—and no intentions of going anywhere with these people. They could well be from those who'd taken her in the first place—they knew she had no memory, wouldn't be able to put this encounter in context. She'd be an idiot to believe the tale this pair spun. "And what do they know about the gym?"

"Spaneas checked with some places the day they lost you," the man said. "Left a nice trail. We would have been all over it if we'd known you were loose—that it was *you* he was checking on." His voice held an honest grimace. "We were a little slow on that one. Only figured it out after they started looking so noisily."

Spaneas? Steve's last name? *Steve* had checked around without telling her?

Of course. It was probably SOP for him when someone new came staggering into the gym. Especially if they fainted.

"Maybe," the woman said, not nearly as casual as her partner, "we didn't realize it was her because we expected her to come to *us* if she shook them off."

"Maybe," Mickey said, sensing the end to their little detente, "I have my reasons." And she was right about the changing nature of things. The woman took a step, a bold one—one that dared Mickey to prove she had the weapons she'd claimed. And if the man seemed to know and respect her, the woman—if she knew Mickey at all—held no such opinion.

Her tough luck. Mickey let fly with a ball bearing, genuine slingshot ammo stolen from Steve. She didn't aim for the parking meter. She put some zing into it.

The woman yelped; she blistered the air, and if she'd been about to go for her gun, she forgot about it now. "*Sonuva*—you *shot*—"

"Oh, I did *not*," Mickey said. Already she had the slingshot reloaded. They might not have any idea what she was using, but now they knew for sure that she had it. "I bruised you. And I told you not to come any closer."

"You should have let me handle this," the man told her, stepping back with some disgust.

"Because you know her?" the woman spat, one hand clapped to her bruised thigh. "She sure as hell doesn't seem to know you. Or maybe she just doesn't like you."

"Or maybe I just need to do this my own way." Now Mickey

backed up, ready to put more distance between them. Right out into the road she went, stepping off the curb, easing between the bumpers of two parked cars. Someone was working late. "You don't have to like that. I don't like it, if you really want to know. But it's the only way to work this one." She rather liked that last bit. Almost as if she had the slightest idea what she was talking about.

"They're not going to allow that, Jane. You're only leaving you and your new asset vulnerable to the Irhaddanians—"

"Oh, let her," the woman snapped, nearly falling as she tested her leg.

For the first time, the man became intense. He turned to his partner, his voice low but still hard to miss. "We've got to know what she told them," he said. "We've got to find out if we're compromised!"

Mickey could have answered that . . . but she didn't think they'd listen. Not here on the street, with Mickey the one in control and her loyalty apparently already in question. *Now,* she thought, as they conferred with an intensity that she suspected to be a trick. The old *pretend to argue and suddenly leap on your quarry* trick.

Unless your quarry had already left.

She took a step back. Another. She cleared the cars; she waited until the argument rose to the kind of fevered pitch that, if she were correct, would lead to the moment of pouncing— and she silently dropped, putting herself behind the car.

The argument stuttered to a stop.

"Where—" the woman said.

"Did you see—?" the man asked.

"Note to self," the woman muttered. "That trick works a lot better in the daylight. And *damn,* my leg hurts. What the hell did she do to me?"

"There's no telling." The man's voice moved, pacing down

the street a few steps. "I told you she's deceptive, all that sweetness and light. The *singing*, for God's sake—all those damned oldies. Why do you think she's so good at what she does? She wouldn't be placed in prime territory if she weren't."

"Blah, blah, blah," the woman snapped. "You think you can stop *singing* her praises long enough to find her? I don't know if I can walk on this leg."

That sounded like a cue. Time to get them away from here. This wasn't exactly secure, as hiding places went. Wouldn't even score in a child's game of hide and seek. Mickey stuck the ball bearing in her cheek and silently felt around for road gravel, choosing the largest piece. She loaded the slingshot, aimed for a high fly ball trajectory, and sent the gravel at the nearest cross street.

. . . And the kids scattered, leaving behind one tearful little girl. Leaving Mickey to emerge from her hiding place in the roadside bushes, having already learned that the mystery assault was much more frightening than any tough face she could have put on. No one believed her tough faces. She was sweet . . . responsible . . . bearing up so well under her mother's death—

She was gonna get nailed if she didn't hold it together, that's what.

She sent out another piece of gravel, letting this one skitter across the distant pavement.

"Probably a rat," the woman muttered. Sour grapes from someone who should have respected the directive to back off and stay back. But she was already hop-running after the man.

Mickey wished she'd run into the man alone. She had the feeling they might have come to some kind of wary understanding—if nothing else, a stall. But she hadn't, and she didn't look back as she crept right on down the street, along the parked car behind her and to the chained sandwich shop sign board beyond it and then to the modernistic sculpture outside the small, upscale plastic surgery clinic—and then she was up and running, silent and fleet.

And by then she was thinking, too.

These people knew about the gym. If they'd been truthful about being separate from those who had taken her, then *those* people knew about the gym, now, too. The Irhaddanians. And just because Mickey wasn't there any longer didn't mean they wouldn't wreak havoc looking for her at her last confirmed location.

Go to the gym, possibly lead the nasty people back there on her trail. Or don't go, don't warn Steve . . . and leave him completely unprepared for the kind of people who employed mad scientists, kidnapped those with whom they wanted to converse, and used trickery and violence to get what they wanted.

Of course, for all she knew, she was that kind of person, too. Certainly the man had held her skills—dubious-sounding skills—in some esteem.

"Any way you look at it, Steve, you lose." She muttered it out loud, and in some way it cinched her decision. For even if she felt the weight of truth behind her words, she wasn't, she discovered, quite smart enough to let the inevitable just simply happen.

Some day we'll find it . . .

But not today. Today—tonight—she'd see about just keeping them alive.

CHAPTER 11

Steve swam out of the depths of a foggy, hallucinatory sleep to a foggy, hallucinatory awareness. The bed, he slowly realized, was jiggling. Tiny little bounces.

Totally atypical of his bed at any time.

"Ise gaiduri," he muttered at it.

The bed giggled. Just a little.

Okay, *that* definitely wasn't right.

His eyes were reluctant, but he forced them open anyway, and found an almost familiar dark form on the edge of his bed—found too, that the giant space of the warehouse apartment was—barely—lit by the small lamp at the entrance.

"There you are." The dark form used an almost familiar voice, too.

And then quite suddenly the foggy, hallucinatory quality of the moment vanished, and he knew exactly who sat here on his bed. The shock of it jolted him instantly, completely awake. He sat straight up, grabbed the sheet to make sure he stayed covered, and for the first time doubted his habit of sleeping in the nude. "That door was locked!"

"Not very well," she said, and sounded apologetic.

"Oh, I get it. Just another one of those things you *do* remember. Breaking and entering."

She crossed her arms—or he thought she did. Too dark to be sure. "If I'd had any idea you were such a grumpy riser, I'd have thrown something at you from a safe distance."

117

All the pains of the previous day slammed into him as his shock faded. He groaned, put a hand to his so very sore ribs—didn't dare touch his pounding skull. The details of the past twenty-four hours jammed themselves into his awareness, and he groaned again at the memory of the situation he'd gotten himself into. At the image of a weirdly masked super-heroine coming to his rescue and then spending a gentle night tending him. *Aurgh.*

"I thought you might feel that way. I brought you some ibuprofen," she said. "Boy, do you have a lot of supplements."

Of course she'd been through his things. Because that made it all so perfect.

Mutely, not trusting his tongue, he held out his hand. She placed several small round pills in his palm, her rough fingertips brushing his skin. He would have swallowed them on spit alone, but she reached to his bedside table and came up with a glass of water he hadn't left there, then settled back on the bed. He glanced at the glow of the clock and found it to be almost midnight. He'd slept most of the afternoon, all of the evening, and still felt like a bear woken in the middle of hibernation.

The water had ice in it. It felt wonderful on his dry throat.

He marshaled his thoughts, hunting for the most concise path to coherency. "What's going on?"

"I used your computer," she told him.

"Again?"

"Again." She shifted on the bed. "Just so you know. I don't want you to think I'm sneaking around. I need your trust right now."

He laughed, sudden and irrepressible, and then clenched his teeth on a little yelp of pain.

"It'll be better once you move around a little." She said it as though she thought moving around might be imminent.

"Just tell me," he said, teeth still gritted.

She took a long, slow breath, exhaling just as slowly. He thought it sounded like surrender. "I found some more people who've been looking for me. And they—and the Irhaddanians—know for sure that I was here. I think they'll come looking. I think they'll expect you to know where I am. I think they're not going to take no for an answer."

"The *Irhaddanians?*" Steve got stuck on the word, tried to make sense of it. "What the hell do the Irhaddanians want with you?"

"That's the part I haven't figured out yet," she admitted. "But there's not much doubt about it. I barely got away—I used your advice. You know, about running away. It worked."

"Somehow I don't think you need my advice." But the words were just buying time while he tried to make sense of it all. "You think they'll come after me? The *Irhaddanians?* The others?"

"Pretty sure," she agreed.

Enough of the darkness. He needed to see her face, to think things through with his eyes wide open. He stretched for the lamp, discovered he'd pushed it aside with the latest hardcover book, and finally reached it.

The sheet slipped.

Mickey said, "Oh."

It would have destroyed his dignity to snatch for cover, so he kept his movement deliberate. She raised her gaze to smile at him—a strange combination of sweetness and appreciation. And then she said, "I'm afraid they'll hurt you." And her smile faded, leaving behind what had been there all along—a newly haunted expression.

Steve shook his head. "You know, I think I need you to start closer to the beginning. As close as you can get."

She hitched herself further onto the bed and faced him, drawing her knees up to rest her chin on them. "There is no begin-

119

ning, Steve. There's only being plunged into the middle of it."

He squelched his impulse for a crabby response. She was right enough. He rubbed a thoughtful hand over his bruised ribs and said, "You woke up handcuffed to a bed and you had no memory. You were drugged with something experimental and the doctor doesn't know if you'll ever remember. And then there's Naia." He watched her, found those clear blue eyes slightly widened.

"You remember that," she murmured. "Naia . . . Naia's the one I have to find."

"And now suddenly a country a zillion miles away is part of it. And another group."

She seemed to find that easier to deal with. "They said I was one of them. That I should come with them so they could get me sorted out." She snorted, a clear indication of the probability of *that*. "For all I know, they're with the first people and they're just taking advantage of my memory loss. Though I have to admit they played it pretty well."

Steve rolled it all together in his mind a moment, then shook his head. "It doesn't come together to make much sense."

"Except," Mickey said, raising her chin from her knees and hitting the word with emphasis, "that this latest group knows I was here. And they said the first people—the Irhaddanians—know it too. The man said, 'Spaneas checked with some places the day they lost you.' " She sent a piercing look his way. "Awfully Greek-sounding, that name. *Spaneas.*"

Guilt pierced him right along with that gaze. "I did," he said, struck by the sudden understanding of where his standard inquiries had led them. Struck by the sudden realization that he believed her. "I always do, when someone lands here. They know me . . . they work with me . . ." The halfway houses, the various low-cost and free clinics, social services . . .

Dammit, *he believed her.*

She sighed, waved away the apology. "You couldn't have known. I sure didn't."

He let a moment pass. Not one in which he was thinking about any of it in particular, but in which he was just *being*. Achy, bruised, and immersed in a strange companionship with a woman who'd broken into his apartment in the middle of the night to sit on his bed. And then, when she did nothing more than rub a finger over her lower lip in what seemed like that same sort of non-thought, he asked, "Where do you go from here?"

"Naia," she said. She drew herself together, her arms wrapping around her legs. "She's in trouble. I don't know what it is, only that I'm involved, and that the Irhaddanians wanted to know about her. She trusts me. I think . . . I *think* I'm somehow responsible for her." She looked at him, wrinkled her nose in a sudden wince. "God, I hope I haven't led her to a life of crime or anything. She doesn't seem the type—" But that notion was apparently too painful, for she dropped it and added, "That's what I was doing on your computer. Naia. Irhaddan. Guess what? The president's daughter, Naia Mejjati, is attending school at Stanford. How's that land on your coincidence scale?"

Good God. What the *hell*—"You've got to be kidding!"

She only lifted one corner of her mouth in a wry little smile, one shoulder in a wry little shrug. "Just so you know," she said. "If I'm really caught up in something international, they're not going to give up. They're not going to leave you alone just because you *might* not know anything."

"Turn your back," Steve told her. At the question on her face, he made a little twirly gesture. "You. Turn your back. If international thugs are going to burst into my home at any moment, I'd really like to be dressed."

"Ah," she said. "That's a shame." But she slipped off the bed and turned her back, and he slid free of the covers to snatch up the nearest pair of jeans. At the sound of the zip and snap, she turned to face him, wearing that same sweet, appreciative look at his naked torso.

Steve plunged his hand in a random drawer and groped for a shirt. "Should I even ask what you were doing this evening in the first place?" She'd met up with the second group—her people?—somehow.

"Different kind of breaking and entering," she said. "I went back to where I woke up. It was abandoned . . . but they—whoever they were—were watching." She hesitated long enough so he turned, loose cotton weave pullover in hand. She said, "It was all there, by the way. All the parts I remembered."

"Okay," he said, and caught her eye. "I'm in, Mickey. I get it. You're not off your meds. You're just the most extraordinary woman I've ever met, in the most extraordinary circumstances I never imagined."

She exhaled relief. "Then you'll find a safe place to wait this out. You'll take your own advice and run away."

Wait this out? When he'd seen so much of it? When for once in his life he'd been given a stray who wasn't doomed simply because of who she was? "I didn't say that."

She tossed her head in annoyance, understanding the implication immediately. "You don't want to be with *me*. I've got a thing or two to remember before I can move forward. Naia . . . pottery shelves . . ." She trailed off, and shook her head again—this time in annoyance at herself. "I'm headed out for another night of harvesting muggers—I've got to hurry or I'll miss prime time. Even if you *wanted* to be involved in that—in any of it—you're not up for it."

"I can afford a hotel room," Steve informed her. "Maybe not two of them, but we can find something with two beds—"

For the first time, she seemed to lose her composure. "It's not your problem!" And then she whirled away so he saw nothing but her stiff, tense back, her arms at her side and her fists clenched with frustration. "Except of course it is. I've *made* it your problem."

"No," he said, surprising himself. "I mean, yes. But I could go off and find myself a room somewhere, Mickey. I just don't want to. I want to help. It might not be much, but a good night's sleep is something—and it might just improve that memory of yours. You can harvest muggers another time."

"Why?" The frustrated word sounded torn from her; she still didn't turn to look at him. "Why would you? Why do you *care?*"

That was easy enough. He'd seen the need on her face when she talked of Naia—the need to make things all right. He knew that feeling well enough. He asked, "Why do *you?*"

For a moment he thought it was the wrong thing to say. Her shoulders didn't relax; her fists didn't unclench. And then quite suddenly it all happened at once, and she walked to his refrigerator as though she owned it. "Let's bring food, then. We're too late for room service, and I'm starving."

"All right," he said, and found that he, too, had let go of a tension that had made his bruises ache—found that his voice had softened to a satisfied murmur. "Let's bring food."

Mickey had her hand on the door—the one she'd found too easy to pick with a cotter pin from an old weight set downstairs—before she heard the brief rustle of noise from downstairs. Steve literally ran into her, laden with tote bags of food and his own version of an overnight bag—a stuffed backpack.

But the words of question died forming on his lips, and he caught her eye in query. She tipped her head—*listen*—and he did. It took a moment, but the noise repeated.

They backed away from the door. "You left the place unlocked?" he asked her, just short of accusation—but he kept his voice low without being warned.

She shook her head, distracted . . . her gaze on the wall of the open floor plan that held his practice targets. "*You* left it unlocked," she informed him. "I only had to pick my way into your apartment, not the whole gym."

He closed his eyes and groaned. "I was so out of it when I got back here . . ."

He still looked out of it. And his shirt might cover the bruises on his torso, but she'd seen them only moments before and she knew what he was dealing with. "Think ahead, not behind," she told him, and then grinned. "Of course, that's easy for me to say. What do I have but *ahead?*"

He stared at her for one taken aback instant, and then returned the favor, taking her completely by surprise when he wrapped one hand around the back of her head and pulled her in to kiss her forehead. While she still blinked, he said, "You're a breath of . . . *something,* Mickey Finn. Let's think ahead."

"Cool." She nodded at the end of the room with all the pointy things in it. "You as good with that stuff as I think you might be?" Something downstairs crashed; Steve winced. So did Mickey, though she kept it inside. "Guess they haven't found the light switches. What about it?"

He shook his head, just once. "I started targeting when I was a kid. After Zander got sick. It was either that or take out my teenage angst on kneading bread dough, and that was too damned close to what they had Zander doing before they took him seriously."

"In other words," she said softly, "you never considered you might use your skills on someone else one day."

"No," he breathed. "I never did."

"Can you?" She asked it seriously. "Because I can cover us. But I still need your help to get out of here."

"Ohh, yeah," he said. "They crossed that line when they came onto my personal turf." He appeared to give it second thought.

"Unless it's a stray cat?"

She almost laughed. *Almost.* "We should be so lucky. Grab some gear. And grab me another brace of knives—?"

He shot her a sharp look, though he'd dropped the tote bags and didn't hesitate in his silent journey to the other side of the lofty room. Oops. He hadn't noticed yet, she supposed, that she'd already been here. Too busy being beaten and sleeping it off. She shrugged and returned to the door, giving the tote bags a regretful glance on the way. She suspected they'd be jettisoned before all was said and done. Probably not even make it out the door.

The quiet clank of carefully handled metal served as background noise while Mickey listened at the door. Murmurs she couldn't hear, a few disagreeing words—they'd found the right switch, and the stairwell flooded with light. Yup, they were coming up. Not casually discouraged . . . not plain old thieves hunting on a pilfer-and-run. She glanced behind, found Steve behind her, already handing her a brace of knives—bigger than those she'd taken the first time. She hefted them. "Sweet," she said, her voice barely a whisper. He'd strung a bow for himself, and had the quiver hanging off his shoulder. She understood then that if he was going to do this, it wouldn't be halfway.

She put her head close to his, her mouth close to his ear. "Move back with me and flank the door. Keep an angle, so we aren't in each other's way. Hit 'em hard and fast—and then go through them."

"Shock and awe?" Steve murmured.

"Shock and awe and run away," she corrected. She watched him head for position—and then, with footsteps audible on the stairs, she yanked the cord for little lamp—the only light that entry switch controlled.

"Here," Steve murmured, anticipating her need to orient on him in the darkness, and she put herself into place—the slingshot unfolded and ready in her back pocket, ball bearings waiting in her lower lip, and the knives in hand. In the darkness, she didn't expect to cause serious injury . . . she didn't *want* to cause serious injury. But a little chaos would be just the thing—and if it made the intruders think twice about following them, that would be fine, too.

The footsteps hesitated outside the door; shadows blocked the faint stream of light coming in from outside. Two male voices whispered in hasty conversation . . . not in accord. Not quite sure of their plan. Stretching the damned moment out.

Mickey hummed the *Jaws* theme under her breath. Steve desperately stifled his amused reaction, arrows clinking faintly in their quiver.

And then the men decided on the bold approach. They threw the door open and strode into the darkness, silhouetted by the stairway light. One of them slapped futilely at the wall, finding the expected switch and not getting any response from it.

That's all the time Mickey gave them.

She made her first throw count, feeling the heft of the knife, judging its balance—and even then knowing that too much rode on luck. Overhand, smooth and swift, she released straight and true at the end of the arc, letting the knife handle slip unhindered through her fingers. The blade's impact came heavy and muffled, a distinctive and unforgettable wet thump.

Steve might have heard it; he certainly heard the man's reaction. The twang of the string sang loudly in the darkened room; the thump of impact came tidier than that of the knife. As close as he was, a full draw would have sent an arrow the better part of the way through a man's body.

One man staggered against the light; the other threw himself down, a deliberate movement. Gunshot split the room, the noise staggering Mickey even though she'd half expected it. *"Go!"* she told Steve, throwing three more knives one after the other and reaching for the slingshot even as she ran over the man on the floor—literally ran over him, feeling the give of flesh beneath her sneakers. She and Steve collided in the doorway and burst through it together, leaping down the stairs two and three at a time until Mickey jumped the last five, landing in a crouch and twisting back just in time to see a man stagger through the second-floor doorway, leading with his gun. She snagged Steve's arm and bolted around the corner of the enclosed stairwell, her ears ringing from a second gunshot and a third that was purely wasted on plaster.

For an instant she found herself disoriented, blinking in the strong light, but Steve had his bearings and took the lead, heading down the back hallway for the alley door.

That door slammed outward, blocked by another large body. Mickey had a reeling moment of déjà vu—this was the man she'd collided with outside the building during her first escape, and this time he was ready for her. Ready for Steve, too, who had no room to draw the bow in this hallway.

"Down!" she cried, dropping a bearing into the slingshot pocket and pulling it back at the same time, low at her hip where she had the most power. At this distance, aim was no issue.

Steve threw himself to the side as another damned gunshot rattled Mickey's head—she had no idea if Steve had been hit and no idea how he couldn't have been, but she loosed the ball bearing on the fly, diving at the other wall on the way. *Stay on the move, split the targets—*

The man's head jerked back; his arms windmilled as he lost his balance, teetering back, gun waving.

Mickey didn't waste time on finesse. While Steve pushed away from the wall, she bounced past him and hit the teetering man feet first, riding him right out the door and then flinging herself aside, into the corner where the dumpster met the back of the building. "Wait!" she called back to Steve, and took the moment to assess the alley and all the shadows where the city light didn't reach. But nothing out there moved, not even in response to the man who now rolled around on his back, hands covering his face. Safe enough, for the little time they could spare. She returned to the man, wrenched the semi-auto out of his hand without paying attention to his groans, and gestured Steve out.

Iron fingers clamped around her ankle as Steve leaped out the door right over the man; Mickey reacted with decisive callousness, stomping her other foot on his already damaged face and making no attempt to keep from going down—she simply rolled, coming right back to her feet and already grabbing Steve's arm, tugging him away from the open door, the cursing man, and the clatter of noise from inside that meant one of the two invaders was coming to join the fray.

They made it only to the end of the alley before reaching a dark shape on the ground, one Mickey barely managed to vault as Steve dodged around it. With a gasp of both effort and shock, she recognized the man from the underpass, the one who had given her a hard time. He seemed entirely out of place here, as though two worlds had inexplicably collided.

And just that fast, she understood. *Betrayal.* The poster at the police community bulletin board. The man hadn't wanted her in his world, and he'd found a way to get rid of her—to gather up a reward in the doing of it. He just hadn't counted on who he was dealing with—or he'd else gotten wise to their nature and they'd realized it.

This time it was Steve who pulled Mickey onward. "C'mon," he said, panting with effort, the bow and quiver turning his dark shape into something bizarre. "We can't—"

It was all he needed to say. Mickey tore herself away from the body and put herself into a serious sprint, running down the cross-alley with Steve beside her and everything she knew of her past and present pounding at her heels.

CHAPTER 12

"They *knew* I'd been there," Mickey said. "What did he say to them to bring them back? *Why?*"

They hadn't spoken during their flight across city blocks, breaking pattern to reach the hotels near the convention center. Nice hotels; pricey. Willing to take them even at this hour. Steve put a room on his credit card without batting an eye, and Mickey . . .

Mickey somehow felt right at home. The classy furnishings, the padded carpet . . . *the whisper of silk and chiffon, the strut of high heels, the caress of beautifully draping cloth and a hint of expensive perfume.*

Whoa. She shook herself out of the sensory conflict, putting herself back into the sneakers, lightweight drawstring yoga pants, and sporty top that she'd been in all day. Back into a hotel that was nice, but not opulent . . . following Steve Spaneas into an elevator to their hotel room after evading capture, stumbling over the dead man who had probably betrayed them, and bolting through the city streets with such unrelenting drive that she still felt breathless. No conversation, no debate about how to proceed, just hasty, somehow tacit retreat to this place.

The room had two beds with mints on the pillows and nothing else worth notice. Steve dropped his backpack and bow on the bed—the hotel clerk had been very careful not to look at the bow—and Mickey . . .

Mickey's things were still at Hotel Fleabag.

She sat. Steve sat across from her. And for a long, silent moment they only regarded one another in silence, until Mickey absorbed the signs of pain drawing on Steve's Mediterranean-cast features and the lingering disbelief in his eyes.

Mickey thought she should probably feel the same . . . but somehow it hadn't taken her by surprise at all. Not the violence, not the death, not the betrayal.

That's it, then. I don't want to remember who I really am. I don't think I'm going to like me.

She broke their silence with quiet words. "You knew him, didn't you? I'm sorry."

Steve shook his head; he didn't look as though he'd truly absorbed any of what had just happened to them. "He was a hermit more than anything . . . just didn't fit in, and liked the freedom of that life. He got odd jobs regularly . . . he isn't one of the ones I worried about—" He cut himself short, there, as though that were the crux of it—and Mickey thought she understood. Steve worried about them all; had seen too many of them go down. Sad endings, difficult destinies. But this was one he hadn't expected.

She mused, "I just met him the one time. I took some stuff to the underpass, after I left you at the hotel . . . this morning." Only this morning? "He grilled me. And he said—"

He'd said she was sweet on Steve.

He wasn't so shell-shocked that he didn't notice she'd stopped—or the significance of it. He caught her gaze; he stood, filling the small space between the two beds.

She let him loom over her. In a moment he'd feel silly and sit back down; Steve Spaneas wasn't the kind of guy who used size against someone—or who often had the opportunity. "I think," she said carefully, "he may have felt he had to make a choice. He—"

"Anthony," Steve supplied, and he'd already taken a step

131

back, looking almost confused to find himself pulling intimidation tactics.

"Anthony . . . he was concerned about me. That I was trouble. He could have seen me on that poster, and felt that having people looking for me would be a problem for the underpass people. Or someone from our cast of characters might have come looking for me. And he knew I was swe—I mean, he had accused me of being sweet on you—he had no reason to keep that a secret." It seemed obvious to her, but this caring man wasn't getting it. Couldn't think that way. She tried again. "It's possible that the Irhaddanians weren't coming after *me*. That they weren't expecting me to be there at all."

He looked stricken, those dark deep eyes widening; he finally sat again. "You think he told them they should *use* me—"

Mickey was the one to get up; she found herself half-kneeling beside him, taking one hand in hers. "Steve. He's not—he wasn't—used to playing these games. There's no reason he would think that way. More likely he mentioned it and the Irhaddanians took it from there."

"Then why—" he stopped, turned his head away, his jaw working. "*Why?*"

She tightened her hand over his. "We may never know. Could be they killed him just because he'd talked to them, could identify them if anything happened to you. Could be they said enough so he realized what they were up to and came to warn you."

He took a sudden deep breath. "That works for me. I'm going to go with it. And if you hear otherwise—"

"I'm not expecting to," she told him. She didn't add that it wasn't because she felt that scenario to be correct . . . it was because she simply never expected to learn anything else about it. In her own heart, she felt the man she'd met at the underpass was perfectly capable of doing and saying whatever he thought would keep him safe—keep the whole underpass area safe. He'd had no way to understand the kind of people he was dealing with.

"So now they're after me," Steve mused. "Not just you anymore."

"Looks that way." She rubbed a thumb over his, suddenly realized what she was doing, and backed off to reclaim her seat on the bed. "Just a guess. But they had no reason to think I'd be at the gym, and they came loaded for bear. Makes me think it's a good guess."

Wearily, he reached down to pull his sneakers off, standing to toss them at the chair in the corner. "I suppose I should be flattered. Three of them."

"Well," she said, and looked him up and down most obviously. "You do teach self-defense for a living. And work out regularly. And have lots of pointy weapons."

And she really, really, hadn't meant to be looking just below waist level when she said that.

He was kind; he merely raised one eyebrow at her and let it pass. "Then where do we go from here?"

She tried to keep her voice upbeat. "A couple of days here should do it, I'd think. Close the gym, keep your people safe." He didn't look happy at the idea, but he didn't protest. "It's me they're really after, and I don't think they'll spend a lot of time on a failed strategy. They seemed to be in a real hurry to get the information they wanted."

"And exactly what was that?" He yanked the covers down, scattering mints, his brusque movement the only clue to his state of mind.

She shrugged. "What has Naia said to you? Where do you see Naia? Who does she spend time with? How did you meet Naia? How do you feel about Naia? Is she important to you?" Another shrug. "Honestly, I got the feeling they wanted to ask me something more directly, but as soon as they realized I couldn't remember anything—even before they really believed it—they started playing coy. Trying to get answers without giving anything away."

"And of course you have no idea what they were really driving at." He picked up a pillow, scrunching it in his hands.

Mickey winced. Wouldn't want to be that pillow right now. "I think it's obvious I'm involved with Naia somehow, and that they're concerned about what Naia might have told me. How those pieces fit into the larger picture . . . not a clue."

He gave the pillow a blank look and tossed it aside. "Any plans for *getting* a clue?"

Her throat suddenly felt clogged. "Steve," she said, "I'm so sorry. I never meant to get you involved in anything like this when I asked to stay. I had no idea—"

He gave a short laugh, bitter-edged. "That's the whole problem, isn't it? Doesn't answer the question, though. Where do we go from here?"

She tipped her head at him, puzzled. "I thought I had. Just stay here a couple of days . . . by then they should be trying something else. I probably shouldn't even stay the night, but I'm so tired . . . I'll clear out tomorrow morning and keep poking around."

"No," he said, and his voice was as hard as she'd ever heard it. Suddenly he loomed over her again, and this time he meant every bit of it. This time he pulled her up by the arms, and pulled her close. Close enough so he could look straight in her eyes, showing her every bit of determination there. "You don't get it. I'm past running away. It's good for the moment . . . it's good for the kids. But not for me. Not this time."

As if he deserved to be dragged further into a mess she couldn't even define—didn't even know in which direction lay safety, or if he'd be on the side of good guys or bad guys. "Steve—"

"No," he said, a word heavy with finality. "Now . . . where do we go from here?"

She didn't have an answer for him. They'd gone to bed without such things, sleeping in the unfamiliar silences of the hotel room with mere feet separating the beds and an overwhelming and awkward awareness of each other's presence. Mickey felt it; she heard it in his voice. But soon enough his breathing deepened, and the sound of it lulled her into a light sleep.

Not for long.

She woke straight into alertness, so alert that she felt for the knives she'd left on the bedside table. But moments of listening revealed nothing other than Steve's deep breathing, his occasional soft snore. Moments of listening revealed that the noise was all in her head, panicked clamorings of responsibility and need.

A man was dead in her wake.

NaiaNaiaNaia . . .

She'd learned very little about Naia on the web. Stanford was close-mouthed about her, and wisely so—Irhaddan's president wouldn't allow his daughter to attend a school where she was easily exposed to examination and speculation. Stanford had already established its ability to keep high-profile students away from the limelight—various actors, another president's daughter—they'd been vulnerable, too, and they'd been protected.

From basic news sources she only gathered that the girl had been home-schooled and yet passed her college prep tests with flying colors, that she returned to her country at every break, and that although she wasn't worldly, she was plenty intelligent.

The perfect asset.

Mickey stiffened, her hands clenching around the covers. The perfect asset? What did that mean? What part of her had said that?

And thinking about it, as usual, made every trace of the memory flee into the inaccessible recesses of her mind.

She could have screamed. *Would* have screamed, if not for her sleeping companion—a man drawn into Mickey's shifting world of too many dangers and too few answers.

She shoved the covers aside, baring her legs to the cool air-conditioned room. She wore her stretchy sport top, but had rinsed the bottoms out and devoutly hoped they would dry before morning. Because come morning . . . she had to do something. *Anything.* And for that she needed a hook . . . something that would help her answer Steve's question of the night before. *Where do we go from here?*

That's how she found herself on his bed, a queen-size with plenty of room for her to ease beside him and sit cross-legged on top of the covers. On second thought she pulled a stray pillow onto her lap, and then she just sat there. Getting here had been so easy, so natural—but waking him up was another matter.

Finally, she whispered into the darkness. "Steve. Wake up."

He slept on.

No wonder. Still recuperating from that beating, and she'd dragged him across town on foot. Quietly, she leaned over to rap a knuckle against the headboard, not far from his ear.

His hand flashed up to close around her wrist. Her startled gasp turned into a grin quickly enough. Steve, for all his caring save-the-world ways, underestimated himself when it came to his physical nature. "Shh," she said, all too aware of what those first, disoriented moments of wakefulness could be like. "It's Mickey."

Slowly, he released her. "You're on my bed *again?*"

"I am," she confirmed.

"You woke me up *again?*"

"I totally did."

Silence followed, into which he finally sighed.

"But this time you're wearing something," she pointed out, most helpfully. And then winced at the pained noise he made as he pushed himself up to sit beside her. The bed shifted beneath her and darned if it didn't feel almost companionable.

"What's up?" he said, and the words were muffled as he rubbed a hand down the side of his face and reached for the bedside light.

Mickey would have preferred the darkness. If she was hidden from herself, she should be able to hide from everyone. Too bad it wasn't working out that way. She squinted as her eyes adjusted. "I can't sleep."

Yeah, that had come out well. "I mean . . . there's just so much going on in my head, and I can't reach it. If I go after it, it slides away. I thought . . . maybe if we talked . . . or maybe if we did word association."

His reaction was more perceptive than she expected. "You remembered something else?"

"Something," she admitted. "It just doesn't make sense on its own. I was thinking of Naia—who she is, both as a figurehead and as a person." *Huge dark eyes, fearful but trusting.* "And I thought that she'd be the perfect asset. And then I had no idea what I meant."

His eyes narrowed, as though it meant something to him. "Irhaddan," he said, making it a question. Word association.

"Big mean guys." Nothing new there.

"Foreign."

"Embassy." Well, obvious enough to anyone who lived near San Francisco, which housed a number of embassies; the society pages were always listing one event or another . . . "Antiques," she added slowly.

"Foreign antiques?" He shook his head, letting it pass. "Gun."

"SIG P22 . . . 6." Dismayed, she barely spoke the last number. She had a gun. She must have a gun.

He didn't give her any time to think about it. "Antiques."

That brightened her. "Champagne!"

He snorted. "You . . . you're one of a kind, Mickey Finn."

But her grin barely made it to her face, replaced by a big fat lump in her throat. "Alone," she whispered, keeping up the game. "Champagne and silk and indescribably good food and . . . a cat."

"Station."

"Chief," she said, and made a face at him. "What kind of sense . . . ?"

He didn't answer directly. "Dead."

"Drop." *Sturdy shelves divided into niches and half-finished pottery projects, brick wall looming high behind them, diffuse light of a cavernous room, carefree laughter . . .* "Pottery?" She let herself flop backward, legs still crossed, and barely missed the headboard. "This is pointless."

"I'm not so sure." And his words sounded so careful that Mickey raised her head to look at him and then tried to sit up, but the bed wasn't firm enough and she only floundered.

Steve took her hand and pulled her upright, and there she was, ruffled and frustrated and knee to knee with him. He looked down at their hands and put hers on the bed, releasing it to give his own hand a puzzled kind of glance. And then he said, "I lived with a paranoid schizophrenic when I was growing up. I spent a lot of time hanging with him on the street . . . hanging with him in clinics and hospitals. There were your average number of tin foil hats, alien abduction concerns, and the governmentally persecuted. I did my share of reading . . . it was a kind of self-defense, you know?"

"Reading," she repeated blankly.

"Sure. I figured if the topic of conversation was going to be government conspiracies, I'd damned well have something to talk about. It was a while ago, but not so long that your words don't mean anything to me. Station chief. That's CIA. Dead drop—standard spy stuff. Foreign embassies—your basic spy breeding grounds."

Mickey groaned. "So not the innocent victim." She flopped back again.

This time he didn't hesitate; he pulled her upright, and didn't let go of her hand. "That doesn't mean you're guilty, either. You really think you're part of the problem? Why not that you're trying to *solve* the problem?"

She pulled her hand free and covered her face—pure cowardly retreat. "Because," she said, and her voice barely made it to the audible range, "it would be so awful if I was wrong."

And again he captured her hands, pulling them away from her face to cup them in his as he leaned close. "Okay, then," he said, startling her with his intensity. "I'll just have to hope for the both of us."

"But—"

"Just this once," he told her, fiercely enough so she wondered which of them he was trying to convince. "Just *one more time.*"

Mickey woke in a strange arrangement of arms and bedcovers, pillow optional. She took a deep, slow breath, not surprised to find herself surrounded by the scent of a certain Greek self-defense instructor. On top of the covers, but he'd flipped the bedspread back over her so she both slept on it and slept under it. Under her cheek, his arm gave an involuntary twitch.

Sunlight streamed through the carelessly closed curtains; a squint at the hotel alarm clock told her they'd slept well into the morning. Through the room's door, she heard the sound of a vacuum, a brusque knock on a nearby door. "Housekeeping!"

Oh, please. Just a few more moments. Not being chased, not trying to remember . . . not being alone. Just being with this intense, caring man who'd seen so many unhappy endings and yet who still thought he could carry her through this.

He had no idea what he'd gotten into. How could he? Mickey didn't.

But she was beginning to suspect.

Just a few more moments . . .

Steve took a sudden deep breath, a waking breath. He stiffened—that moment of realization. Mickey smiled into his arm and said in a low voice, "Oh my God! I've woken up in a strange bed with some woman! I don't even know her name!"

He relaxed, his laugh nothing more than a gust of warm air on her neck. "That's okay," he told her, his voice morning rough. "She doesn't know it, either."

She rolled away from him and off the bed, rueful to leave the nest he'd made for her. But this wasn't a day she could wait for . . . this was a day she had to go out and chase down. "Dibs on the shower," she said, stretching mightily. She turned, not surprised to find him watching, and affected great shock. "Good God," she said. "All that beard *overnight?*"

He gathered his dignity. "Most of it was there last night. You just didn't notice."

"Mostly we were moving too fast," she agreed. "You want the bathroom before I declare it off-limits, you'd better hurry."

He took her seriously enough, and vacated the bed. She put the Do Not Disturb sign on the door and plunged into the bathroom as soon as he left the door open for her, peeling off her shirt and underwear and deciding to wash them right along with her. With luck, she could recover her things from hotel fleabag, but until then she'd get clean when she had the chance. A quick scrub with overly floral hotel soap and shampoo, and she dug out the toothpaste from the compact kit Steve had left in the bathroom, scrubbing it over her teeth with the corner of a washcloth. Putting her wet clothes back on rated right up there with puddles of dead worms after rain, but at least the pants were dry.

Steve knocked on the door even as she attempted to finger comb her straight hair into something styled; the image regarding her in the mirror wasn't quite right. Cut-rate clothes, top-rate haircut.

Tendrils of hair against her neck, the slight tug of an up-do against her scalp, champagne sharp on her tongue . . .

"You have any scissors?" she asked, still staring at herself. Bright eyes . . . too bright. Too memorable. She needed shaded lenses or sunglasses.

"If you're decent, open up. I got you a touristy T-shirt to put on. That outfit of yours is a little . . . eye-catching."

Great minds think alike, she decided. Time to tone down the amnesiac so the amnesiac could go hunting. She opened the door. "Scissors?"

He handed her a heather grey shirt with a colorful sun logo and *San Jose* in a fanciful font. "Cuticle scissors, I think," he said, his expression full of doubt.

"They'll do," Mickey told him.

CHAPTER 13

"I can't believe you did that." Steve looked at Mickey, looked at the mess of hair in the sink, looked back to the cuticle-scissor hack-job on Mickey's caramel brown hair.

"Hey," she said airily. "I left enough to trim into something decent when this is all done. And it's not that bad. It's just not what it was."

"It's not what it was," he agreed, and had to grin at her. It wasn't so bad at that . . . and he couldn't help but appreciate that she'd simply done what needed to be done. "Suppose I should grow a beard?"

She snorted. "That'll take what . . . another two days at most?" She pulled the T-shirt he'd brought right on over the obviously wet stretchy sports top, much to his relief.

With dignity, he said, "It takes at least three days."

"Well, never mind then." She rinsed out the sink and vacated the bathroom, gesturing that it was all his.

He closed the door, had a sudden thought, and popped back out again. She looked back at him in surprise, and he said, "Promise you won't take off. Promise I won't find myself alone in this room when I come back out."

Only the faintest flicker of annoyance crossed her face. Yeah, she'd been thinking about it . . . but she wasn't going to make a big deal of it. "I suppose if I don't promise, then you're not going to take a shower."

He smiled most meaningfully.

142

She flopped back on her bed. The one she *hadn't* slept in. He took it as surrender and returned to the bathroom.

Didn't mean he didn't make it quick. Or that he didn't nick himself three times with the haste of his shaving. When he turned the water off he could tell the television was on, but didn't find it reassuring. In a sudden surge of concern, he yanked the bathroom door open—

To the sight of Mickey dancing on the bed in cheerleader fashion, singing lyrics that included her own name. That old Hey Mickey song.

He sagged against the door in relief.

Then he retreated back into the bathroom. He combed his hair, dutifully patient with the tangled curls, and he gave it a part that would hold for about five minutes. Then he fumbled loudly with the doorknob, and emerged to find Mickey sitting in the chair in the corner, slightly flushed but completely relaxed, swinging her foot. "Hey," she said, and turned the television off with a click of the remote. "Guilty pleasure movie. *Bring It On.* You know it?"

He gave a single, baffled shake of his head, and moved to his backpack—stuffing what little he'd taken out right back in. Mickey reached for the thick phone book she'd left on the table and began flipping through yellow pages. By the time Steve made it over there to look over her shoulder, she'd found the pottery listings. She glanced back at him, smiled, and said, "Wherever it is . . . there's a *lot* of pottery."

"Not someone's basement?"

"Not unless they live in the Batcave. *Huge.* Reminds me more of your place than anything."

"Pottery Co-Op," he said instantly, not even thinking about the words. She was already flipping to the suggested alternate listing of *Ceramic Arts*, and there it was, big as life—under the *Schools* subheading. Pottery Co-Op. Not San Jose, but Palo

Alto. "They get a lot of students there."

"You dated someone," she guessed, stretching to reach for the hotel guest information book.

Steve nudged it closer. "I did," he said. "Once upon a time. Looking for breakfast?"

"Gonna grab breakfast on the way. Looking for public transportation. VTA mean anything to you? How about Caltrain?" She shook her head at herself. "I guess I really do live around here. God, I hope someone's feeding that cat."

He ignored the last, not having any words of comfort or wisdom to offer even if he assumed she'd remembered something about a cat. "VTA does connect with Caltrain to reach Palo Alto. But wouldn't you rather hitch a ride?"

She snorted. "That's all I need, get myself into a bad situation hitching along the freeway. Then I'd—" She looked up at him, quite suddenly. "You have a car?"

He only smiled.

Mickey liked motorcycles, she discovered. It didn't feel familiar, hugged up behind Steve with a helmet encasing her head and occasionally knocking up against his. But she liked it. She wrapped her arms around his stomach and enjoyed the play of muscles as he maneuvered them through the streets and onto the Bayshore Freeway.

She tried to avoid the bruises.

The bike was a practical street bike, a lightweight Suzuki that took neat turns; Steve maneuvered it with casual skill. He'd had it stashed at a friend's near the gym, and a quick taxi ride got them there. They stopped by Mickey's fleabag hotel of choice and grabbed her modest grocery-bag luggage now stashed in the bike's saddlebags; she wore Steve's backpack.

All neat and tidy, packed together on the bike. Tooling north on the Bayshore Freeway, heading for Palo Alto.

Why not San Francisco beyond? Why not south, to Yuma and Arizona, and into the dramatic geography of northern Arizona and Utah?

Why not *anywhere?*

It would be so easy.

It would solve so many problems.

At least until the day when she finally remembered everything, and understood anew the consequences of her flight.

A man had already died. Naia, daughter of Irhaddan's president, stood in harm's way.

So no, there'd be no riding right past Palo Alto; no turning around to head south. Not even if Steve would have done it.

He wouldn't have.

"Hey," he said, turning to look at her as they idled at a stop light at the end of their exit. His body twisted under her hands. "You okay?"

"Fine," she told him, wondering *how did he—?* And then she realized how tightly she'd been gripping him—over those bruises no less—and forced herself to relax. "Sorry."

But she didn't stay relaxed. As they headed down the Oregon Expressway and then on Alma Street toward the Caltrain station, her anxiety only became more intense. Inexplicable, but not to be rationalized away—or ignored. Finally Steve pulled over to the curb, putting his foot down to balance them. "Mickey," he said. "I can't drive this way." But when he turned to her, his faint annoyance dropped away, replaced by concern. "You're as pale as a ghost! Look, Bowden Park is right here—we can take a minute—Mickey?"

But Mickey found herself swamped in sensation. Dread sat uneasily in her stomach; anticipation skittered along her spine and made her skin tingle. The same fear that made her fingers clench around Steve's sore ribs turned her knees into Jello. And just as he looked at her even more sharply, as he turned the handlebars to take them to the park, she made herself say, "No. We're in the right place. That's what all this means." Inexplicably breathless, she forced every bit of strength into her voice to say, "Let's go."

Naia met her opposition at the door of her apartment: Badra, and the often-present Fadil Hisami.

This time, the often-present Fadil Hisami looked somewhat battered; he walked with a limp. But he was no less imposing for it.

In fact, Naia took one look at his face, at Badra's face, and knew that something had changed. She felt it as a certainty deep within, as though there wasn't actually anything to think about at all. No decisions to make, because they were already made.

So very similar to the evening she'd realized she'd truly made her choice to work with Anna.

She'd been in Irhaddan for spring break . . . surrounded by the welcoming familiarities of home. The arid climate honed scents into whisper-thin blades of sensation, bringing out the spice oils, the fragrance of the gardens both inside and outside their home. A veritable palace of a home it was, with airy hallways and dark, rounded shadows. Mosaics ran along the top of the walls and down the corners, work that had much influence on her own pottery. Cunningly concealed fans kept the air moving, fresh against her face.

The evening's reception had been held in Naia's honor—a celebration of her visit, and an invitation for all those heads of state, sons of the long-wealthy, and male cousins of politicos to express their interest in and admiration of the president's daughter.

Of course, circumstances required that she go veiled, even here in her own home. They required that she stare modestly at the hands folded in her lap while her educational accomplishments were feted. She'd had to compose a poem—her father read it, considering himself quite the orator—and she'd stuck to safe subjects, as instructed. Devotion to family, love of country, desire to please.

It had been easier than expected, to write such a poem. She forced herself to look deeply, to write from the heart. To write true.

She discovered that all the things Anna had seen in her, had admired in her, were truly there. She relearned how she loved this place; she understood how much she wanted to support her father. And she understood all over again that her opportunities to do so publicly were limited in the extreme.

She'd been glad when the reception divided, sending the women to the room set aside for them while the men stuffed pipes with their rankest tobacco and puffed themselves into a nicotine haze. It hadn't been hard to wander away from the women. She could hear the musicians strike up light background music—the jingle of the daff, the reedy tones of the mizwiz, and the nimbly plucked strings of the qanun.

She went the other way. Into the darker, closer hallways, where offices and studies sprouted. It was a man's domain, to be sure . . . but not off limits to the women who lived here, especially on this night when the men were otherwise occupied.

It was a good place to think of loyalty to one's country . . . and exactly what that might mean.

Anna said that a woman had to work how she could. If she didn't have a man to work through—and she lived in a culture where that was the norm—then she had to find other ways. Ways that felt right even though they might seem to obscure motivation.

She'd said that if Naia's father wouldn't listen to her, then perhaps the enemies of her father's enemies would. That such a route of action would weaken her father's enemies just the same.

She entered her father's study. This wasn't his public study, the place where papers were signed and visiting dignitaries were greeted. This was his private place. It held his beloved maps— tubes and sheaves and wall-hangings everywhere—and it held the most discreet of advisory meetings. Here he scribbled out his forming thoughts; here he kept his secrets. It smelled of his favorite spice and had wood furnishings, wood wainscoting—all rich southern hardwoods that gleamed in a deep shade just shy of purple.

Since her conversations with Anna, Naia had become more interested in this room—in the manner of thoughts that passed through her father's head while he worked here. She'd gone ahead with the dead-drop dry run only the week before, but she still wasn't sure she'd ever fill that space with anything of significance—with anything she learned here at home.

She trailed her fingers over the edge of the desk, unhooking her veil to drop to one side. She would, she thought, replenish the spice oils while she was here. In that way, her father would know she was thinking of him.

And so it was that she was in the closet when she heard a hand upon the doorknob. And so it was that her recent thoughts led her to stay there, instead of coming out to greet the new arrivals as would have been perfectly appropriate.

And so it was that she heard her father's most trusted advisor discussing treasonous matters with a man purported to be an imports expert from a nearby country. She heard them laugh, scorning her father, and she listened closely when their voices dropped . . . and that's when she learned that the most trusted advisor was also feeding false information to the United States.

If the States wanted illicit weapons of mass destruction, they need look no further than this man. He was providing nearby countries with the opportunity to store such things here in these less scrutinized lands.

And so it was that Naia made the decision to spy on those within her own country. The feeling of it—the certainty in her chest mixed with flutter everywhere else—had surprised her.

Just as it surprised her now, looking at Badra and Fadil Hisami and knowing something had changed. She was no longer flirting with playing the game; things had gone deadly earnest. She might well not get a second chance if she played poorly . . . and she hardly knew enough to play well.

She pretended she was Anna. She stepped aside for Badra and Hisami, looking them each in the eye, failing to greet them as she should. "What's wrong?"

Neither tried to pretend there was nothing. Badra's lips thinned in disapproval before she said, "We have concerns that someone inappropriate might try to contact you. Such a person would lie to you and upset you . . . and might well be a danger to you."

Naia didn't need to pretend her distress. She stepped back again, letting her briefcase thump to the floor. "Here? Does my father know?"

The man would have lied; he was halfway through a nod when Badra said, "Not yet. We don't want him to worry. If you're sent back home, it would reflect badly on your father's image. It would seem as though he couldn't control his own daughter. Unfortunately, that is very close to what has happened. Had you not been so free with your friendships and behavior here, you would not be in this position."

Naia should have been shamed by those words. Instead she blinked at the audacity of them, at just how many ways Badra had tried to manipulate her in one short speech. *It's a good thing I was free with my friendships. Anna is the one who taught me to look past your ways.*

And still, she didn't think Badra knew precisely what was

149

happening. She thought the woman had simply fallen back on her old methods of control when faced with the uncertainty of the orders she'd been given.

Hisami, however . . .

Hisami was another story. He gave her the coldest of looks as he said, "It is necessary to tighten your security. For the next few days, you will not attend classes; lectures will be taped for you. Your instructors have been informed of the situation."

"This decision is already made?" Naia couldn't hide her surprise. Even her father wouldn't treat her so.

But her father didn't know.

She thought perhaps her father would never know.

Unless she could break out of the prison of her apartment to contact Anna.

"You're sure," Steve said. He'd seen Mickey exhausted, drugged, flying into action with a tank top on her head, and dancing on the bed. He'd never seen this shocky look on her face.

She looked blankly at him, as though surprised they would even have this conversation. "I'm certain. This is the place."

Her surprise made him think twice. "What are we talking about here? We're looking for your connection with Naia, right?"

She laughed, small and wry, and there was something on her face that made him think of those first vulnerable moments he'd seen her. "Oh. Right. We were, weren't we?"

"Mickey." It was as much a warning as a question, and he left the handlebars to fend for themselves even as he put a second foot to the pavement to stabilize the bike. They weren't going anywhere until he understood what was happening with her.

"I don't know yet if we found the connection with Naia, but I think so. What I know is . . . this area is where it happened.

Where they took me." She shuddered, and then gave him a smile as wry as her laugh. "I can't imagine wanting anything more than to succumb to the animal urge to flee. Good thing I've got a brain, I guess."

"It's not such a bad thing to listen to your gut," Steve said, suppressing the need to cradle her face in his hand. Wouldn't work anyway, not with the motorcycle helmet.

"Going in there is the only way we're going to find answers," Mickey said, and it sounded like she was trying to convince herself.

Or as if she already knew, and just had to find a way to face it.

"Do it," she said. "Take us to the pottery place."

He tried to read the best option in her eyes, but she'd closed them. "Mickey—"

"Do it!" she said sharply. "I *can't*. I need you to—"

He got it, then—he got that every moment they sat here just stretched out her experience of their approach. He turned back to the bike, grabbed the first opportunity, and accelerated into traffic. Her arms again wrapped painfully around his bruised ribs.

This time he said nothing.

CHAPTER 14

The pottery co-op loomed large even in an area filled with warehouses. Old, brick, several stories tall . . . it had square jutting towers on either end, giving it an old-world look, and the red brick was trimmed with limestone crenellations on the corners and base. Its parking lot was a cozy space behind the building, outlined with greenery and half full of cars—both the ostentatious and the junker.

Steve's motorcycle tucked away quite neatly in a tiny spot beside the privacy-fence enclosed trash bin, and after he cut the engine they sat in silence for a moment. Mickey pried her hands away from his sides and hugged her arms, rubbing her hands over goose bumps.

To his credit, Steve didn't remind her that they didn't *have* to go in.

Because really, they did.

Mickey dismounted the bike with all the vigor of a little old lady, then gave herself a vigorous shake—a dog shake. She had her—Steve's—slingshot. He had his bow, broken down and stashed in a saddlebag where it had poked her in the back of the thigh the whole time. She even still had the small set of knives. She touched them, currently strapped on the back of her shoulder over the sports shirt and under the baggy San Jose T-shirt.

Steve grinned at the gesture. "You want me to string up the bow?"

"*That'd* be inconspicuous," she told him, but it was just the thing to get her kick-started into moving. He hastened to catch up as she headed for the entrance—a door set off to the side of a short row of loading bays. *Pottery Warehouse* was the actual name of the place, carved into an understated plaque by the door.

They entered into a cavernous space—the entire warehouse, left open and filled with rows of low, convenient shelving, display nooks, and tables. The second floor loomed over only part of the building, a loft floor on two sides with a narrow door opening to stairs along the back of the building. The stairs, she knew quite suddenly, had an exterior exit as well.

The third floor was complete, forming a ceiling high above them. And while the tracks and pulleys and catwalks were a reminder of what had once been a working warehouse, the chains and hoists had been removed.

"Wow," Steve said. He wandered into the store, reaching for but not quite touching an exquisite vase. "All the potters in northern California must send their stuff here."

"And the classes . . ." Mickey looked up to the loft. "That's where we want to go."

They excused themselves from the approaching sales floor monitor; a nod at the class area was all it took. And then they were through the door and into the tight area of the bottom landing, the exit door looming on the other side. Mickey staggered under the sudden onslaught of feelings. More than feelings—reactions, bursting out from deep within. *Danger and strike out! and the build up of an angry scream—*

She made a noise in her throat, a grunt of impact. Steve turned to her, touching her—too fast. She struck. A lightning blow to his abused solar plexus and then she had her arm against his throat, pushing him back against the wall and cutting off his air when she'd just knocked it right out of him. Not

Steve, not here in this place—only the enemy. Only those who wanted to hurt her. Her vision filled with the past, leaving nothing of the present.

Nothing of the real man she was choking to death, a knife already finding its way to prick just below his breastbone—just at the angle it would take to twist upward and pierce his heart.

"—*Mickey*—" the man said, and it meant nothing to her. Not the voice, not the name. Not the feel of the body she pressed against.

"C'mon, easy, Mick—"

That there was nothing of aggression in that voice made her hesitate, just for the merest instant. Made her back off some of the pressure at his throat.

"Hey, Mickey," he croaked, words barely scraping by—never mind the notes he attempted, the Mickey song she'd been singing only that morning. "Hey Mick—you're so—"

No. No, that wasn't right.

"Mickey—" Pleading, now. And with the kind of desperation that said he couldn't wait much longer. That he'd act. That neither of them would walk away in one piece, and maybe not at all.

The here and now came flooding back; she gasped with the impact of it. He easily pushed her away—only long enough to wrest the knife away and toss it behind her to clatter on the stairs. Then he drew her back, holding her up when her knees would have given way with the realization of it all. What she'd almost done. What she *could* have done.

And he just held her. Through the shuddering, through the weakness left by the storm of feelings from the past, ambushing her as much as she'd ambushed him. "I'm sorry," she said finally, mumbling into his shoulder. "I'm so sorry."

He didn't say it was okay. He said, "No one's hurt." But when she drew back to look at him, she saw his doubt. His renewed realization that just maybe the happy endings were still out of his reach, and that they always would be. In that moment, she would have done anything to smooth away the look in his eye.

But when she reached to touch his face, he flinched. Only the tiniest bit, but it was enough. Mickey gave herself a mental kick and pulled herself together, a deep breath and then another, and suddenly she was standing apart from him. She retrieved the knife and returned it to its sheath, and she couldn't look at him as she said again, "I'm sorry."

He cleared his throat. It didn't do anything to hide the aftereffects of what she'd done. "Tell me those were memories. That at least we know more than we did."

"Well," she said wryly, "I think we can be pretty sure this is where they took me." The violence had left her drained . . . and yet the need to act, to *react,* lingered. "Let's not hang around, okay?"

No need to tell him twice. He led the way up the stairs, leaving Mickey to wrestle with her guilt in his wake.

By the time she reached the second floor, he'd had plenty of time to wander into the room. She just stood there a moment, momentarily overwhelmed by the place. It, too, came with feelings—hints of laughter, the welcome scent of wet clay, the visual clutter of the project shelves. The floor itself was full of kick wheels and electric wheels, work stations and tables. Jars of clay working tools dotted the surfaces, and splashes of glaze had found their way to nearly every table and even some of the floor. Cabinets full of tools and glazes lined the wall next to the project wall and the whole thing looked out over the first floor, a bird's eye view of juried work from established artists.

Only a handful of people were at work, several of them clustered together and one woman off to the side, inventorying glazes. Steve wandered toward her, while Mickey found herself drawn to the project shelves. Slow and steady, as if nothing else in the room existed. She stopped before a niche with an outrageously cheerful vase, unglazed daisies and a dozen stem ports; she ran her hands over it. Closed her eyes and knew it.

This is mine.

But her attention quickly shifted to the lopsided vase nearby, a deliberately flawed creation. She reached for it . . . reached past it, her fingers taking over as long as she didn't think too hard about it. Fingertips on rough brick, a tiny nick in the stone that drew her attention, the memory of a brick sliding and then suddenly it was out. So easily, so silently, that Mickey startled herself and couldn't help a glance around to see if anyone noticed.

The woman beside Steve caught her movement and smiled, lifting a hand in greeting without breaking away from her conversation.

Good God, she had to get out of here. She couldn't afford to connect with someone who knew her—someone who would start asking questions. She fumbled the brick, fingers dipping inside to make contact with paper. And suddenly she was all efficiency, palming the paper, replacing the brick, and straightening both her vase and Naia's. She lingered at the firing schedule just to make it look like she'd had a purpose in stopping by, and then she headed out of the room.

Not downstairs, not yet. Upstairs, where she could hesitate on the steep stairs and pull the note from her hand.

Need help/advice—blown?

Tiny, precise lettering with graceful curves. Familiar lettering.

Naia. Naia, reaching out for help. Who knew how long she'd been waiting? Since the first day Mickey had been taken? Since yesterday?

Too long.

And still, she didn't know how to reach Naia. The university and her government had kept her too closely guarded. In her spy guise Mickey no doubt had access to any such information as a matter of course; for now she was on her own.

You could go looking for the pair who found you at the CapAd .Com building, she told herself. Surely the place was still under surveillance.

Right. Except all the reasons she hadn't trusted them the first time still very much applied. She thought they were telling the truth . . . but even so, they wouldn't trust her any more than she would trust them. Not after the way she'd bolted from them—not with so much time unaccounted for. And being on the same side didn't mean having the exact same interests.

And that meant she had to hope Naia would come here.

She sat on the stairs, rubbing her eyes—and shook her head. Waiting . . . whoever she was, it wasn't her style. She needed to *act.* To take care of the young woman who was counting on her.

Fine, then. This place must have an office. If Naia took classes here, then she'd given them some kind of contact information.

Mickey peeked back into the classroom to find Steve still in conversation—flirting, by the body language—with the woman by the glazes. Okay then. Up she went, to check out the third floor.

But the third floor was no joy, not when it came to offices and filing cabinets and records. The area had been nominally divided—walls that didn't reach the high ceiling—but held nothing more than old furniture, construction material, and boxes so aged they looked brittle enough to fall apart if anyone got a notion to move them. It was a child's dream attic, lit by huge banks of dirty windows and full of treasure chests and odd bits of this and that. Over here, the chains that had been removed from the main warehouse. Over there, a set of shelves with the shelves themselves leaning drunkenly inside the frame. A pile of old magazines . . . a rat bait box, long emptied and now lined with dust.

Nothing. If she wanted to look for Naia's sign-up information, she'd have to do a little B&E after hours.

But as she turned to go, Mickey hesitated. She looked back at the room . . . she considered.

She needed a place to hide out, a place that didn't threaten anyone else. Not the homeless, not Steve, not even the proprietor of a fleabag hotel. And if she hung out here . . .

It was just possible Naia would come to her. And in the meantime, she could use the after-hours to look around for those files. It wouldn't be breaking and entering so much as breaking and sleeping.

She looked around the room again. "Hey," she said to it. "Home sweet hideout."

She took the resounding silence as approval, and went to wait for Steve in the stairwell.

Mickey sat in the stairwell between the second and third floors, elbows on knees and chin propped in her hands. She didn't wait long before Steve appeared in the landing outside the second floor, looking down the stairs for her. She said, "Were you really singing the Mickey song?"

He jerked around, saw her sitting relaxed and patient, and offered something between a grin and grimace. "Such as it was."

"You heard me in the hotel."

He looked a little wary. "Maybe."

Mickey laughed. "Hey, no biggie. Being watched has never stopped me."

That got his attention, all right. "Really?" And then he cleared his throat and seemed to remember the circumstances of their presence here. "Hey," he said. "I learned something useful."

She regarded him from her lofty height, chin still propped. "Do tell."

"The woman in there is one of the teachers. She didn't recognize you at first, because of the hair thing. She really wasn't keen on the hair thing. But then she said you were—"

Mickey sat bolt upright, both hands shoved out in a warding gesture. He stopped short—for a moment he looked like he might retreat, for which she didn't blame him. She said, "I don't think I want to know."

He moved closer, putting a foot on the first step. Brave of him. "I don't think I get it."

It had been a gut reaction, and she had to think it through. "What if it just sets me off? Totally messes with my head? I can't afford that right now. I've got to be able to think through what's happening. Make good choices."

And yeah, he totally got that. How could he not, with his throat still reddened and his voice still hoarse from the last time something *just set her off?* "Maybe later," he agreed.

Except—

"No," she said, surprising herself—surprising him. "If I know who I am . . . if I remember . . . maybe we can find Naia. Warn her. *Save* her." It was worth the chance. It had to be worth the chance.

He watched her, giving her the opportunity to change her mind. No doubt he was thinking of those moments in the stairwell, the moments in the gym. When she *had* lost herself. Completely and totally lost herself. But she waited, and he finally said, "Pleased to meet you, Anna Hutchinson."

Anna Hutchinson.

Nothing.

Disappointment gripped her, bitter and twisting in her stomach. *Nothing.* Her name was Anna Hutchinson, and it meant no more than Jane A. Dreidler. No more than Mickey

Finn. "*Anna . . .*" she repeated out loud, and let it fade away, offering him a helpless, frustrated expression.

"Give it time," he said gently. "Don't think too hard about it. And maybe now that we have a name, we can hunt down your address."

Right. As easy as that. She didn't think so. Nothing about this had been easy. She shook her head, both acquiescence and doubt. *Dammit. Nothing.* She was Anna, and it meant *nothing.*

He moved ahead for her, pulling her out of that particular emotional black hole. "You learn anything?"

She pulled the note from her lap. Such feminine, precise handwriting . . . such a concise plea. *Need help.* How long had this been sitting in the dead drop? She held it out to him. "I don't know. It might be too late already."

He took it, running his thumb over those words and then shaking his head. She could see it on his face . . . the *what the hell have I gotten into* of it all was finally hitting.

Hard to believe it had taken this long.

He said, "Got a plan?"

She gave him the same wary look he'd given her a moment ago. "Maybe." And as he made a face in acknowledgment of that faint cleverness, she said, "This place is my plan. I just scouted out the third floor. It's unused, mostly. And it's got everything I need, right down to a working bathroom." A disgusting bathroom, but a working one. "It's got two potential exits, plenty of room to plunk down a camp mattress, good solid moorings near the fourth floor exit for ropes—"

"Ropes?" he said, startled.

"Exit number one. Rappel right out of trouble."

"Oh," he said. "Right. Of course. What was I thinking?"

She decided against mentioning that exit number two was an old elevator shaft in one of the towers, and that the elevator seemed to be stuck between the first and second floors.

She cleared her throat. "What I want," she said. "What I *hope*—is that Naia will come back here to check on the dead drop. If she hasn't given up yet. Right now . . . this is my only connection to her. I'd like the chance to do a little more Internet surfing . . . maybe early evening, after this place closes. Could find some clues there. But I'll plan to stay here. I needed a place to hide out, anyway. I have to get some gear, though."

"We can use my credit card for that," he offered.

"*We?* This is where the whole *we* thing ends. You need to—"

"Hide out." He gave her a pointed look. "I'm sure there's room."

"It's not safe," she blurted, and instantly regretted it. What guy—what *self-defense instructor*—was going to walk away from a challenge like that? "Look—whatever my world is about, I don't think I want it rubbing off on you. And I sure as hell don't need the distraction—"

He perked up at that one, damn him. "I'm a distraction?"

Cranky, she said, "Don't let it go to your head." And then she rubbed the heel of her hand across her eyes, huffing out a breath of weary frustration. "I don't think I can deal with it if you get hurt, okay? And you've *already* been hurt, from the last time I tried to leave you out of it and you didn't cooperate."

"I can be like that," he admitted. "Just ask the kids."

She wasn't getting through to him.

She wasn't getting through to him at *all*.

Where he found the strength to keep on hoping—after all he'd seen of her, after she'd gone after him in this very stairwell, lost in the throes of what had been—she couldn't imagine. And she didn't know how to fight it. "I just mean . . . look, I don't know when it will happen again. When something will trigger me." She looked at him, grabbing his gaze with enough intensity so his eyes widened slightly. "I don't get any warning. I don't have a safety. I could go off on you *whenever*."

He raised his brows, leaning against the stairwell in a way that pretty much blocked this particular exit—filling it, somehow, even though she wouldn't have said he had the size to do it. "Then I better be around to pick up the pieces, don't you think?"

She leaped to her feet, quite suddenly, towering over him. He didn't flinch—she was completely under control if you didn't count that fraying temper—and he didn't let go of her gaze. She was the one who had made that particular connection, and now she was caught in it.

Caught in his decision, too. Sure, she could evade him. She could evade him any time she wanted to. But that wouldn't keep him from coming after her, and who knows how long it would take him to stumble into the line of fire.

So she did the only thing she *could* do. She stamped her foot and she said, "Dammit!"

And Steve just grinned.

"Check this one out," Mickey said, leaning away from the computer monitor so Steve—who sat at the computer beside hers—could see. The Internet café bustled around them, full of tourists and foreign exchange students. A handful of languages pattered against Mickey's ears . . . she wasn't sure if she should be surprised that she understood most of them. Japanese, Spanish, Farsi, French . . . Steve seemed oblivious, though it was obvious enough to Mickey that he spoke Greek. His own speech had just the slightest of blurring around some of the consonants, and she suspected he'd learned Greek before English.

Together they could—

She blinked, shook her head in the most infinitesimal way, and refocused on the monitor. Steve had already absorbed the gist of the editorial she'd shown him, one from the San Francisco paper. *Irhaddan Leadership Confused From Within.* The body of the piece offered all sorts of implications that President Mejjati had recently lost consistency—that he needed to be replaced. His most staunch supporter was a man named Mounir Farooqi.

"Mounir Farooqi," Mickey mused out loud.

"You know him?" Steve gave her a sharp look.

"Just another one of those brain tickles." Disgruntled, she gave up when another moment of thinking resulted in no astonishing revelations. "It's probably important . . . but we'll just have to keep it in mind."

"Okay, then check out this site." He tipped the monitor in her direction. "This is the Stanford student paper. Got some editorial types discussing privileged foreign students, making the point that they don't add anything to the student body experience if they go reclusive—and what's the point of schooling in a foreign country if you don't experience the country?"

"But Naia wasn't like that," she objected, then hesitated, thinking about that—about why she'd said it. *Because it's true, that's why.* She had to trust her reactions—otherwise she'd paralyze herself into inaction.

"I'm thinking something changed," Steve said . . . one of those trying-to-break-it-gently voices. "The article mentions bodyguards."

"Good," Mickey said. "If she's taken steps to protect herself—"

"Unless they aren't bodyguards," Steve pointed out. "Because wouldn't that just make it clear she thinks she should be a target? Wouldn't you have taught her better than that?"

She could only hope.

"Watchdogs," she groaned. "What's the date on that thing?"

"It's today's." Steve ran his thumb around the rim of the foam cup that had held his long-gone specialty coffee. "It references a 'certain lecture hall' from yesterday."

A whoosh of relief ran all the breath out of Mickey's lungs. "She's okay, then. At least within the past couple of days . . ."

"And we know someone we can ask about her. He knows her lecture hall, at least—I bet he knows the class. It could be a connection point."

She gave him a skeptical look. "You're awfully good at this. Should I be worried that you're a plant?"

He laughed, short and humorless. "Let's just say I have a lot of experience in tracking down Zander. Not at the end—he was fairly predictable by then. But when it had just started. When we still had—"

"Hope," she finished for him softly.

He highlighted the editor's name and hit the CONTROL-C hotkey combo with more force than Mickey suspected he'd meant to. "I can email the person who wrote this," he said. "I've got a throw-away account as a spam trap."

Mickey nodded. "Do it," she said. "And then let's go shopping. How much cash do you have?"

That stopped him short. "You think they're tracing my credit card?"

"By now?" She shrugged. "They might be. I'd rather not take the chance. We can get what we can for the night . . . and then later I'll go harvesting." At his skeptical look, she gave him a beatific smile. "I've still got the tank top with the holes," she said. "And maybe I'll sing for them."

Chapter 15

He'd thought, for that one moment, that he was dead. He'd felt the prick of that blade against his skin. He might have been stronger than Mickey, he might be the one who knew who he was and who he'd been . . .

But she'd been quicker.

And dammit, she'd been more skilled.

Amazing, how quickly she'd come back to herself after that. Turned back into the Mickey he knew . . . what little he knew of her.

That's plenty. He knew of her grit, of her refusal to bow down to odds so overwhelming that some deity, somewhere, was having a god-sized laugh at it all. He knew she didn't give herself enough credit for who she was—everything he'd seen about her spoke of her compassion and loyalty, but all she saw was her ability to hurt, her willingness to be mixed up in the spy games that had brought them to this place.

Then again, she had a point there.

And then there was this. Sitting on his motorcycle, ready to be the getaway vehicle if needed. He didn't even have his bow; his role would be to scoot them out of there and nothing more.

Mickey sat pillion behind him, separating her latest take into *cop drop* and *assimilate* piles.

He twisted to look at her in the late evening darkness. "This doesn't bother you?" For this, at least, was something he didn't quite understand.

She didn't pretend not to understand. "The original victims are getting more back than they would if I weren't doing it."

"Unless you interrupted the mugging as it was going down. Stopped it."

She stopped her sorting, and stowed the grocery bag for the cop drop. And she sighed. It was a sad sound, but he couldn't tell if she was reacting to the situation or his words. "Let's pretend I try. What do you suppose would happen?"

"Mugger loses out," Steve said promptly, but suddenly he wasn't sure he liked where this was going.

"I'll give you that one," she agreed, scratching an itch beneath the shirt on her head. " 'Trembling in fear, mugger thinks of Tank Top Woman's fast-growing rep and runs away.' But it's not the only scenario."

"Scenario," he repeated, and wondered if that was her background coming through or just one of those words any average Tank Top Woman would use.

"Then there's the mugger who, rightly deducing that Tank Top Woman isn't going to do anything worse than ping the hell out of him, takes out his righteous anger on the muggee, shooting him or her dead."

Steve made a grmphing noise.

"Or the muggee, who, sensing help is at hand, tries to play the hero and bang—"

"Okay, okay." Steve held up his hands in surrender. "So I guess the real question is why these guys are still dinging this neighborhood."

"Two nights ago, I was only an aberration. Tonight might make them think . . . but I doubt I'll be back after this." She considered her words a moment, and then straightened in a cheerful way that alerted him. "Not unless I'm in the mood."

He growled. "Now you're just tweaking me."

She patted his shoulder, flipping open his backpack so she

could drop her gleanings inside. "Maybe," she said airily, and dismounted the bike to regard him with head tipped. "Maybe mostly."

He growled again and she laughed lightly, fading into the darkness and off to patrol the streets. She headed off toward a small patch of bars that were just beginning to disgorge their ripe-for-trouble customers. Steve shook his head in the darkness, amazed at her knack of finding the right situations, of spotting the right potential victims. Whatever she truly did in her real life as Anna Hutchinson, he bet she was good at it.

He prepared for another long wait. Tonight they'd return to the Pottery Warehouse . . . tomorrow morning, they'd do more shopping—they hadn't been able to afford her rappelling gear, for starters—and he'd check his email. And then . . . he wasn't sure. They couldn't wait in the warehouse for Naia forever, and their records had proved bemusingly elusive. Mickey had muttered something about breaking back into the CapAd.Com building, hoping to shake loose the surveillance again—if it still existed. Or hoping to find more memories.

She wouldn't sit around hoping for something to fall in her lap, that much Steve knew for sure. That much, he'd already seen.

Something popped in the distance. Again. And twice more, in quick succession. Steve stopped breathing—listening. *Might not have anything to do with her.*

Except as far as he could see, action followed Mickey like a faithful dog. *Of* course *it has something to do with her!* The only question was whether he waited here or went to check on her—and after a few moments of infuriating indecision, he realized that if he needed to go to her, it was already too late.

He'd wait.

It would kill him, but he'd wait. He'd stay where she knew to find him. He fidgeted, went for the ignition key, and let his hand drop away.

And then he heard the footsteps. Fleet, light . . . on the run.

He started the bike and pulled out into the open before he even saw her—and when he saw her, he also saw the others. Not close, but coming. Half a dozen of them—heads bobbing, arms pumping, gun metal glinting briefly in the streetlights.

"Go!" she gasped, still fifty yards away, ripping the tank top off her head and glancing back on the run. "Go, *go!*"

She couldn't mean it.

Except she'd said it.

He got it, a sudden light-bulb of understanding—she wanted him already rolling. He eased off the clutch and put the Suzuki in motion, pushing off with first one foot, then the other—and then she was there, flinging herself onto the back of the bike, wrapping her arms around him and ducking her head against the backpack he wore. He didn't need encouragement—he gunned the engine hard, slipping the back tire a little in spite of the rolling start.

Something popped behind them—a closer, louder pop than before. "Shit!" he muttered, ducking in spite of the fact that it would have been too late anyway. Mickey ducked right down with him, and they rode low and fast, squealing through streets as one creature—man, woman, and bike.

Within a few blocks they straightened, but Mickey didn't release her tight hold on him.

Damned if he didn't like it that way.

They'd been waiting for her. Or if not waiting, ready. And in the middle of his little slingshot-inspired mugger dance, her latest target had managed to hit an instant-dial on his cell phone and yelp a few words into it.

By the time back-up arrived, Mickey had his recent take and was on the run, but . . .

It had been a close thing.

"You are a crazy woman," Steve had said, and he'd said it as though even he wasn't quite sure how he meant it. Then when they'd reached the co-op and he'd discovered she'd thought ahead, jimmying the rarely used outside door to the stairwell so it wouldn't lock and they could easily gain after-hours access, it seemed like a weird last straw. "I can't believe," he'd said, "that this is the way you live your life."

"I don't think it is," she'd said, her voice rather small.

Though she thought it was probably how she lived her life when things went wrong.

Never like this.

Surely not.

Even though she seemed perfectly prepared to deal with it.

And now she lay on a surprisingly comfortable camp mattress in a huge, dusty space, and every time she closed her eyes she saw nothing but the old man's face as he was being mugged, and thought about how she could have stopped him from facing such cruelty, stopped him from facing mortality that was clearly all too close already.

Steve wasn't far away but he wasn't close, either. He'd reached his limit; he needed space. He needed to recharge.

She could understand that. She was exhausted herself, and wanted nothing more than a deep, long sleep. It was just . . .

Every time she closed her damned eyes, she saw that old man's face.

"Hey," said Steve, so softly she barely heard it. "You okay?"

She hadn't even known he was awake. And she almost said *sure,* but it was far too blithe a response to someone who had earned every bit of her respect. "What makes you ask?"

He took long enough that she thought he wasn't going to answer, but he eventually admitted, "The way you keep forgetting to breathe."

"Oh." Breathing. Right.

He shifted on the air mattress, crinkling. They had only the light survival blankets—impressively effective, especially in this mild climate, but also noisy. He said, "This was one night I didn't expect to have trouble sleeping."

He'd been tired, she knew. And even if he *wasn't* far away . . . she wished he was closer. An unfamiliar feeling built inside her—sad and bittersweet. *Lonely.* Not even memories to keep her company, only this unceasing need to fix things. *Poor me,* she told herself, but the sarcasm didn't jar anything loose.

Okay, so it really *did* suck to be stuck in the middle of life and death and spy games with no memories to turn to. No established resources. Just mugger harvesting and the unrelenting help of a man who had finally realized he had no idea what he'd gotten himself into. That for all his history of helping, all his work toward out-of-reach happy endings, Mickey had landed in his lap with a whole new world of problems.

He sighed. "Still not breathing."

"I must be," she protested. "I'd pass out if I wasn't." But she felt the tightness in her throat, the emptiness in her chest. She might be breathing, but she certainly wasn't doing it on a regular basis.

He crinkled again—enough to make her look. He'd sat up. "What's wrong?"

She didn't think about it; she crawled right off her mattress and sat next to him on his, cross-legged on tubes of air and slightly unstable. He didn't seem surprised. He opened his blanket and pulled her in, putting his arm around her. Their knees bumped.

Something about that sad and bittersweet feeling quite abruptly faded. But it made way for other things, and quite abruptly—

"Are you crying?" he asked, suspicion in his voice.

"No!" she said, and her voice was unconvincingly thick. Didn't even convince herself. "It's just . . . that old man—"

He stilled in surprise. "We talked about that. It was too risky to interfere, right? I thought you were okay with that."

Asperity replaced the unwelcome and unfamiliar heat of tears. "I had to be, didn't I?" And then she hushed, for he didn't deserve sharp words. But he gave her shoulders a little squeeze, and she sighed. "I just have this feeling . . . that I should have been able to protect him."

"Why?"

"Because that's what I've always done," she said promptly . . . and then had to stop and consider her words. Consider what few memories she'd regained—and fall back into them. The darkness made it easy; his presence beside her made it easy. "Everything I've remembered—okay, everything but the cat— tells me it's what I've always done. The slingshot . . ." She knew there had been a time when she hadn't used one. She just couldn't imagine it right now. "My mother—"

"You remember your mother?"

"I remember . . ." Mickey closed her eyes, even in the darkness. "I remember that she looked a little like me. And that she died when I wasn't very old."

"I'm sorry."

"It was a long time ago," she said, not thinking of layers of grief still buried somewhere in her mind. Thinking instead of how fiercely she'd protected her sister. "My sister—I have one of those, too, somewhere—didn't deal with it well. She became the strange one. Every school has one, you know."

"There but for the grace of God," Steve said, his voice distracted enough to let her know he'd gone back to his own memories. "I teetered on that path. Got too distracted by just trying to deal with Zander's sidetrips."

"I didn't hurt anyone. It's just . . . they never knew if I was lurking. And they never knew what I'd put in that slingshot next. Rotten plums . . . I think those were my favorites."

"Nice," Steve said, admiring. "You sound like a good sister."

"Oh, yes," Mickey said. "A very good sister. Protective."

"Ah," he said. "I get it. It's what you've always done. Right."

"And there was this thing in school . . ." she said, letting it trail away as she hunted something more substantial than mere wisps of images.

His hand moved from her shoulder to the back of her neck, stroking what was left of her hair. *It's not that bad*, she told herself. And she'd stopped getting those surprised looks as people took in her state of dress versus her hairstyle. He said, "High school?"

"College, I think. It feels small and private . . . lots of overseas students. I'd say it was outside of DC, but I can't tell you why."

"So you're a college girl."

"Not you? I mean—"

He chuckled. "I get it. No, I never went. Too much else going on in my life. I took some business courses. They come in handy."

"Mm." She tipped her head so he could reach the other side of her neck. Purr. He could just touch her like that all night long. "There was this . . . incident. I'd think it had been a dream—a nightmare—if I hadn't been awake when it came to me. Actually, I guess I went looking."

"When?" he asked in surprise. Understandably . . . she hadn't made a big deal of hunting her memories once she'd decided to follow her gut instinct.

"The CapAd.Com building. When I broke in and didn't come up with anything. End of my trail, y'know? So I gave it some thought." She searched for some way to tell him of those memories, and then shook her head. "*I* wouldn't believe . . ."

"I've seen Tank Top Woman," Steve said. He'd turned to look

at her in the darkness; his breath was warm on her ear. "I guess I can believe anything."

She straightened just long enough to strike a superhero pose—from the waist up, anyway. But it didn't last—not with those memories poking at her. "College," she said. "Foreign students—exclusive ones. I guess someone was important enough to get nabbed or something. Whatever. It went wrong. I ended up in the middle of it . . . hostages, dead instructor . . ." *Frightened faces, splattered blood, anger so thick it might smother her—*

Steve's hand tightened on the back of her neck. "Breathe," he said.

She did, deep and long. "At the time I didn't think it was a big deal," she said. "I was just as scared as any of them." *Dried blood, a dead woman on the floor and partially covered with a lemon yellow raincoat, shoulder-length grey hair fanning across the plushly carpeted floor.* "It's just . . . there was no one else there. No one in charge. And someone had to—"

"—Protect everyone," Steve finished.

"Something like that," she said it wryly. "More like . . . stall. Calm things down. I just talked to them, that's all. Convinced them that the college would do anything to make sure we were all right, and that they could get whatever they wanted. I don't know what they thought I was . . . why they believed me."

Glass shattering, explosive light, tear gas and choking and more shrieking and there she was, a blur of motion and a shove and one of the gunmen went right out that second story window—

"What happened? Do you know?" His hand on her neck had grown tense, waiting for the end to a story that might not have one.

She shrugged and patted his knee, leaving her hand there. Reassuring *him.* "The FBI hostage rescue team took out one of them. The other, I think . . ." No, she *knew.* "There was tear gas . . . confusion. I pushed him out the window."

Steve thought about that a moment. "I get the feeling you weren't on the first floor."

She shook her head. Definitely not the first floor. "That event feels pivotal to me. As though my childhood set me up for it, but it set me up for . . . whoever I am now."

"You know, we could follow up on that. A web search. College, DC, hostages . . ."

She shook her head, but softened the negative reaction by squeezing his knee slightly. "It's not about me right now, Steve. It's about tracking down Naia. She's in trouble . . . and she wouldn't be, not unless she had something to tell me." She stopped, thought about the words that had just come out. "Yeah, I'll stick with that. She's got something to talk about. Otherwise they'd just keep an eye on her, make sure she wasn't in a position to learn what she shouldn't—at least until they knew one way or the other."

"I'll buy that," Steve murmured, but in a voice that indicated he knew he was totally over his head.

Mickey buried her face in her hands, if only briefly. "What I don't get," she said, "is . . . if I have this need to take care of people . . . how the hell did I end up being who I am?"

"We covered that," Steve said. "I don't think you're giving yourself enough credit. There's nothing you've done that didn't have justice in it. Hard things, yes. But—"

"Tell you what," Mickey interrupted. "You just keep believing that. You believe in it for both of us. It'll free me to do whatever needs to be done." *Whatever.* She hadn't killed anyone yet. But she had the feeling she could, if she needed to.

"You know," Steve said, and his hand moved from the her nape to stroke loose hair away from her face, "it seems to me that it's only fair if someone protects *you* now and then. So that's our story for the rest of the night, okay?"

Mickey couldn't let go that easily. "Even if it means protecting me from who I really am?"

"Even if," he breathed, and somehow he'd moved closer, and those words brushed warm air against her cheek. She turned to him, surprised, and knew she'd only managed to put herself within trembling distance of him—and when he spoke again, his lips barely brushed hers. "How about it?"

She tensed. "You don't know," she said. "You *can't* know—" And finally, in a whisper, "I just don't want you to be sorry."

"Never that."

Then again . . . "It *would* be a shame," she said, knowing his mouth was still *right there,* just close enough to tickle her lips as she spoke, "if we had all this swashbuckling adventure and the guy didn't get to kiss the girl."

"Shut up," he said, and kissed her.

Not, as she might have thought, a sweepingly romantic kiss, a Han Solo and Princess Leia kiss. No, it was a Steve Spaneas kiss, full of all his compassion, deep and achingly sweet and apparently endless and yet not quite endless enough.

"Oh," she said, more like the gasp for air it was. "Right. *Breathe.*"

He laughed, more than a little breathless himself. "Now. Come curl up beside me and let's see what we can do about that sleep."

"But—"

"Later," he said. "Because I need to believe we'll have one."

She touched her fingers to her lips. *Achingly sweet.* The kind of kiss that deserved a *later.* "Later," she agreed, and tucked herself against him. *Please, let there be a later.*

CHAPTER 16

Steve wouldn't have said the two of them could sleep through the night on that small air mattress—not and get any real sleep. He wouldn't have said he could wake up in the morning, intensely aware of her body spooned up against his, and be satisfied just to have had the night, hoping for their chance at a later.

Not that he failed to react to her; not that she failed to perceive it. He'd seen that sleepy smile.

But she'd made it plain what she needed. And somewhere inside himself, those needs resonated. So he nuzzled her neck a few times, wallowed briefly in the feel of her as she stretched against him and then rolled away in a tangle of crinkly silver blankets.

She'd brushed her teeth first thing—bottled water was their friend—changed clothes into a similar low-key, sporty outfit, shoved their gear out of sight, and been waiting for him at the stairwell by the time he managed his own morning ablutions. A quick slink down the stairs and they were out in the open.

With his bike at hand they wasted no time getting the day started; he dropped her off at a sporting goods store and headed for the Internet café. The menu was limited, but orange juice and an egg muffin wannabe combo did the trick. He thought guiltily of Mickey, but she'd been happy enough with her granola bars.

Mickey.

No, it was Anna. Anna Hutchinson. *Ahn-na,* the pottery instructor had said, along with commentary on how well-liked she was.

So Steve had been good. He spent a few moments to check the reporting on Anthony's death and found nothing. At first he truly didn't believe it—he looked for twenty minutes longer than he should have, certain he was missing something.

And then his brother's voice—a voice that hadn't found its way into his thoughts for a startling number of years now—said quite practically, *they cleaned up after themselves.* It was the kind of statement Steve would have dismissed when his brother was alive—but right now it struck him as exactly right. They'd cleaned up so thoroughly that no one but those involved knew it had happened at all. And who would miss Anthony, or report him missing, aside from his homeless neighbors?

He forced himself away from the subject—from even letting the bitter afterthought of it taint his progress—and delved into Naia and Irhaddan, hunting for any piece of information that would make it all make sense. He discovered a recent *Times* article about UN weapons inspections—that certain Mid-East countries had been declared weapons-free in spite of everyone's belief that they had been manufacturing and acquiring them. Irhaddan was mentioned simply because it was one of the few countries never under any suspicion.

Huh. Well, WMD was always worth some attention, but it didn't seem as though it could be related to Naia's situation.

He couldn't find any photos of Naia, not even old ones. He did find plenty of photos of her father, an older man with much dignity who seemed to do a decent job of keeping his country stable with massive instability all around them. He found photos of the man with his contemporaries, most of whom appeared more than once and some of whom always seemed to be on hand—mostly Mounir Farooqi, the man Mickey had known.

He found a number of articles praising the president for his temperate ways, and more than one that praised his decision to send his daughter overseas, acknowledging the personal difficulties this created for the man.

So Naia was clearly a figurehead. A private, protected figurehead.

Steve's brain felt like it was tied in knots. So Mickey and Naia were somehow involved in a spy game—one in which the agencies were still an unknown. None of it made sense—especially the encounter with the pair outside the CapAd.Com building. They'd used CIA terms . . . but the CIA didn't work on native soil. Didn't spy on its own. And Steve, for whatever research he'd done to deal with his brother's street friends once upon a time, had no truly special insight into the various agencies. Who did what, where they did it, how publicly they did it . . . he knew enough to throw around a few terms. The end.

And then there was Naia. Protected, private . . . she had somehow acquired importance in this game.

What the hell could be so important in relation to Irhaddan? They were one of the few countries in that area *not* being a problem or a threat—*not* under close scrutiny with regard to WMD.

Oh.

Idiot.

What would be important to a country with certain freedoms and reputations would be to keep those freedoms and that reputation. And the Irhaddanians—the ones who had killed Anthony, who had come for him and Mickey at the gym—they acted like men with a lot to lose.

So the Irhaddanians had something they wanted kept quiet, and Naia knew it, and Naia was working with Mickey.

He wanted to believe that this meant Mickey was working for U.S. interests. The Good Guys, not the Bad Guys. She could be

FBI; she could be . . . well, something he didn't even know about.

No one who cares so much about protecting others would work against her own country.

He believed that. He was even satisfied to leave it at that.

Mickey wouldn't be.

Then let's find out more about Mickey.

Steve went hunting for Anna Hutchinson. He threw in keywords like hostage and college, and it didn't take him long. Ten years earlier the Internet hadn't quite been the archival tool of its current incarnation, but an event like that . . .

There were anniversaries. Memorials. Various ceremonies, lingering like aftershocks through the years.

He found a few photos from that time—longer hair, same bright eyes, the rest of her looking young and shell-shocked. He found reference to her role in the incident. He learned that she'd been hurt. She hadn't mentioned it; maybe she didn't know. Otherwise, nothing new to be learned. Only what she'd said.

Except he hadn't realized it would be such a relief to find that confirmation. For her sake, and for his.

He took the moment, breathed deeply a few times. His Mickey—right here in phosphor history. Lost her mother, protected her sister, took on gunmen . . . and danced with brooms and on beds.

His Mickey.

I am such an idiot. I know better than to believe in this.

And still, on a whim, he did a People Search. No phone or address for Anna Hutchinson here in Northern California. But he went to the regular search engine and linked her name to Palo Alto, San Jose, San Francisco . . .

Bingo.

A simple one-page website, a simple one-screen front page. It looked like the online business card it was. Classy, simple, with just a hint of "if you have to ask, you don't need to know."

Antiques. She sold antiques out of San Francisco. If he interpreted the display correctly, she was also an antique hunter—the person to go to with those special requests.

He had to admire the beauty of it. It meant travel; it meant she had an excuse for being anywhere she needed to be. It meant that dropping out of sight wasn't a problem—she need answer to no boss, and no set work schedule. It meant, from the exclusive look of the website, that she had clients in the very upper strata of San Francisco society—second only to DC when it came to the number of foreign embassies in residence.

He bet she went to a lot of parties.

The discovery left only the question of who she worked for—*truly* worked for. And it didn't really matter which combination of letters she reported to—CIA, NSA, NCIS, FBI, or even Homeland Security—it only mattered that they originated in the U.S. That she wasn't somehow cultivating Naia to influence Irhaddan against the States.

In which case, the men who had killed Anthony and shot up the gym might well be the good guys.

"Screw *that*," he said out loud, garnering a glance from the neighboring table. He offered a sheepish shrug in response and checked his email one last time. Nothing—again—from the editor he'd written the day before.

So in spite of what he'd learned, he hadn't advanced their plan. Mickey's identity didn't matter so much as her memory, and she'd already told him she didn't want to force anything— didn't want to distract herself from the matter at hand. At some point they could use the contact info on the website to track down her office, but she didn't consider it a priority. And his research into Irhaddan had netted nothing but speculation.

That, he could tell her. She had an uncanny knack for follow-

180

ing her leftover instincts to a decision . . . she might well have an opinion on his speculating.

And now? He had his own life to see to. The gym to check on. His people to worry about. And no one better to give him answers than Dawnisha.

He logged off his email, dumped the browser cache, and emptied the URL history cache. Finally paranoid at that.

His brother would have laughed.

Naia hooked the diminutive headset over her ears, not the least bit certain she could concentrate on the art history lecture podcast when she was still a prisoner in her own apartment.

They wouldn't tell her anything more. They made sure Badra was there at all times, preserving appearances and Naia's virtue. They spoke among themselves when they thought she couldn't hear—and they were right. The most she gleaned from any of it was that Badra was no happier about the situation than Naia, and that the men felt it would be necessary only until the situation was contained.

What did that mean, exactly?

In her ears, her professor droned on about the Parthenon. Naia typed a few desultory notes . . . highlighted a phrase in the open textbook beside her laptop. Most college students sprawled hither and yon for such work, using furniture in creative ways. Naia sat properly at a tidy desk, as dressed and presentable as if she'd been in the classroom itself.

Partly because of Badra, of course. But partly just because it made her feel more in control.

She turned the textbook page; her eyes strayed to her laptop screen. Her email icon had appeared in the tool bar. She swapped out program windows to check her automatically downloaded mail.

Two pieces of junk, one email from a casual friend wondering if she was okay or just ditching class this week, and one email from someone she didn't recognize . . . but the subject header made her look twice. *Someone's looking for you?*, question mark and all.

She glanced up to see if Badra was paying any attention, and found the woman embroidering the edges of a hijab, her culturally jarring PDA on the arm of her chair as though she were multi-tasking something. Badra, it seemed, had plenty on her mind. Naia opened the email.

. . . Don't know me . . . student newspaper . . . editorial . . . email from someone . . . interested in contacting you. But he didn't, it seemed, give out other people's email info without permission. Come to that, he shouldn't have had hers in the first place. Very few people did.

No, she wouldn't read too much into that. She'd been tidy with her email, but she'd given it out to enough people so that asking in the right place would result in the information. For the moment, she'd assume this was just what it looked like—someone who respected her privacy enough to contact her rather than just handing out her email address when asked. The editor had pasted in the original query; she didn't recognize that email address, either. kickr@gmail.com. The text was no more enlightening. The author knew her, had lost track of her, would like to reconnect. Hoped the newspaper editor could help. The author pointed out that he . . . or she . . . knew Naia well enough to read between the lines of who he'd been talking about in that editorial, and professed concern that she hadn't been seen.

Nothing terribly exciting. Nothing to catch her eye. Until the author of the letter signed off. The email signature included only an initial—*A.*—followed by the email address and a title, *Community Interface, Pottery Warehouse.*

The Pottery Warehouse had no such position. It had no one whose first name began with A. on staff.

But it had her dead drop.

It had Anna.

Swiftly, Naia deleted the email. The security detail hadn't demanded to inspect her computer yet, but she thought it was just a matter of time. And though there was nothing overtly incriminating about this email or any other, she quickly emptied her mailbox trash—and with a grim satisfaction, she put her government-grade data chew-and-destroy program to work on those files.

When Badra looked up again, Naia had rewound the podcast to the point at which her attention had diverged, highlighter in hand. But she was no longer Naia the student.

She was Naia who'd had enough . . . and who now had somewhere to go.

She met Badra's gaze and smiled.

Mickey disembarked the bus as close to the pottery warehouse as she could, and carried the considerable results of her morning shopping spree the rest of the way. She hid the purchases in the prickly and unwelcoming evergreen shrubbery. A glance at the class schedule showed a nice gap at dinner time, and that would be the best time to haul this stuff to the third floor.

Then, because she was running out of time, she gave herself the luxury of picking up a cab at the Caltrain station, and directed the driver to the Internet café. This bemused them both, as she did it in his native Russian when she ran into trouble with English.

Huh.

Steve wasn't by any of the computer stations in the bright, contemporary café; she found him at the short bank of high-tech public phones along the wall, startled to see her. And beneath the startle was worry and no little turmoil. He gestured her over.

She got a few double-takes from the other customers as she threaded her way through the tables, since her current look was meant to blend in with a slightly more downtrodden crowd. But this was a college town, and those who noticed her did little more than shrug and return to work. Here, she probably would have blended better if she'd added electric blue and pink to her hair and turned herself punk.

"Dawnisha," he was saying. "I can't—" Frustration then. "But everyone's okay?" He met Mickey's eyes, shook his head slightly. She didn't take it as a response to his conversation with Dawnisha—more like frustration, part two. "Okay, good. Just keep your distance from the place. Don't mess with these guys. Anyone who comes up against them should just say what you know—that I've taken off for a while."

He looked up at the ceiling; Mickey thought he was grinding his teeth. "Of *course* I think everyone there can take care of their own neighborhood. But these guys . . . they're cold. It's not about honor or family or proving themselves to some gang—it's bigger than that, and they don't *care* who gets in their way. You hearing me? This is one of those times where running is the best option. What do you think I've done?" He made an expressively exasperated gesture that looked like it had come from an Old World relative. "Look, Dawnisha . . . it comes down to this. If anything happens to anyone there, it'll be my fault. I don't think I can live with that. Don't make me, okay?"

After that he seemed to relax a little; he made only a few more comments, promised to come back as soon as he could, and hung up. When he turned to Mickey he looked as though he'd gone ten rounds with a heavyweight.

"You're not running," she observed. "You're ducking and dodging so you can find the right opening to strike back."

"I don't think that would have made much of an argument."

"Everything's okay, though? Hey, guess what—I speak Russian."

"Among other things, I imagine." Steve took her arm, a gentle guidance that she allowed. "Dawnisha doesn't think they've been there since you pulled me out of my loft. I think I convinced her that no one should screw with them." He rubbed his lower lip, a disgruntled gesture. "She didn't believe me about Anthony. Not at first."

"Surely someone found him—and we left the gym wide open."

"*We* did," Steve pointed out. "They were still there."

Of course. She felt foolish, walking out into the late morning sunshine without a clue in the world. "They cleaned up," she said, voicing his unspoken conclusion. And then, "It's just as well. The cops won't be looking for *us*, either. They won't know I stabbed . . . I shot . . ."

She'd been so busy with everything else . . . she'd thought more about that old man's expression than she had about the two men she'd been willing to kill. *Might* have killed, for all of that. And she found herself surprisingly able to put them aside. They'd come after *her*; they'd made their own troubles. The old man . . . he'd deserved none of it. So she cleared her throat and said, "It's just as well."

"Anthony deserves better."

"He does," she agreed, following him down the sidewalk to the bike. "We'll make sure he gets better, too. Before this is over."

It seemed to reassure him and bring him back to the moment at the same time. He looked at his bike, the one he'd strode to with such purpose, and he said somewhat sheepishly, "So, um, where are we going?"

"I want to give your email more time to stir things up before I go looking, and that leaves us with a block of free time." She checked her nails, an affected gesture. Even when she'd arrived at Steve's, they'd been without color.

Unlike her toenails.

Her concentration somewhat fractured but a whisper of memory concerning a struggle over foam toe separators and the cat, she added, "I considered a manicure but I think we should go big box shopping instead. Maybe there's a grocery store closer to the underpass than the one I used the first time—I don't think we're going to fit the half of it in your saddlebags."

He brightened considerably as he regarded her. "I like it."

She shrugged, not quite comfortable with that gaze. "It's part of the deal. Steal from the rich, give to the poor. Some of it, at least. Same as last time."

"Did you?" he asked. "Is Mosquito still there?"

She shook her head, smiling. "Don't remember much from that night, do you?"

"I'll take that to mean yes," he told her with some dignity. He handed her the extra helmet, strapped on his own, and waited for her climb on behind him.

She gave in to the impulse to spread her fingers wide over his chest and stomach, touching as much of him as possible—when, with the sedate pace they traveled, there wasn't all that much excuse to touch any of him at all.

Once at the store, Mickey also gave in to the impulse to buy some items not strictly practical. Toaster pastries, some pretty hair clips. She crammed her cart full and stuffed a few last things into the bike saddlebags. "Meet you there," she said, and pushed the cart on out of the lot, looking forward to the big downhill section.

Steve had gathered an audience by the time she got there. The place seemed almost familiar to her by now—the vast lines of concrete, the sound of traffic far overhead, the haphazard signs of humanity here below. The underpass was cool, the air slightly dampened there; the acrid smell of smoke from someone's nighttime fire still hung in the air.

With some reluctance, they broke away from Steve to greet Mickey, pulling her cart into the shadow of the bridge. "Hey," she said. "Looks better than he did the other night, doesn't he?"

"It was dark," said an older woman, quite practically. "Who knows?"

"Where's Mosquito?" Steve asked, joining the group from the other side.

The older woman gave Mickey a sideways glance. "It's not a good day. He's inside."

Inside *what?* One of the refrigerator box homes dug into the sloping sides of the underpass culvert? One of the metal corrugated storm pipes sticking out of either side of the underpass area? Some hidden spot by the riverside?

Maybe just inside his own head.

Mickey pushed the cart forward, and that turned out to be the signal; the assembled denizens of the underpass dove in.

When Meth Woman approached just a tad on the late side, Mickey pulled out some of the hair clips she'd saved aside. Meth Woman tore into the package and clipped her hair away from her face with much relief as she gestured Steve over.

"What's up, Missy?" Steve said, familiar enough with this place, with its people, to be easy with such questions.

Missy looked around, making sure the others were engrossed with the cart. "I'm worried about Anthony. There were people here yesterday. Wanted to know if we'd seen someone who didn't belong. We didn't say nothin', 'course. None of us talks to people who have that look in their eye. You know, the one that says they want to make the way the world is run? And like we don't fit in it anywhere?"

"I've seen it," Steve said.

"So then they started waving around money. But we know that trick. You put it together with those expressions? Never turns out right."

"But . . . Anthony talked to them?"

She nodded. "Not at first. But they started making threats. So Anthony said he'd get them off our backs. I don't know what he told them. He took their money and that was it." But she looked troubled, and she looked away, and she said, "That *shoulda* been it. But he couldn't just leave it. He said he was going to warn you, Steve. He said he ought to have lied about that part."

"That part," Steve repeated blankly.

"Oh, *you* know," Missy said, and smirked a little at Mickey. "How she's sweet on you."

Steve looked over at Mickey, eyebrows raised. She shrugged, very *hey, watcha gonna do?* "Later," he told her.

"I thought we'd already established that," she responded sweetly.

Missy waved a hand between them. "Hey, Anthony?"

Right. Anthony. Mickey glanced at Steve in a grim, tacit game of *you're it*. And Steve said simply, "Anthony was trying to do the right thing, Missy. But it looks like they found him first."

Missy's lips thinned; her eyes shone and she blinked fast a few times and looked away. She muttered something; a curse, Mickey thought, at Anthony's stupidity. When she turned back, her face was hard. Street hard. "I guess we'd best be moving on from this place for a while, then."

"That might be best," Steve said. "Not for long."

Damned well better not be. Mickey didn't have patience for much more of it. "Can you describe the men?"

Missy made a face that indicated she hadn't really cared. "Foreign, like I said. They had funny little caps—not like a Jewish thing, but not a whole lot more. One had a big fat mustache, one had a big fat nose. They were big. They were dressed too nice. Didn't see guns, but I bet they had 'em."

"Who doesn't," Steve grumbled, grumpy in a way that made Missy nudge Mickey and grin. But even as Mickey grinned in response, the other woman lost her smile, lost all her animation. She froze, except for her eyes. First they darted around, a little wild thing in search of escape, and then they got stuck, staring. Dreading.

Mickey had a good idea what Missy was looking at. Her spine prickled . . . someone might as well have been drawing a target on it. Steve had only to turn his head slightly, and his widened eyes pretty much confirmed Mickey's suspicions.

They'd returned. They'd failed to nail Mickey the night before and they'd come back to their little treasure trove of information.

But they were only looking at her back. They had no way of knowing who she was. So she eyed the distance between Steve and his bike parked back under the bridge, and she eyed the distance to the various cover opportunities—the bridge support structures, the galvanized pipe tunnels, the trees planted out and beyond the underpass.

The bike had the disassembled bow. She wondered how fast she could put it together. How fast *Steve* could put it to-gether . . . and put it to use.

And she made sure he saw her wondering—that he followed her gaze toward the bike. And then she drew a deep breath and, because it pleased her sense of dark irony, chose a song from *Cats.* *"Mem'rieeeees!"* she belted out, startling Missy as she drew the woman in for a few dramatic, swaying dance steps—and then shoved her away, toward one of those drain tunnels. "Lala la la la *lalaaaaahhh!"* Missy didn't quite get it, but she didn't hesitate to retreat, either. Dancing, swooping, Mickey bumped into Steve just long enough to shove him, muttering, "Get the bow!" A grand swoopy gesture let her pluck a knife from the harness still hidden beneath her oversized T-shirt; she palmed it, twirled around, and faltered in assumed confusion when she faced the two men.

They weren't the men she'd seen at the CapAd.Com. These men were more outwardly foreign, from the cut of their baggy suits to the headgear Missy had described. They were less suave . . . and more purposeful. They may have been at the gym the night before . . . she'd never gotten a good look in the darkness. She drew herself up to regard them with great dignity. "Oh," she said. "Were you invited? This is opening night, you know."

They spared each other only a glance. They showed no concern for those who had scattered before them—and no doubt that they'd found their target. They came on.

Boy, she hoped Steve was fast with that bow.

CHAPTER 17

"Tickets," Mickey said, gesturing grandly to the Irhaddan intruders with the hand that didn't hold the knife. "You must have tickets."

They didn't so much as blink. No curiosity, no interest, no concern. One said to the other, "Don't play games with her, just get her. I don't know why Hisami had so much trouble." And he spoke in Irhaddanian, which Mickey hadn't expected to understand.

But she did.

And because she knew better than to think too hard about it, she instantly replied in kind. "They had trouble because they thought just like you do, you jerks! What makes you think you can get away with this kind of blundering, goonish behavior on U.S. soil?"

Behind her came the muffled noises of flight, the cry of someone falling, the scuffle as that person scrambled up again. "C'mon, c'mon!" voices urged, and Mickey knew the underpass people weren't all safe yet—couldn't believe Steve had had the time to put his bow together, grab his quiver, and take cover behind the nearest corrugated storm pipe, the only place that offered him both angle and range.

When the men exchanged a glance and moved for her, she stepped into it—still buying time. She would have walked right between them if they hadn't grabbed her upper arms, leaving them with the awkward necessity of turning around as a single unit in order to escort her backwards from the underpass.

And that's all they figured they had to do, she realized, and was insulted all over again. Just walk in, grab her arms, and walk right out again. "Am I supposed to make little squeally, frightened girly noises while you're at it?" she demanded in English, not concerned that they might have trouble with her slang and her sarcasm or even her train of thought.

In fact, they did no more than exchange another glance, very much *what did you expect?* They'd probably known about her bad reaction to the super cocktail; they'd certainly gotten an eyeful of her *Cats* performance. And now, meaty fingers closed hard on her biceps, they thought they had her.

Steve's voice, strained or not, was music to her ears. "Hey, fellas."

Mickey's words under her breath came in a sing-songy rhythm. "You're gonna be sor-ry." One of them gave her a quick series of jerks, as though she were nothing more than a doll. But Steve's words meant that everyone was under cover—that he was ready to go. She tensed—

"Let her go, now," Steve said. He should have just unloaded a couple of arrows into them. Too much of a nice guy, dammit. Mickey . . . probably not so much of a nice girl. Under these circumstances, she would have—

The guy on her right grunted . . . staggered. Mickey jerked her head around and got a glimpse of fletching jutting into the air from the other side of the man. *Whoop! Go Steve!*

The guy on her left went for his gun, reaching inside his loose suit jacket. Mickey wrenched her arm loose from the wounded man—he, too, groped for a gun, and the two shouted at one another in quick, hard phrases that Mickey couldn't follow. And loud. Way too loud.

And they weren't paying nearly enough attention to her.

She slammed her heel behind the wounded man's knee—

already off balance, he went down hard, screaming as he landed on the arrow. The second man turned to her in annoyance, ready to slap her down with a gun-filled hand. *Shoot him too!* she thought at Steve, but knew they were too close now, too unpredictable.

She shifted the knife in her hand so it protruded out beyond her palm, and she slashed backwards, taking him on with the same arm he'd thought immobilized. *Speed is everything . . .* She scored him across the ribs, the blade so sharp he probably wasn't even sure what she'd done. But it threw him off anyway, and the pistol landed across her shoulder instead of on her head.

Mickey staggered under it—but didn't back off, not for an instant. Using his own grip on her as a fulcrum, she went for his ribs again—biting more deeply this time, metal skidding off bone and then jamming between ribs. This time he felt it—he roared at the insult and tossed her away as though she were weightless. She felt like human skeet, expecting to hear the report of his gun, feel the impact of a bullet—

Oof. Just the impact of the ground, rattling her head. She rolled with it, reaching over her numbed shoulder for a second knife—only to run smack into the black barrel of a gun. The wounded man's Glock 36, jammed right into her face as she came to her knees, heading for her feet—but stopping, sinking back, gone from hunter to hunted and frozen with the very visceral fear of that gaping .45 barrel.

An arrow quite suddenly sprouted from the man's chest, blooming in Mickey's peripheral vision. She dove away as the gun went off; the acid burn of the bullet cut across her neck, kicking her right back into high gear. She rolled upright to the tattoo of gunfire reverberating around the underpass—*shooting at Steve, a bullet pinging off metal*—and brought her arm back as she rose, flinging the knife in one smooth motion, letting the handle slip through her fingers with a whisper of cool metal.

It pinned the second man's lapel to his chest even as he turned to sight in on her. Steve's arrow followed close behind, a much more lethal wound, and the pistol sagged in the man's hand as he looked down at himself. Mickey launched herself up, kicking the gun away and just as quickly gathering it up, one hand at her neck just to make sure she wasn't gushing blood.

Leakage, yes. Gushing, no.

She turned back to the first man, grabbing up his gun as well. Neither man had long to live without help and she hesitated there. "Aw, dammit," she finally muttered, and patted the man down for a cell phone. Found it, too, and opened it up, putting it in his hand. "Call your people," she told him, speaking in his own language. Damn, she'd have to get out of here fast.

She returned to the second man—he reached for her, grasping, as though he still thought he could get his hands on her. She ignored him, yanking her knives free, then went for Steve's arrows. My, my, wasn't she just neat and tidy?

But weapons could be traced. Fingerprints, tool marks, manufacturers . . . they were evidence. If the cops got here before the Irhaddanians, Mickey wanted none of this in their hands. She only hoped the Irhaddanians would do as thorough a job cleaning up here as they had in at the gym. "You good?" she yelled toward Steve, not quite ready to turn away from the fallen men. One more arrow . . .

But he didn't answer right away, and she repeated her call, interrupting herself with a grunt of effort as the final arrow came free.

"Mickey," he said, his voice uncertain, and that's when she finally whirled to look at him—to see he wasn't alone. To see that the two Irhaddanians hadn't been alone, either. A third man stood behind Steve—and he had Mosquito cringing at his side, swatting air with distinct, crooning grunts of effort that made for a constant if syncopated *wuhwuh wuh wuh* in the background. Steve stood with his hands away from his sides, the bow discarded, his spine in such an unnatural posture of attention that Mickey knew damned well he had a gun jammed into his back.

She straightened, letting her gathered weapons slip through her fingers to clatter on the ground. One blade in the harness, that's all she had left. She didn't wait for the man's demands. "Your friends are dying," she told him, using his own language.

"A tongue such as yours should speak only your own ugly language and sing your own ugly songs," he said in English. "Don't make that mistake again. You need no tongue to write the information we need."

Steve half-turned to give the man a horrified look, but instantly jerked and straightened.

Mickey said, "What does it matter what Naia has told me, if I can't remember it? That would be your fault, by the way. Your people—or those working for your people—are the ones who did that to me. Talk to that woman."

The man spat off to the side. Mickey hadn't realized that anyone did that anymore. Mosquito reacted in horror, swatting and slapping, whining frantically as he tried to break away. The man had only a grip on his shirt, but it was sufficient to hold Mosquito's uncoordinated efforts. "They assure me they can reverse that problem."

Not according to what Mickey had overheard the doctor saying. Of course, the bitch who'd questioned her about Naia was probably desperate about now. Would probably say anything. The Irhaddanians had hired her to do a job, and she'd messed it up in a big way.

"These men are yours, I think," the man said, giving

Mosquito a little shake, giving Steve a little jab. "Come with me, if you want them to live."

And Mickey, hands away from her sides, stepped toward the shadow of the underpass.

"Mickey—!" Steve gave her a horrified look—a look that said he'd seen too many action movies where the hero never bows to the inevitable. Never loses.

Not that she was done yet. But she wasn't playing this out with their lives, only with hers.

"*Mickey—!*"

"Nothing to talk about, Steve," she told him—quite evenly, she thought—and walked to the edge of the shadow. If the cops were going to be here, she thought there'd be some sign of them by now. A siren. A prowling cruiser. She said to the man, "I'm coming. But I need to talk to him first." And nodded at Steve.

The man snorted. "Talk," he said, his English heavily accented even on single-word sentences. "Right here." And he gave Steve another nudge with the gun just to remind them both that he could. Mosquito, whining and cringing in his grip, was clearly starting to annoy him.

"Run," Mickey said to Steve. "As soon as he lets you go, just run." And here was the risk—the chance that the man's English was no better than it sounded, and Mickey's bet that he wouldn't be able to follow simple pig-Latin. "He's going to ill-kay you oth-bay anyway—ab-gray a un-gay." Either of them, still in the pile of discarded weapons. She had no idea if he knew guns, but she hadn't set the safeties on either before she'd been forced to discard them.

"But—"

She didn't let him finish that—*what about you?* She put a finger to his lips, tracing them. She hadn't expected her hand to be bloody; she hadn't expected it to be trembling. She leaned in to kiss him—a strangely erotic hands-off kiss, arms still halfway to "hands in the air" position. At first he was frozen, shocked—and then he kissed her back with more greed than she'd known he had, pouring enough into that kiss to make it feel like full body contact.

She wanted to get lost in it.

Of course, that would kill them both. She pulled back enough to finish what she'd started, whispering against his mouth, "You got it? I'll try to distract him. Get the damned guns and take him out before he gets *you*."

He didn't have time to answer—instead of prodding him, this time the man yanked him back. Out of contact, out of range.

Mickey caught Steve's eye, and she saw the understanding there. Maybe they'd make it . . . maybe not. But he'd try.

"Take your idiot friend," the man said, thrusting Mosquito forward. Mosquito stumbled into Steve, and Steve just barely kept them both upright.

He'd have to leave Mosquito behind if he was going to reach the guns in time.

But Steve didn't. He righted the man, he took the time to say, "We're going inside now, Mosquito. Behind the walls." It made no particular sense to Mickey, but Mosquito straightened, standing under his own power, understanding briefly surfacing in his eyes. "Let's go, then."

And Mickey stood, the very figure of bereft defeat, hugging her upper arms and shoulders in a crooked embrace, one hand just shy of the burn across her neck.

And not so far from the knife at that.

She watched them go, her gaze lingering on Steve as though it were the last time she'd see him—and watching, from the corner of her eye, as the man followed their progress, Mosquito's stumblings and Steve's efforts to hurry him along. She saw when the man lifted his chin slightly; she knew what would follow. *The gun.*

She moved. She snatched the final blade from the shoulder harness, slashing outward with the same motion, whirling into the follow-through. Right across his neck, a mirror image of her own wound—but much deeper.

His gun discharged—not once but twice, finishing what he'd been about to start. Mickey kicked it out of his hand and when he grabbed for her—not quite aware of the severity of his wound—she met his reaching hand with the knife, jamming it right through his palm. He stared stupidly at it a moment, as if he couldn't understand why such a peripheral wound would leach his strength so quickly—and then he realized. He had just enough time to dab his fingers in the arterial spurt of his own blood before his knees slowly gave way.

Mickey stepped on his hand and yanked her knife away. "You shouldn't have dissed *Cats.*" But her voice was grim, and she thought she'd never get clean again no matter how many showers she took.

Never.

And then she looked over to Steve, to find him whole and yet his expression still stunned, still reeling—and Mosquito in his arms, slowly slipping toward the ground.

Looked like she was playing with other lives after all.

She wanted to run to him. But she couldn't help Mosquito and she couldn't take away Steve's pain—and she *could* watch their backs. Get them ready to run. And chase away any of the underpass people who were left.

First, to call someone who *could* help Mosquito—for the wound still bled, and that meant he was still alive. She appropriated a cell phone from the dead man, calling in a quick 9-1-1 and then hanging up when she wasn't supposed to. No one from the underpass was in evidence as she turned to the bike, scooping up Steve's bow and not quite ready to break it down yet.

She slung the quiver over her shoulder and hung the bow there much more awkwardly. At the bike she checked the saddlebags—empty, other than a few personal items and Steve's now-flaccid backpack. She flipped the kickstand back and wheeled the bike toward Steve, but not without hesitating to shout to the palpably fearful silence of the underpass, "Steve was telling you to leave this place for a while—you'd best do it. I won't be back—I won't cause you any more trouble. I—" she stopped, knowing the words were inadequate to the point of absurdity, but in the end she couldn't walk away without saying it. "I'm sorry."

Silence greeted this remark, as well it might. She thought she heard a sob—of grief or fear, she didn't know. They were still here somewhere, she knew that much—gone to ground, probably already bundling up their belongings and their new acquisitions and ready to bolt the moment the coast seemed clear.

She pushed the bike out into the sunshine, squinting resentfully. Too bright and cheerful by far. But it didn't slow her—she couldn't afford for it to slow her. Off to the side, she gathered up her little cache of dropped weapons, cleaning the knives and jamming them home at her shoulder. Into the quiver went the arrows; into the saddlebags went the guns. Swiftly, matter-of-factly. Behind her, the scuffle and whisper told her that some of the underpass occupants had re-emerged, and were taking her advice. Someone commandeered the new cart; she heard the quickly diminishing squeak of wheels.

Steve sat on the ground just as he'd gone down, Mosquito half on his lap, his hands pressing desperately on the chest wound. Mickey couldn't even imagine how he felt. One man from his world dead, another possibly dying . . . and he'd shot two men, one of whom still whispered desperately into his cell phone as he inched away from his dead or dying buddy.

Dead or dying. Steve had done that. And as much as Mickey's throat burned with the awareness of how effectively she'd handled her encounters, she knew that somewhere along the line, she'd made the choice to become that person. She'd taken on that responsibility—she'd trained for it. Steve *hadn't.* Steve had trained for saving the world—or his little corner of it. His target practice had been a refuge from his efforts, not part of those efforts.

She couldn't imagine him picking up his bow to blow off a little steam ever again.

"Steve," she said, and felt just as she had with the street people . . . there were no adequate words. She'd gotten him involved, and now his life would never be the same.

If he even got to keep that.

She cleared her throat. "Steve, we have to go."

He looked at her without comprehension, lifting that dark-lashed gaze to reveal all the things she expected, and more.

"We won't be alone long. We've got to—"

"What?" he demanded. "Leave him? Like we left Anthony, and now no one but us even knows he was killed?"

"I called for help," she said. "And for Anthony . . . when this is over—"

Anger sparked to the surface. "Is it going to be over, Mickey? Or is this just the beginning?"

Both. "I'm sorry," she whispered, and winced when it made not a dent on his grief. Then again, she hadn't expected it to.

The wounded man was the one to get her attention—to raise new alarm. He stopped talking on the phone, dropped it, and scrabbled to get away. But Steve's arrow must have hit an artery; the man was pale and shocky and managed approximately half a step before staggering down to a crawl.

That part didn't worry Mickey. What worried her was *why*—

and she immediately went looking for the cause.

And found it. Behind her, at the overpass . . . someone had parked just beyond the bridge, and two people now navigated the steep slope of the overpass at that point. Not wanting to lose any time, those two.

Neither did Mickey. She dropped the bow and quiver, and dove for the saddlebags. By the time she had her hands on a gun—the one with the most cartridges in the magazine, she hoped—the two were close enough so she could see they weren't cops, weren't from Irhaddan. No, it was her two friends from the night she'd broken into CapAd.Com.

She wasn't sure this was any better.

She put herself in front of Steve, legs braced in a no-nonsense stance and the gun at the ready in a two-handed grip.

"Hey, *hey*," the man said, and put his hands half in the air. But he didn't drop the little snub-nose he held, and his partner didn't drop her sleek little semi-auto. "I thought we'd established that we're all friends here."

"Friends would have knocked," Mickey said.

"We didn't want to startle you."

"That *is* thoughtful. But as long as you're here, you can play clean-up. I'm sure you have the resources for that. Though you should know there's help coming for the wounded."

The woman looked around in a mixture of disgust and frustration. "Dammit, did you have to be so messy?"

"I like to think of *them* as the messy ones," Mickey told her. "Though they cleaned up the mess at the gym pretty well. You know about that, right?"

They exchanged a glance. "We suspected," the man said finally. "Look, we really need you to come in and talk to us. We understand that something's happened so you no longer trust us, but it's obvious you're not working for Irhaddan—"

"You *think?*" Mickey said. "And I'd love to chat, but I'm

busy." *Busy getting ready to take this fight back to Irhaddan. All the way back.*

"I'm afraid we're going to insist," the man said. Bold talk for someone who was still a third of the way up a steep bank, his gun nowhere near taking aim.

And Steve said, "No, you're not." And when he stood behind Mickey, he already had the bow drawn.

"Steve," she said, alarmed.

"Doesn't look like I have much to lose," he said. "And I'm damned tired of being someone's playing piece."

"There's always more to lose," she told him sharply, aching to turn her gaze away from the two under her sights, and knowing she couldn't. "If they're really CIA, that's a tangle you'll never get out of."

"At least *my* paranoia would be real," he said, his voice hard; it sounded as thought it came through clenched teeth.

The woman interrupted their exchange with surprised annoyance. "Of *course* we're CIA. *You're* CIA, for God's sake. What the hell—"

"She doesn't remember," the man said, dawning realization offsetting his partner's strong words. "That's what that was all about outside CapAd. She doesn't the hell remember."

"I don't the hell remember," Mickey agreed, but inside she felt as taut as the bowstring Steve had drawn. "And I don't the hell know how you—or *I*—can be CIA and working on U.S. turf."

"Oh, for—" The woman had lost none of her abrasive edge. "Foreign Services, Dreidler."

Mickey shook her head, a small gesture, and added a shrug. "Means nothing. Sorry. Like I said, we've got to go. And Steve's had a really bad day. I'm not about to let you near him, and I don't suggest you try to get near *me*. We're going to take the bike, and—"

"Foreign Services," the man said. "We work *here,* but we target foreign citizens. Our assets. Lately you've been working someone new—we've figured out that much. And I can tell you we've pretty much guessed who, thanks to the Irhaddanian involvement."

Naia.

Mickey hated that this was making sense. It meant she couldn't just walk away . . . and it meant she had to. It meant she was one of the good guys . . . and it meant she'd somehow lured a naive young woman into spying on her own family and risking her life to do so, which in her newly unsullied mind also made her one of the bad guys.

"Look," the man said. "We don't work in a vacuum. The FBI works closely with us, and they *know* there's something going on. If they find you—if they take you into custody—they're not going to give you the benefit of the doubt. They'd just love to use you as proof that we're as wildcard as they say we are. Don't even talk about Homeland Security—"

"Then I guess you'd better clean up this mess really well," Mickey said. They couldn't stay, not with sirens rising in the background, not even if it tore Steve apart to leave Mosquito alone. "You'd better make sure Mosquito gets the best of care." She lifted her chin in a gesture Steve could barely see, but one he acted on. He withdrew, leaving a cold spot at her back in spite of the day's warmth. In a moment, the bike started—and then discussion was impossible.

Mickey didn't need discussion to know that if they were telling the truth, they'd no more shoot her than they would tattoo *CIA Officer* on their foreheads. And if they weren't . . .

Best to know the truth now.

CHAPTER 18

Steve knew the feeling.

Mickey had a stunned look on her face. Now that they had handily escaped the CIA officers and no one else currently had sights on them, Steve supposed she could finally afford to have that stunned look on her face. "CIA," she said, having slipped off the motorcycle as Steve killed the engine outside the Internet café, twisting tail-shaking miles later. One more email check before they proceeded—and from the look on Mickey's face, she planned to proceed with vigor. "*CIA.* Hell of it is, I still don't know if that makes me one of the bad guys or one of the good guys." And her bright eyes darkened with pain, the way they did every time she thought of the woman Naia.

Yeah, Steve knew the feeling.

He'd always thought of himself as a good guy. As one of the problem solvers, not the problem starters.

Now he wasn't so sure.

"I need to wash my hands," he said grimly. "And you should wash that . . ."

"Hard to say *bullet wound* with a straight face, isn't it?" She wrinkled her nose. "Flesh wound, maybe?"

"No John Wayne impressions," he said, but she'd gotten him to smile. It didn't last long. Not with Mosquito's blood still on his hands and clothes.

Sorry, Zander. I'm not doing so well by your friends.

Not that Mickey had meant any harm, giving supplies directly to the underpass occupants; she'd certainly known better than to give them the mugger harvest directly. Missy would have OD'd on meth largesse, Jake would have finished destroying his liver, and Mosquito . . .

Mosquito would have given his share to Missy and Jake.

If he'd thought it was a bad idea, he'd have stopped Mickey. Maybe he *should* have thought it was a bad idea. Maybe he should have thought about it harder. He just hadn't expected the Irhaddanians to come after them in broad daylight.

Then again, neither had Mickey. And for the CIA to follow—

"Hey," he said, turning back to her as he tucked his helmet over a handlebar and took hers to do the same. "How the hell did they find us?"

"They hit paydirt with Anthony," Mickey said, nonplussed by the obvious. "Thought they'd try again. Not bad thinking, as it turned out."

"I mean the CIA," Steve said, trying to keep the impatience from his voice. It wasn't her fault; she'd been as surprised as he had. And she was the reason they'd gotten away.

"Oh," she said. "Hey, they're *CIA*. Who the hell knows how—" But she stopped, confusion on her face, and looked away. Shame, he might have said. She said, "I guess I *should* know. I guess I'm CIA, too. Them are us."

"Not at the moment," he said, not expecting his own ferocity. And then his mind's eye flashed back to the underpass, where in a heartbeat she'd gone from cheerful and laughing to deadly. She hadn't faltered; she hadn't needed time to plan her strategy. And when she'd taken action she'd been swift and unhesitating, and on this day she'd killed at least one man herself. She'd been deadly with the blade in her hand, with the blade thrown, or even with her hands empty. . . .

And now she stood beside his bike, watching him with worried eyes, an ugly, ugly gouge across her neck just where it made him think of *what might have been*. His hand reached out of its own volition, touching her neck beside the wound, and then moving to trace the line of her jaw. And then quite suddenly he'd closed the distance, giving her only enough time to widen her eyes before he kissed her—hard and thorough, driven by something greedy that didn't seem as though it could ever be slaked. But she met his need with her own, and he drank from her—

Until he broke away so abruptly that they both gasped, and he thought she might pull him right back in. Breathing heavily, staring at each other like a befuddled Romeo and Juliet—until someone across the street applauded, a sardonic sounding and well-spaced clap . . . clap . . . clap.

Mickey, being Mickey, turned around and took a bow. A bow with a flourish.

Steve had no such capacity. But he took several deep breaths. He wiped the back of his hand across his mouth, and he pretended she didn't strike him anew when she turned back with her cheeks flushed and her lips just-kissed. "Right," she said, and if she looked longingly at his mouth, she didn't let it stop her from squaring her shoulders, reaching into the saddlebags for his backpack, and straightening with purpose. "Time to wash up."

They ducked through the café, and Mickey hoped that those inside were so immersed in their Internet activity that she and Steve wouldn't be worth looking at—because if they were, they'd be worth a second look, too. She only had that point confirmed when she made it into the bathroom and discovered the splash of blood at the neckline of her T-shirt, drying to dark around the edges but still bright in the middle. And soaked through, so turning the thing inside out would do no good at all. And taking it off meant exposing the knife harness at her shoulder.

In the end she took it off, feeling exposed in the sport top. She removed the harness as well, and wrapped it within the shirt. She'd damn well better hope to avoid any new encounters until she rearmed herself.

I was trying to help. *To turn dirty money to good use.* And to take the sting out of using it for her own purposes, if she was brutally honest with herself. If she'd thought about it, she'd have known she was bringing trouble down on those vulnerable people.

Yeah, right. She stared at herself in the mirror, as though she could find some secret, hidden knowledge in the bright blue eyes that stared back at her. Choppy hair, blood staining her neck in a thin, uneven pattern, the hollows of her face and collarbones already filling in since her first arrival at the gym. She had to have been out for several days in the aftermath of that chemical knock-out drug to have lost that weight. They hadn't had the facilities to do more than keep her hydrated—or possibly even the desire.

Mickey grabbed a rough brown paper towel and wetted it under the faucet, scrubbing roughly at the sensitive skin on her neck. There'd be no answers in the mirror. No answers in her own mind. Just as she'd failed to anticipate what had happened to Anthony and Mosquito, she would continue to fail in this operation. She was working off her gut and her instinct, and it had gotten her a long way . . . but it couldn't do everything. The longer this kept up, the more chance she had of walking them right into trouble again.

Her neck stung; she eased up her ministrations, re-soaking the towel to dab at the edges of the wound. It was already crusty. They'd have to pick up some triple antibiotic on the way back to the warehouse.

And oh, yeah, some .45mm ammo for the two Glock 36s they'd acquired.

Because Mickey didn't intend to wait around for someone else to take the next step. The longer this dragged on, the stronger the chances that she'd stumble into a situation she couldn't get out of—or that she'd expose other people to that situation.

Other people. *Steve.*

She dried her neck, patting down the sport top where the water had run down on it. When another woman entered the bathroom and stopped short at the sight of her, Mickey gave her a rueful shrug. "Wicked nail file accident," she said, and breezed back out of the bathroom.

She discovered Steve at a computer station, his hair wet in a finger-combed way that turned the curls wickedly ruffled. His face had the same scrubbed-clean flush as her own, and his hands, stilled at the keyboard, no longer spoke of Mosquito's questionable fate. He'd turned his T-shirt inside-out, and though he now looked as though he needed his mother to dress him, the blood didn't show. He glanced up at her arrival and nodded at the screen. "Some interesting headlines about some crazy person who seems to be taking down muggers. The police are calling it vigilantism and making stern noises. That's just the teaser headline of the day, though. Check this out."

But Mickey's thoughts were latched onto action, and the immediate future. She said, "We need to stop at a sporting goods store. And I need to borrow your bike. This has gone far—"

"Mickey." He looked away from the screen long enough to raise his brow and truly get her attention. She didn't want to listen; she didn't want to lose the least bit of the internal momentum she'd built up. *Go. Do something. Fix it. Stop what's happening.*

But she stopped in mid-word, her fingers tightening on the shirt and knife bundle until she could feel the details of leather and metal through the cotton. He was in this as much as she;

his efforts here deserved respect. As soon as saw that he had her attention, he leaned back in his chair, ignoring the screen much as she had. "You know, Irhaddan has a unique position in this country, relative to those countries around it. It's the one country in that region that isn't under constant scrutiny when it comes to weapons. The president makes no bones about it—they're small, and they're relatively homogenous in population. They have little internal strife, no religious wars, and they want no part of the violent heritage of everyone around them."

In spite of herself, Mickey smiled. "Homogenous," she said. "No one uses that word in casual conversation."

"Hey, I read a lot," he said, pretending offense. It didn't last long; neither of them were up to any real banter. "I saw it in an article this morning. Point is, it's a pretty quiet little place. Their hardships come from the spotty use of modern conveniences and medicine and education, and that's partly thanks to the shifting population around their borders—they're getting crowded by refugees from their neighbors. People who want to raise their families without getting involved in suicide bombings and random automatic gunfire. So Irhaddan . . . it's really not a weapons of mass destruction kind of place. The president is clear about that."

"I don't follow you." And she didn't. She was too focused on the here and now. San Jose. Today. Stopping this. She thought she could cause a pretty big ruckus at CapAd.Com. She thought she might just march on down to the Irhaddan embassy and make a public demand to speak to Naia. She wasn't sure either of those things was the least bit wise, but it was all overridden by that overwhelming need to—

Fix it. Stop it. Make it better.

"So if you wanted to hide some nice WMDs, where would you do it? In the place where you have to dodge inspections and constant spy eyes, or in a place no one worries about?"

"I can't believe Mejjati would—" Mickey stopped herself. So she had an opinion about that, did she?

Steve noted it, glancing sharply at her, but let it pass. "What if the president doesn't know?" He lowered his voice, going from casual conversation fodder to something more pointed. "What if you really are with Foreign Services, and what if you've talked a young woman with unique access into keeping her eyes open for you because the CIA is beginning to suspect what the president doesn't know?"

Mickey felt an odd rush of relief. "Then I wouldn't have talked her into spying on her own father. In a way . . . she would be working *for* him. Protecting him."

Steve shrugged, offering enough reservation so Mickey knew he didn't buy any hint of altruism on the CIA's part. "Look," he said. "We've got a lot of information. We know who you are. I know you couldn't trust those two at the underpass, but they didn't shoot us, right? Kinda backs up their story. Don't you think we should somehow call—-"

"No," Mickey said, more sharply than she'd meant to. "They'd lock us away in isolated rooms until they could be sure we were playing things straight. They'd do what they think is best for the States, not for Naia. We don't go to the authorities—*any* authorities—until Naia is safe."

Steve gave her an even look. "I don't know if that's truly in her best interest," he said. "I can't argue with you . . . they'll snatch us up and throw us under bright lamps until they're happy they've gotten all the answers. But if Naia still has information, surely they'd—"

"No," Mickey said, simply enough. "Agency turf wars, bad communications, international pressure . . . those things will all come before Naia. Especially if they think they can get their intel another way, now that they're alert for it."

He absently touched his shirt, there in the spot where it must have felt damp against his skin; the dark stain almost showed through. "I guess . . ." he said, his thoughts taking him inward, "I guess even if they responded, they wouldn't do it in time." And then he indicated the monitor again. She leaned over his shoulder and tapped the shift key to disengage the screensaver and read the email on display there.

Dear A:

Thank you for your interest. I am indisposed but well. I still love working on my pottery and will come as soon as I have the opportunity. I am pleased that my piece is being fired tonight.

Naia

And Mickey felt an instant jolt of fear. "They've got to be monitoring her email. She's got to know—"

"She does," he said. "Look at what she's written. She's trying to make them think she's putting A. off. And I think she'll try to meet you tonight. Meet *us.*"

She frowned at him, wanted to tell him there'd be no *us* about it, not if they were getting into the thick of it. But rather than get off track just then, she said, "It can't work. They've got to realize—"

"It *might*," he said. "Look—what is it they want to know? What Naia's told you. They aren't sure of her one way or another. They need irrefutable proof before they act. They may not even believe it themselves. She's an isolated young woman from a culture that keeps its women behind closed doors. What if they don't suspect her of active involvement—what if they think it's all your doing, that you've siphoned information from her? They won't expect active spy games from her."

The frown deepened into a scowl. "That's an awful lot of *iffing*. With too much riding on it."

"And nothing to lose from being at that warehouse this evening. Because you know what? I looked at that firing schedule yesterday. Her stuff's not on it."

"And her piece . . . isn't ready." Mickey pressed the heels of her hands against her eyes, a wave of self-recrimination battering up against her. "I'm such an idiot. I should be the one figuring out these details."

"You've got a lot on your mind," Steve said. And then, when she lifted her hands to give him a silent *oh, please*, he added, all innocence, "Or a lot *off* your mind, whichever way you want to look at it. The point is . . . I think she'll be there tonight. So no, you can't borrow the bike. I think you should be there tonight too."

"And if she doesn't show?" *If she's dead, if she can't get away, if that's not what she meant in the first place—*

"Then tomorrow, you can borrow the bike."

"It's a Glock 36," Mickey said, holding the gun on display in one hand. It sat there comfortably. Too comfortably. And she knew . . .

She knew far too much about it.

"The magazine holds six rounds; there's one in the chamber. Only thing you have to do to fire it is pull the trigger—it's got a heavy pull, though. It'll take you by surprise the first couple of times."

"I hope it always takes me by surprise," Steve muttered. He sat beside her on her air mattress, both of them cross-legged. The spoils from Mickey's shopping excursions were spread out before them—ropes and carabineers and harnesses, a new knife or two, a handful of broad-head hunting arrows. He was to stay out of sight, she'd told him—he was her secret weapon—and thanks to the silence of the bow, he could do some damage before they located him. But once that happened, he'd need to know how to use the gun.

"This is the magazine catch, in case you need to reload. We've got a couple of extras now. This model sometimes doesn't quite let go of the magazine, so don't expect it to come shooting out like in the movies."

"Right," he said, and his voice still very much indicated his disbelief that he was even having this conversation. But when she checked his expression, she found his eyes deep and dark and loaded with determination. She reminded herself . . . this was a man who taught self-defense for a living. Who knew his body; knew his capabilities. Who could pose for a sculptor any day, beautifully formed and proportioned and muscled.

It was his heart she worried about.

She quit biting her lip and cleared her throat. "Here's the thing—it's a lightweight gun, and it's shooting .45 ammo. That means lots of recoil. Don't go for the *blamblamblam* style of shooting—your gun's just going to kick higher and higher. Aim a little lower than you think you should." She chewed on her lower lip a moment, wondering if she'd told him enough—wondering if she'd remembered everything.

Didn't really matter. She'd told him what she could. "Here," she said. "This one's yours."

He took it. He turned it over in his hands and said, "You know I'm not going to hit anything, no matter how much advice you give me."

Probably not. And probably just as well that way. She said, "It'll be covering fire." And then she said, "You're sure—"

He held up one hand. "Mickey. Do you really think I'm going to just walk away?"

She opened her mouth for a flippant response, and decided he deserved better. Looked at him, then—looked closely. Late afternoon light barely lit the third floor of the warehouse, hindered by the dirt-filmed windows, but it was enough to see that his dark brows and impossible lashes framed eyes that couldn't have been more sincere. Totally aware of what he'd done, of how his life was changing with each passing moment. He couldn't go back to the gym right now even if he wanted to . . . but she didn't think he'd go even if he could.

He met her scrutiny unfazed. "It's not just about you anymore, Mickey. And even if it was—if it always had been—this is one I want to see to the end. This is one where the people I care about—where the *person* I care about—is going to *win*, dammit."

She wasn't so sure the odds supported such determination. But she understood. He'd lost too much to look at it any other way. Anthony and now maybe Mosquito, the satisfying world he'd created for himself . . . and quite possibly everything he'd ever thought he was. Or hoped he'd be.

All because she'd lost herself more thoroughly than he'd ever imagined before she'd stumbled into his gym.

So maybe she owed him the chance to help make this a win.

Without planning it, she said, "Every morning I wake up not knowing. Have you ever done that? You wake up and you have no idea where you are, what day it is, how you got there . . . and then you grasp at glimmers of remembering, until suddenly there you are in your own home, in your own bed, and it's Tuesday, and you've got coffee on a timer in your own kitchen and things you plan to do that day." She added a box of ammo to the semi-automatic she'd just given him, as matter-of-factly as though they did this every day. "But that never happens to me. I never wake up all the way. I fake it through each day, wondering when I'll know how I got here in the first place."

"Antiques," Steve said, and winced, looking as though he hadn't truly intended to say anything at all. But he'd said it with such certainty—

"You *found* me?" And then, "You found me and you didn't *tell* me?"

"You said—"

She'd said she didn't want to know. That it would muddle her thinking, confusing two different issues. That if it didn't trigger the right memories, it would only get in the way of thinking through the situation—of figuring out how to find Naia and keep her safe. So she shook her head, sharply. "I know. I said I didn't—" But she couldn't finish the thought, too overrun by new ones. "You know more than my name? You know who I am? What I do? At least, what the world thinks . . ." She stopped again, trying to order her thoughts. Fat chance of that. "Antiques?"

He nodded, watching her with wary caution. She couldn't blame him . . . she'd already shown that mixing past and present could trigger brittle reactions. He added, "High end antiques, from what I can tell. Exclusive. Commissions. Finder's fees and treasure hunts."

She'd been right. The table, the vase, the candlesticks—even the cat. She'd been right. She'd found that little piece of herself, by herself.

"Hey, *hey*," Steve said. "You're not—you *are*—"

Crying. She was crying. "Happy!" she choked, and offered him a watery smile. And she meant it. As much as the emotion had ambushed her, she meant it. Because maybe one of these days . . .

She'd wake up not knowing, and she'd grasp at glimmers of remembering . . . and she'd find them.

Steve must have understood, for he put his arm around her shoulders and drew her in, and there in the midst of weapons and gear and hopes and escape plans, they sat together in silence. They listened to the noises below—the scraping of chairs and increased conversation and laughter, drifting up the stairwell to tell them the late afternoon class had ended. Shifting them closer to the evening, when they hoped for Naia to appear. They waited for the noise of the class exodus to fade away, and then in tacit accord, shifted away from one another.

The air felt cool on Mickey's side and shoulder where she'd been so comfortable against him; reality felt cold against her bones. She said, "Let's talk about rappelling."

CHAPTER 19

Naia thought she might be ill. She sat at her desk, dressed as though she'd actually gone to classes, the room tidy and clean around her, ostensibly typing notes for her art history architectural comparisons paper. And quite, quite sure she was going to be sick. *Hasbun Allah wa ni'am al-wakil.* Words of solace, and she clung to them.

It's going to happen, Anna had told her when she asked about being in a tight situation. *But you have the power to turn it into nothing. To keep it unrealized.*

Out in the small living room, the television muttered, set to the sports station Fadil Hisami liked to watch. Badra worked her embroidery, patiently fulfilling her duties as she thought Naia's father would desire.

Except Naia's father would never imprison her like this. He might well choose to confine her to the apartment—for her own safety, to prevent misunderstandings, even in censure. But not without speaking to her about it. Not without making sure she understood why.

No, this wasn't coming from her father at all. It wasn't something he'd want, no matter what Fadil Hisami said. And that meant he probably knew nothing of this situation.

Fadil still limped. Once she'd seen blood staining his trousers. It gave her a grim satisfaction she hadn't known she could feel at someone else's misfortune. But now . . . now it meant he wouldn't be as fast as normal. It meant she might be faster.

And it meant she had reason to be faster.

Her stomach turned.

Fear is good; we should listen to what it tells us, and then use it— but not be used by it. So put that part of yourself away. Close it into a little bubble of elsewhere.

Naia imagined a bubble of elsewhere. She imagined her fear floating off in that bubble. She pictured it clearly, floating off into the dark recesses of her inner self. She returned to her work and hit *print,* and as soon as the page was done, fed it back for the second side. When it was done she folded it into a tiny rectangle, and while she folded it, she electronically shredded the file. No getting that one back.

Hisami's cell phone burbled; Naia started. Fear flooded her— animal fear, heart-pounding, gut-churning—

For the care with which she was being treated would last only so long as it was expedient. And once she made this move, she would no longer be expedient at all. She would kick the situation into a crisis for those behind it.

And those behind it had a lot to lose.

She clapped her hand over her mouth, willing her stomach to stop heaving even as she pushed away from the desk and turned toward the hall.

"Naia?" Badra called to her. "Is everything well?"

Had she gasped? Made a sound of distress? She didn't even know. She swallowed—or tried to. A second time she succeeded. She pretended she was Anna. Anna, who knew what she was doing, and who had somehow disappeared from Naia's world . . . until that email. She knew—she *knew*—the email had something to do with Anna. She had to believe it, if she was going to make this move. "Everything's fine," she called. "I'm just finishing up on these notes." Notes that weren't about art history at all, but which detailed the conversation she'd overheard in Irhaddan. Not so very long ago, and yet . . .

Lifetimes.

But even if she didn't find Anna this evening, she'd leave the notes in the dead drop. She should have done it earlier, but she'd been arrogant enough to think she could continue to bluff her way past Hisami's people until she'd gotten advice from Anna.

No longer.

She made herself get up from the chair to stand in the doorway where Badra could see her. She wasn't Naia at all . . . she was Anna's courage, Anna's confidence. "I'm just finishing up on these notes. I'd like to take a shower and have some dinner. You don't think there would be a problem with ordering Chinese food, do you? There's a place not far from here run by a nice family . . ."

Badra looked to Hisami, who looked away from the television long enough to give her his standard disapproval. "Order something appropriate," he commanded her, reminding her of her faith's dietary restrictions. As if she needed *him* to tell her how to make such choices. Annoyance reinforced her faltering resolve.

"Of course," she told him, as respectful as she'd ever been. She put Anna's courage into her legs and moved briskly for the bedroom, where she pulled out a casual long-sleeved lilac shirt and the matching wide-legged fleece pants. An evening lounge set, and one Badra had often seen her wear when she was in for the night. She spoke briefly to Badra with the clothing in her arms, and then she headed for the bathroom, where she closed and locked the door.

She rustled the shower curtain, turning the water on full. And then, under the cover of the flushing toilet, she pulled the screen from the window and poked her head out.

The fire escape from the bedroom wasn't so very far away.

Or so she tried to tell herself.

"That didn't take long." Mickey climbed over the lip of the third floor, out the elevator shaft and the doors they'd jammed open. She dumped the colorful mountain climbing rope in a coil at her feet and unclipped it from the carabineer at the front of the Swiss seat she wore.

Elevator shaft. Perfect clandestine location for teaching someone how to rappel. And when Steve climbed out of the shaft behind her, his grin spread across a dirt-smudged face. Before she knew it, he'd wrapped his arms around her waist and hoisted her up, swinging her around once before letting her slide down his body—oh, my, yes—and stopping her when her toes barely touched the floor. "What—" she started to say, but he silenced her with a quick, hard kiss. When she could speak again, she laughed. "Had fun, did you?"

"If it's legal to have fun when I'm practicing to escape the ultimate international thugs . . ." He grinned. "Yeah, I had fun. And I will *always* let you climb out ahead of me. The view is amazing."

She gave him the slightest shove in an insincere suggestion to behave himself, but made no real attempt to pull away. "You did great. I don't want to use our little escape route, but we're in good shape in case we get trapped up here." They'd also pried the second floor doors open enough to provide a crack of light; the elevator was stuck just below, and Mickey could just barely stand on the top of the car and see over the shelves that had been placed in front of the doors from the other side. Observation post Number One—except she wouldn't use the rope this evening—she'd simply climb the wooden rungs snugged up against the side of the shaft for maintenance purposes.

But before then, she needed to rig the ropes off the tower

roof—one floor up on a spiral staircase that led past the tower-only fourth floor, a tiny area that seemed to be there for the sole purpose of providing sheltered access to the elevator machinery.

She hoped Naia wasn't afraid of heights.

She stopped next to the air mattresses, rifling their stash of food for protein bars and a toaster pastry—she'd always preferred them cold, anyway.

"Hey," she said out loud. She held the toaster pastry out so Steve could behold its significance. "Check it out. I like them cold."

"That's nice," he offered, expression crooked with doubt.

She laughed. "I mean, I *know* I like them cold. See? Haven't taken a bite yet."

"Ah." He nodded sagely. "The mysteries of you, revealed."

"Exactly." She took a big bite, and found the lukewarm bottled water sitting crookedly on her mattress. "Leave that harness on. I know it's a Village People kind of fashion statement, but if we've got to run for it, we'll have enough trouble getting Naia harnessed up and ready to go."

He looked down at himself. "Village People. That about sums it up. You gonna break into song any time soon?"

"You never know," she told him primly, and jammed the power bar into her back pocket to eat along the way, grabbing the fingerless climbing gloves she'd dropped on the mattress. "I'm gonna get this stuff set up. Keep an eye on the stairs, will you? She said evening . . . it's a little early, but I don't want to chance missing her."

He stopped with a power bar halfway to his mouth, face still smudged. "And if she shows?"

Maybe she'd tell him about that smudge; maybe she'd just enjoy the touch of ruffian it added to his unruly hair. "Don't approach unless it looks like she's leaving. But I shouldn't be that long." Just long enough to secure the ropes. *Please, let there be some nice convenient projections. Pipes, metal framing . . . I'll take anything.*

"Okay." He shrugged, visibly deciding he could deal with Naia, and headed for the stairwell. The bounce, Mickey was glad to see, was back in his step. For the moment, he had put the afternoon—the killing—behind them. Like Mickey, focusing more on the future than the past.

She waited until she'd turned away before she let her smile fade. Steve, ever the hopeful . . . ever looking for that happy ending. In spite of her precautions and escape plans, it probably hadn't truly sunk in that the evening could hold just as much violence as the afternoon. That she was preparing for more than just a sly departure.

For if Naia made it here, she wasn't likely to come alone.

Good thing I'm not afraid of heights. Mickey crouched on the steeply slanted tower roof, the ropes coiled neatly at her feet, the cluster of warehouses spread out before her. None of them had the character of this one; none of them rose as tall. This had been one of the first, and had gone on to a new purpose while the others still greeted big trucks and boldly colored delivery vehicles. The constant rumble of diesel engines had faded as evening came on; now she looked out over a quiet neighborhood.

The other direction held the Caltrain station, barely visible. Next to it, the park to which Steve had almost taken her. It looked like a nice place. *Some other time.* And down the block, nearly hidden by carefully tended urban trees, the bus stop she'd been using.

Not a bad view. And it came with a peaceful sense of distance from it all. "Bet I used to climb trees, too," Mickey told the air around her. *Bet I used to climb trees with that slingshot . . .*

But staying up here was a luxury, and she'd left Steve on his own, lurking in the stairwell in the spot they'd chosen as casting the fewest, faintest shadows—probably wishing he could call the hospital to ask about Mosquito, and knowing they wouldn't tell him anything. So she returned to roof access—a quaint old trap door—surveyed the ropes one more time, and told them, "No offense, but I hope we don't meet again."

The ropes had no apparent opinion on the matter. But Mickey left the door open just in case—one less thing to do if the time came. She backed down the iron rungs that served for a ladder and into the tower's fourth floor, a square little room filled with the impressive gears and motor of the elevator. Down the spiral metal stairs and into the vast third floor . . . she found herself looking at the space anew, falling into a mindset that seemed both fresh and familiar at the same time. Good cover over there behind that pillar, too much junk to trip over there, someone's old half-finished wall over there. Their stuff was tucked away, as it had been from the start—she'd never left them exposed, but found a nook behind unused wallboard, buckets of spackling, tubs of nails . . .

This must be what Steve's loft space looked like before he'd finished it. Once empty and echoing, now so obviously an apartment—a place he'd turned into home. A place the Irhaddanians had driven him from—

Just for now, she told herself.

"You there?" she said to the stairwell.

He didn't answer.

Had she been up there that long? Long enough for something to go down out here? She headed for the wall, skimming alongside it to approach the stairwell; the Glock found its way to her hand, and she wasn't even sure how. She held it low, staying unobtrusive as she took a quick peek and retreat into the stairwell, leaning against the wall to process what she'd seen.

Nothing, that's what. No one.

But she heard voices. Steve's voice, a woman's voice. And the woman was scared . . . desperate. Her voice was a beautiful liquid tone nonetheless and—

Tell me about Naia.

Beautiful almond eyes fringed with darkest lashes—eyes wide with fear in dark olive skin, long swoop of a refined nose, mouth dropped open and about to protest—

Tell me about Naia.

"Get a grip," Mickey muttered to herself, but by then her heart was pounding, adrenaline flushing through her system and beyond her control. Because this was it. She'd found Naia . . . or Naia had found her. And Naia would have her answers. Naia would be safe—somehow, Mickey would keep her safe—and then they could unravel this mess.

Except Naia's voice had risen—was heading for ultimatum.

Mickey abandoned her stealth mode and ran down the stairs, leaping the last three to skid along painted wood flooring before righting herself and grabbing the door frame into the classroom. There she froze, taking an instant to assess the situation—Steve with his arms out, a placating gesture, his gun stuffed into his back pocket at his most excellent posterior. Naia, as wild as a trapped deer in an incongruous lilac lounging outfit, her back to the project shelves near the dead drop. Steve hadn't closed on her, hadn't come within striking range. Too much training for that. But whatever he'd said to her, she hadn't bought it. Her hands groped behind her, feeling for the nearest project, ready to fling and run.

Brave girl, brought up protected and isolated and demure, ready to fight for her life.

"Naia," she said quietly, and her voice cut through Steve's

desperate words, cut through Naia's rejection of him. "Naia, I'm here."

Naia jerked around to face the doorway, not quite believing—not until she saw Mickey standing there. Steve faded back, taking himself out of the equation as far as he could. "Anna!" Naia took a step forward as if she couldn't quite allow herself to believe it. "*Alhamdulillah!* Anna! Where have you been!" But even with that she abandoned her defensive posture and ran to Mickey, embracing her with a fervor that betrayed the depth of her fear. Mickey—startled, devoid of any true context for Naia's relationship with her, returned the embrace. But not, apparently, as Naia expected, for she pulled back and gave Mickey a searching look. "Anna? What is wrong?"

Of course, then the absurdity of what she'd said hit her, and before Mickey could respond she said, "Oh, I know—all this is wrong. There is serious trouble for us. But I can tell . . . there's something else . . ." And then she glanced at Steve. "You told him—?"

Mickey shook her head, suddenly weary. "It's a long story."

"That's the understatement of the year," Steve muttered, not quite loudly enough to truly interrupt them, though Naia shot a look in his direction. She'd changed since Mickey had last seen her. Less trusting . . . less gentle. Up close, her clothes were hard used—otherwise lightly worn garments with tears and stains.

She broke away from Mickey and went to the dead drop, retrieving a tightly folded paper. "Here," she said. "This is what it's all about."

Mickey took it, unfolding it to discover a double-sided printout, tiny font crammed to the margins, impossible to skim. She didn't even try. Naia said, "A man in my father's cabinet has been using him—using our people."

"Mounir Farooqi," Steve said abruptly. "He's storing weapons of mass destruction, isn't he?"

Mickey felt her jaw drop. Naia looked at Steve as though a speaking fungus would have surprised her less.

He shrugged. "Hey. I did some research this morning. I meant to tell you," he added, looking at Mickey, "but then . . . I got distracted."

Right. By the gunplay. By killing people. By having Mosquito die in his arms. But she couldn't stop herself from saying, "You found that information *on the Web?*"

"I inferred it," he said. "From what's on the Web and what's going on here. You have to have both pieces."

"Still. That's . . ." She shook her head. "I'm damned impressed."

"Anna," Naia all but wailed, "what's going on? Who *is* this man? What happened to . . . your *hair?*"

Right back to the *long story* situation. "His name is Steve," Mickey said, for the first time really hearing how Naia addressed her. Not Anna, as Steve had said it. *Ahna.* But it still brought no instant flash of memory; no sudden revelation of her past.

"Mickey?" Steve took a step toward her, reaching—

But Naia wasn't ready for that. She glared him off. Gentle Naia, glaring off a self-defense expert. It brought Mickey back to herself, even as Naia demanded, "And why does he call you *Mickey?*"

Just get it over fast, like ripping a band-aid. "You know we're compromised, yes?" She barely waited for Naia's nod. "They came after me. I don't know all the details. I know they got me; they drugged me with something. It damaged my memory. I got away from them, but . . . I didn't remember—I *don't* remember—anything about myself. I've been trying to reconstruct it all. Steve has been helping." Understatement. Steve had held her together, whether he knew it or not. "We had to call me something, so . . . Mickey."

Naia gave her a dubious look. "As in the *mouse?*"

Mickey choked on a laugh. "I suppose so."

"We've been trying to find you," Steve said, and this time he did move closer. "We didn't have a lot to go on. But Mickey knew you were in trouble, so . . ."

"Fill me in," Mickey said. She gestured at Naia's clothing. "What's been happening? How did you get this intel?"

"Fill you in?"

"The big picture. We met . . . where?"

"A party," Naia said. "You go to lots of parties. Everyone wants you there. You sell them fabulous antiques, and you entertain them. You told me once that's why you're so good at your real job. The CIA job. Because no one ever suspects you could be more than a light-hearted society girl."

"Really?" Steve said. "Gee, do you think it's the singing, or the dancing?"

Mickey gathered her dignity. "Never mind him. So we met at a party—not too long ago?"

"This spring. We . . . you have been a good friend. And then . . . this." She gestured at the dead drop. "I went home before summer classes started. I saw things . . . differently. And I overheard Mounir Farooqi. I intended to tell you when I came home, but then Badra—my chaperone, you would call her— started acting differently. And I felt watched. I had to be careful. It took me a while to leave my first note. I think you found it." She gestured at the dead drop. "*Someone* did."

"That was us," Mickey confirmed. And, unbidden and unexpected, "Hey, do I have a cat?"

Bemused, Naia nodded. Mickey bit back a spurt of glee that no one would understand. *I remembered the cat!*

"What about the editorial in the university paper?" Steve asked. "Sounds like someone put you on a short leash. You stopped going to classes."

She nodded. "They confined me to my apartment. I had to break out—I climbed out a window and to the fire escape. By now they've discovered that I'm gone. I take long showers, but not *this* long."

The words hit Mickey hard, cold steel trickling down her spine. "Dammit, I should have asked about that first thing. We've got to get out of here."

Naia shook her head. "But they don't know where I've gone."

"They watched you for weeks," Mickey said. "They're going to have a pretty good damned idea where to look."

"I'm sorry, I—"

"No," Mickey cut her off, more sharply than she'd meant to. "It's not your fault. You shouldn't have been alone in this." She folded the paper and tucked it inside her sport top, the closest thing she had to a bra. Not the best option—it was sure to be damp before all was said and done. But right now, the only option. "Let's go. We need to grab the ammo and gear and get out of here."

"Where?" Steve said. He didn't add, as he could have, *how?* Because all three of them wouldn't fit on the bike.

"Just get out of here first," Mickey told him. She touched the gun, touched the knives she wore—just because. She saw Steve's hand hesitate over the butt of the Glock before he realized what he was doing and snatched it away.

"But—" Naia said. "What will happen to me now?"

"Later for that, too," Mickey told her. She took the younger woman's arm and nudged her toward the stairs, suppressing her impulse to bolt up them—but a nod at Steve sent him on ahead, and he took those stairs two and three at a time, the usual bounce in his movement magnified. His urgency caught; Naia ran after him—swift little one-at-a-time steps that put Mickey right on her heels.

At the top of the stairs, Mickey moved Naia aside so she

could run in and help Steve gather the things they'd deliberately left out for easy access, stuffing them into Steve's backpack and Mickey's newly bought duffel. Only a matter of moments, and then Mickey slung the duffel over her shoulders and took the lead back downstairs, tugging Naia into position behind her so Steve brought up the rear. She ran down the stairs—lightly this time, single-stepping it and listening hard, for she meant what she'd said to Naia—the Irhaddanians would be here, and sooner rather than later. There weren't that many places that Naia habitually spent her time outside of classes, and of those, this building was the most remote, the most separated from the rest of her life.

They'd come here sooner.

Halfway down the final flight of stairs, she heard the noise—heard the voices. She stopped short, holding up a hand—giving the others time to hear without creating noise of their own.

Naia whispered desperately, "Is there not another class? Maybe they're students—"

Deep, male voices. A few distinct words—recognizable Irhaddanian words. *Bitch* and *foolish girl* and *put an end to this* and *authorize to use final measures* and even Naia understood what that last phrase truly meant. For Steve's benefit, Mickey said simply, "They're here. They're not planning to take prisoners."

"Here?" Steve repeated. "What does that mean, *here? Can we still get out—*"

Below them, shadows blocked the light from the door. The door knob turned.

Mickey reversed course, shooing Naia up the stairs—*pushing* her and shushing her at the same time. Steve took the hint and led the way, his single glance back revealing a tight, tense jaw and complete determination.

And they would have made it. They would have been up on the third floor, out of sight, able to slink out the tower roof—

Doranna Durgin

able to rappel down the side of the building and away to freedom.

If Naia hadn't tripped.

If she hadn't cried out in fear when she tripped.

Shouts of discovery echoed up the stairwell.

Mickey dropped any attempt at silence, hauling Naia to her feet. Steve had turned back to help and she waved him onward. "Go!" she said. "Find cover!" She turned around long enough to unload a round into the stairwell, giving the Irhaddanians something to think about. *It's more than just one frightened young woman.* At the blast of the gun, Naia shrieked again, cowering. "*Go*," Mickey told her. "I've got your back. You're okay."

Not exactly reassuring, not with shouted demands following them through the third floor. Mickey pushed Naia at Steve, clipping out, "Stay with her—find cover!"

"Anna!" Naia reached out to her even as Steve moved in, terrified and pleading all at once. And Mickey got it. She got that Naia wasn't used to physical effort; she got that Naia had used all her bold, all her brave, just to get here.

And she still didn't have time to deal with it. "Trust him, Naia," she said, already heading toward the nearest bucket of nails. "He'll take care of you." And winced inwardly. *Sorry, Steve.* Naia's happy ending shouldn't be his burden to share. And then to Steve, "If we get separated, take her to the FBI." Words that would horrify her CIA compatriots—but he could find the FBI in the phone book, and she had no idea where to find the local CIA station. Some discreet somewhere in San Francisco, no doubt.

"We're not—" he started.

But she'd already turned away, snatching up the nails with a grunt of effort, and sparing the breath only to say, "Take cover!" Already she heard the Irhaddanians on the stairs, barely deterred by her warning shot. She heaved the nails down the stairs, aim-

230

ing high so they bounced off the wall; the men's cries of dismay brought grim satisfaction.

And by then Steve had guided Naia to cover across the room—not nearly close enough to the tower exit, not at a great angle from the doorway, but it was too late to change that now. Mickey found herself scantier cover, closer to the tower, a more direct line with the doorway. If she had to scoot for the tower, she could—but not without leaving Naia and Steve.

Best to get them out while she could. "Get her to the roof," she told Steve. "I'll cover—"

Too late for that. A dark shape peeked around the doorway—then retreated just as fast, encouraged by the wooden shrapnel from Mickey's bullet. She hissed a half-formed curse and took better stock of her immediate surroundings—found Steve's bow. "Just in case!" she said, and skidded it across the wooden floor to him. As low-tech as it seemed, he excelled at using it . . . and had no experience with guns. And especially none with this particular model, which took a significant number of practice rounds to master. *Boy, I wish I didn't know that.*

"You have nowhere to go," one of the men said. "You can't escape from this. Surrender is your best chance."

"Yeah, and *that* was dripping with sincerity," Mickey responded, all the while measuring the distance Naia and Steve would have to run, calculating how exposed they'd be.

Too far. And too much. With this six-cartridge magazine, she couldn't provide enough cover. Maybe if Steve slid his gun—

One man stuck his gun around the corner, just far enough to unload a few rounds at her, eliciting another faint shriek of dismay from Naia. Mickey tucked herself away—and damned if the other man didn't use the cover to target her more carefully. His very first shot proved the inadequate nature of her cover—wallboard, just wallboard—and she squinched herself against the brick even more tightly. *Damn, they sent the smart team.* She flattened on the dusty floor, flat as she could ever get, crooking her gun around the end of the wallboard to return fire without looking.

From there, she could clearly see Steve and Naia. Naia crouched against the opposite wall of the giant space; Steve returned her look with a grave expression that made it clear he knew exactly how bad the situation was. He and Naia were trapped; the men could easily pick away at Mickey until they took her down, and then close in on Steve and Naia. Being hell on wheels in a street fight meant nothing here.

And Mickey was the only one who had a clear run for the way out.

She flinched down as another bullet hit way too close, returning a rapid succession of shots until the slide locked back, already reaching for another magazine. Releasing the first, slamming the second home, she said low and fast, "I'm going out, going to come up on them from behind. Cover me."

And Naia, overwhelmed, following the exchange in a second language, understood only that Mickey was leaving them. "Anna!" she cried. "Anna, no, don't—"

Oh, great, just tell them the whole thing why don't you—

And Steve saw the look on her face, understood it. He imitated the Irhaddan technique, peeking out just long enough to get the angle, then unloading his gun into the stairwell right over Naia's protests.

Mickey ran for it. Low and fast, straight for the back tower, jamming her gun into her pants along the way. Steve ran out of ammo and rounds instantly clipped at her heels, far too—ow! Splinters drove up into her calf, making the muscle spasm in response. The leg went out from beneath her and she flung herself into the tower.

Not at the stairs at all. At the elevator shaft. Still propped open, still nothing but empty air. Her upper body slid right over the lip of the shaft; cool air hit her face.

And then she began to tip, to fall. Behind her, Steve had reloaded—he blasted out six more rounds of cover as she desperately snatched for the ladder directly below her. Momentum carried her out into the shaft as her hands closed around the first wooden rung and she cart-wheeled awkwardly out into the open space, so glad for the climbing gloves as she twisted around the wooden rung, losing skin even so. But not her grip.

Not even when she jerked to a stop, hung in mid-air as though she were a gravity-defying gymnast on the bars, and then slammed down against the shaft wall with all the force of a cracked whip.

Then she lost her grip. Then she slid down against the ladder, hands scrabbling, rungs going *bumpbumpbump* like a washboard road against her body—until once more she jerked to a stop, saved by one precarious handhold. Then another . . . and then her toes, jammed up against the shaft wall.

She didn't realize she'd lost the gun until she heard it clatter to a landing against the top of the permanently stalled elevator. She looked down just in time to see it bounce and skid over the side of the car, the noise of its fall echoing forlornly up the shaft.

"Well, *that* sucks," she muttered, and only then discovered she had a fat lip. If that was the only price she paid for this little ploy, then she'd take it.

Above, Steve and the Irhaddanians exchanged gunfire; Steve was being more careful with his shots now, conserving ammo.

And no wonder. Mickey had the box of cartridges in the backpack.

Not good planning. She jammed her feet against the outsides of the ladder and let herself slide in a barely controlled descent. One of them had the ammo; the other now had the only gun. "Do-over!" she yelled, reaching the second floor elevator doors.

Then Steve's gun stopped firing . . . didn't start again. Naia made a noise of great dismay. Mickey clamped her jaw down on a thrill of fear, hanging tightly to the ladder as she brought up first one leg, then two, to shove against the barely open doors. Old doors, unused doors, sticky doors . . . horizontal with the effort, she worked against the world's most wicked leg press. "Open, dammit," she grunted, feeling the sweat pop on her face. She and Steve had worked together to gain even the few inches they'd had, never thinking to do more than observe from here. The doors creaked and Mickey creaked and one of the men upstairs gave a shout of surprise and the doors *gave*—

Leaving her wrung out and gasping, clinging to the ladder with what was left of her strength while her legs scrabbled feebly at the narrow lip of space where the doors had been. Where the doors mostly still were, except for a space just wide enough that a nimble woman might slip through, driven by the noise of combat above.

Too bad about those shelves still directly in her way.

Mickey contemplated those shelves for only an instant. She'd seen them from the other side; she knew they were sturdy, heavy, and weighed down with giant cubes of clay. She'd used up her brute force strength for the moment.

She let her feet swing back down to the ladder and re-approached the new opening from an upright position, stepping over to stand briefly in the narrow strip of floor before heaving herself up and over the chest-high shelves. She made no attempt to do it gracefully, sliding head-first down the other side to tuck and roll upon hitting the floor.

Boy, she was gonna hurt in the morning.

Just hurry, you fool.

Back to her feet, minus the gun but still with the knives, Mickey ran lightly between the classroom tables, humming *I Need a Hero* under her breath. *Thank you, Bonnie Tyler . . .* Out the door and up the first flight of stairs, hesitating then for a quick *please let them be clueless about where I went* and she peered around the landing to find the two men plastered up against the wall, getting impatient. Brass lay scattered around their feet; they had to be running low on ammo just as Steve was.

She saw, then, what had caused their recent surprise—the arrow sticking out the back of the stairwell, chest height and driven deep. No wonder they looked cautious.

Not cautious enough. She took a quick calculation of distance and angle, and knew the knife throw was nearly impossible. *Doesn't matter. Draw them off, that's what counts.* She moved out, ran up three steps to turn impossible to the merely improbable, and let the first knife fly, aiming low.

Yes! She pumped air in the world's briefest celebration as the knife buried itself in one man's calf. For a startled instant of time she met the other man's gaze—and then the absurdity of the situation overtook her. *CIA amnesiac taunting two men with guns.* She made a little flutter-finger wave and ducked back, holding her breath so she could hear the moment they committed to chasing her.

But they didn't. They exchanged a few angry words in their own language and ignored her, taking the moment to shout more demands at Naia and Steve, giving Mickey the chance to peer back around at them in complete annoyance—and to see that they'd exposed themselves in reacting to Mickey, as one of Steve's arrows thwapped into its target, pinning the man to the wall by a small margin of flesh in his upper arm and a large margin of suit coat.

Mickey took the chance—she gave up another knife, taking one smooth step into the open to fling it upward. Her luck wasn't nearly as good as last time. It bounced off the second man's ankle and halfway back down the stairs—and as she hesitated, Steve let loose with another arrow, one that thwapped into the wall inches from the pinned man's head. Mickey took the opportunity to stretch up, snatch the knife, and run. And just around the doorway, she said lightly in their own language, "We can do this all day. I'm doing fine, how about you?"

It decided them. The pinned man tore away from the wall, cursing with pain, and snapped at his companion, "They've got nowhere to go. We can deal with them once she's dead."

Zoicks. That would be her signal. Mickey sprinted on down the stairs and heard them clattering after her, and over her shoulder she shouted, "Go! All the way!"

She could only hope they would.

But it meant she had to keep things in play down here, had to keep the men from charging back upstairs to discover the exit, from reaching the ropes before Steve and Naia were on the ground. Steve the absolute greenhorn, shepherding Naia the terrified, four stories down.

Definitely had to keep things in play.

CHAPTER 20

Mickey skidded on the welcome mat at the bottom of the stairs and then thoughtfully kicked it back in place for those who followed so hard on her heels. She slammed into the door to the co-op sales floor, a token door of half glass whose knob refused to turn in her grip. With only an instant of remorse, she rammed the butt end of her knife through the window and then reversed it to clear the glass, just enough room for her hand—

Out of time. Their footsteps sounded heavily on the stairs and she threw herself against the small section of wall flanking the bottom step. Directly across from her was the outer door and escape—she had no doubt she could make it.

But then their Irhaddan friends would just head back upstairs to take out Steve and Naia.

They rounded the final landing—not moving quite as well as they might, one man distinctly behind the other and neither slowing—they must have heard the breaking glass, seen the door . . . and assumed she'd gone through. Their mistake. Mickey waited, crouching, weight shifted and ready . . . ready . . .

She met him with a wicked high kick. His feet shot out from under him and he slammed back onto the stairs. She got a glimpse of him tangling with his buddy and then ducked behind the corner again, crouching down low. *Hurry,* she thought at Steve. *Really hurry.*

It was a good game, but it wouldn't last long.

Short, harsh curses cut short to an ominous silence; she imagined them communicating in rapid-fire gestures. And then surprise, here came a gun, lightning fast exposure around the corner at chest level. She didn't give the man a chance to fire it; she darted up with the knife, slashing at exposed knuckles.

She had to give him credit—he didn't drop the gun. He jerked back with a noise that would have been cursing if he'd only been able to get the words out fast enough.

Soon enough they'd figure it out. They had only to rush her two at a time. The only thing holding them back—she rose from her crouch, slamming a roundhouse kick to a vulnerable knee still behind the corner, driving them back further and then dropping back into place—was the question of her gun. They didn't know she'd dropped it.

They'd figure it out soon enough.

Mickey, what have you done? He couldn't believe it. Ushering Naia up to the fourth floor, helping her fasten the Swiss seat, already realizing she was toned but not strong, not accustomed to using her body, he still couldn't believe it. Instructing her on the basics of rappelling that he had only learned a few hours earlier, he couldn't believe it.

Looking at Naia's expression, it was clear she couldn't believe it either.

And Mickey was at the mercy of two angry Irhaddan operatives. *They're here,* she'd said. *And they're not planning to take prisoners.* And what had she done but gone and pulled the tiger by the tail?

Hard.

Well, this was his chance, wasn't it? She'd given that to him. The happy ending for Naia.

Except it was Mickey's happy ending that he'd been following. It was Mickey he wasn't willing to let go.

Best figure out how to do it all.

And hurry.

Steve looked over at Naia, poised at the edge of the roof as he was, her brake hand back around her hip as he'd just shown her, her weight leaning into it only tentatively. "I'm right beside you," he said. "Just take it slow."

Except they had no time. Mickey had no time.

Steve sent Naia an encouraging smile. "Let's go, then."

As if they had all the time in the world . . .

They figured it out.

The air whooshed out of Mickey's lungs as they double-teamed her, avoiding the knife in each hand, flipping her up in mid-air so she smacked down hard on the floor, bruised by the contents of the backpack as well as cold hardwood.

Again.

For an instant, just an instant, she had a clear run at the outer door. A little flip, a little roll, and she could bolt out between them. Neither of them were in perfect shape—scored by her knives, punctured by Steve's arrow, bruised by her recent attentions.

Sometimes, Steve had told his kids, *it's better to run.*

This was definitely one of those times.

But running wasn't an option. Not until she'd given Steve and Naia more time. She knew Naia; knew the young woman would have no natural knack with rappelling. She'd be slow; she'd be tentative. She'd be uncertain, wondering if she should take her chances with Mickey in spite of it all.

So this definitely wasn't one of those times.

A little flip, a little roll—she scrambled to recover the knife she'd lost on impact, and when a big hand reached for it first, didn't hesitate to pin it right to the floor with the knife she still had. The man screamed, then screamed again when his partner lifted her up like so much air, pulling the knife back out.

He threw her against the wall, rattling her bones, rattling her thoughts. She had a brief giddy notion that he should do it again, and maybe she'd get her memory back just like on television—and then someone kicked her.

Again.

Deep fire exploded into life, burning strong inside her. They picked her up; she saw only flashes of movement, light and dark—unfocused and without meaning. Words without meaning slapped against her ears; between him, they shook her, demanding . . . something. She couldn't quite get it.

And abruptly, they dropped her. Dismissed her. Agreed to come back for her. Headed for the stairs. *Too soon.*

Her eyes opened all the way at that. Focused sharply. Saw the glint of steel in the corner. Hidden, just like Anna Hutchinson.

She went for it. Crawling—oozing—across the floor, she went for it. Fingers closed around cool metal, automatically shifting it into throwing position. She dug around inside, came up with the strength to make it up as far as her knees—far enough to free her throwing arm. No time to waste, they were climbing right out of range, no longer as speedy as they'd once been.

She let fly, willing the knife to strike hard and deep between the shoulder blades of the nearest operative. And it struck hard and deep, all right. Hard and deep and *low.*

Ow. That's gotta hurt.

The man whirled on her, yanking the knife free with a fury that told her she'd just made the whole thing personal. He threw the blade away with the abrupt force of that same fury, right through the glass she'd already broken. *Uh-oh.* A thin thread of true alarm made its way through the aches and pains and fuzzy thoughts, and she scrambled backwards, trying to get to her feet at the same time, reaching for the outside door and shoving it open, finally, so fresh air blew cool over drying blood.

Hands yanked her back in. One set held her up . . . the other worked her over, one backhand blow after another, a stomach jab for variety—soon enough she wasn't sure just where he was hitting her. One big pain with the world whirling around her.

They dumped her on the floor and stood glaring down at her, and just as she allowed herself to think she'd surely bought Steve and Naia enough time, she heard the motorcycle start.

She laughed. She spat blood, and she laughed.

And damn them, they understood right away. They scooped her up, one on each arm, and they dragged her right out the door, shouting after the motorcycle.

Mickey looked up just in time to see Steve bring the bike to a stop, horror painting stark lines on his face. Behind him on the bike, Naia twisted around to see them; her lips formed the word *Anna!* and she clutched at Steve. The motorcycle engine cut off.

And one of the Irhaddan operatives got clever. Damned clever. He held Mickey up for display and he said to Steve, "You're making a mistake, Mr. Spaneas. This woman has dragged you into her world of psychoses, just as she dragged Miss Mejjati. If you leave now, with Miss Mejjati, you'll be wanted by every law agency in your own country—and all of those in our country, as well. And for no reason. For a mad woman's games."

"What the hell have you done to her?" Steve's voice held a gritty pain that Mickey hadn't heard before; she stiffened against the grip on her arms, looking for any sign that he'd been hurt.

No, fool, it's you.

Dammit, Steve, you shouldn't have stopped. "Get her out of here," is what she said out loud, but not very loudly at that. Not loudly enough to be heard by anyone but the men at her sides. She tried again, managed to make it louder. "Get her *out of here.*"

241

"Your friend is good," the man said, his English comfortable and smooth. "Very good. She's been sick a long time, and she knows how to deceive—it is how she lives her life. But now we have put a stop to her games, and this, my friend, is the moment you decide if you're going down with her."

"You didn't have to—" He didn't finish, his voice going hoarse, and tried again. "You didn't—"

"We subdued her," the man said, talking fast. He'd have to; his story didn't fit what had happened—not the killings, not the way they'd been shooting at Naia along with the rest of them. "She wasn't cooperative. You've dealt with this before—you should know. They have amazing strength when they're delusional."

"No," Steve said, but doubt laced that one short word.

"Steve . . ." Naia said, horrified. "Steve, no, you can't—"

"You know how convincing some of them can be. How good they are, the ones who learn to justify their delusions to others. That's all this has been. But things have gotten out of hand. We've lost our patience. Our president's daughter sits behind you and we'll stop at nothing to take her to safety. You can go down with this woman, or you can step aside and go back to your own life. Just like that. Over."

They'd done their research, dammit to hell, they'd sure done their research. And even if it couldn't and wouldn't stand up to scrutiny, they'd pushed Steve's biggest emotional button. The look on his face . . . he looked as staggered as she felt. Suddenly doubting it all—trying not to, but faced with too many years of lost causes to do anything but let that doubt in. Naia saw it too, closed her eyes and murmured, *"Astaghfirullah, Astaghfirullah." I seek refuge in God.*

And enough was enough. Mickey found her feet, clumsy though they were, and propped herself up on her own power, swaying between the two men. She ignored their painfully tightened grip; it was nothing compared to the shards of pain in her ribs, over one eye, deep within . . .

She said, "Now, Steve. *Now* you call the cops. So long as you take Naia with you."

"Mickey," he said, looking at her with those deeply troubled eyes, agony of another sort. "Mickey, I—"

"It doesn't matter what you think of me. Take her there. Get the CIA." She winced as one of the men shook her, realizing the impact of her words yet unable to hit her again without losing Steve completely. But she saw Steve's face, and she knew he was already lost to them. After a steady refusal to call on authorities, she had what she always said she'd wanted—Naia's safety—and her demand that Steve find help undercut their entire scenario of Mickey the Mad.

And Steve knew it. *"Mickey,"* he said again.

"There is no need to involve—" one of the men started.

Steve turned on him. "You killed Anthony. You killed Mosquito. You shot at us all—you shot at <u>Naia.</u> No. It's time to run away now." And Steve started the bike. He gave Mickey an impossibly agonized look and turned away.

Good. Go for it. Go make it happen.

The men cursed; they dropped her as the bike skidded out across the parking lot, running a few futile steps after it. Mickey had made it to hands and knees when they looked back at her, and she found herself too bleary to do so much as quail before their mounting anger. "We can finish this later," she suggested indistinctly. "You look like you could use some aspirin. Some nice band-aids. Would you like to hear a song? It's the hey Mickey song. I'm pretty good at it—" But she broke off her babble as they headed for her.

The rising engine noise in the background didn't catch her attention until the men were only a step or two away in spite of her floundering attempts to back away from them. Didn't catch her attention until the motorcycle shot around the end of the building carrying only Steve—Steve, who came strafing past to grab their attention from Mickey.

They turned on him, grabbing for guns that were no longer there, then going for backup—and by then Mickey had enough wits and enough time to reach behind her, snatching up the slingshot from the outside pocket of the backpack, fingers searching the ground for—

There. Big and sharp-edged, gravel from the shrubbery plantings. She loaded the slingshot without unfolding the wrist brace; she pulled the sling back with shaky hands, all the way back— even as one of the men thought to check on her, to suspect that she wasn't done with them yet.

She let fly. Up close and personal and full strength, she let fly. *No kids for you.*

The man screamed. Loud and shrill, and barely pausing for breath. The other operative whirled, gun in hand, too close to miss and aiming directly at her mixed-up head. Mickey froze, halfway to her feet, the slingshot reloaded but not pulled back, looking down the barrel of that semi-automatic, thinking she had no chance of surviving a .45 caliber bullet to the brain, thinking that Steve wouldn't get his happy ending at all—

Except Steve was still coming. And Steve came on fast, brushing the man hard enough so the bike wobbled and the man wobbled and in that split second of inattention, Mickey had him. She released the half-aimed stone and clipped the gun, a .38 revolver, and she surged to her feet with all her remaining strength, kicking the gun aside as it went off, burning a trail all the way up her leg.

This time when Steve came around, he just plain ran the man down.

He cut the engine and toed the kickstand down and leaped off the bike pretty much in one motion, while Mickey found herself on the ground again, not even quite sure how she'd gotten there. She'd acquired the .38 along the way, and had it trained on their new prisoner. "Naia?"

"At the Caltrain, calling nine-one-one as requested. God, Mickey, you look—"

"Alive," she said, struggling for dignity when she could feel enough puffy heat on her face to know exactly how she looked. "I look *alive*."

Steve hesitated next to the Irhaddan operative, who seemed as though he might try to get up until he saw the gun in Mickey's hand. In the background, his partner still offered a high-pitched and unending whine. "What I *meant*," Steve said, enunciating his words carefully, "was it was time for *you* to run away."

And Mickey laughed, and pulled him down to sit by her, ready to lean her weary, battered body against him and wait for help.

No such luck. They both jumped as a nondescript sedan swooped around the corner into the parking lot, coming to a stop with a squeal of brakes and still rocking with the motion of it when the two occupants jumped out, ready for action. *The CIA to the rescue.*

"Tsk," Mickey said. "That's pretty active for native soil."

The sturdy woman gave her partner a cranky look, and tipped her head at the sirens in the background. "See? Let's go. We'll grab her up at the police station, nice and procedural."

"Wait," Steve said, stopping them from a departure as abrupt as their arrival. "You were—you saw—" and finally his arm tightened around Mickey's shoulder and he blurted, "How is Mosquito?"

The case officers exchanged a glance, and then the man said, somewhat guardedly, "It's hard to tell. He seems to have been affected—"

"But he's *alive*?" Steve said, sudden hope infusing his voice.

The agent relaxed. "Yes, he'll be fine. His care is being covered."

Mickey found she had her own questions. "And the woman?" she demanded. "Did you find—?"

The female agent offered grim satisfaction. "A specialized contractor," she said. "Abduction and interrogation for hire, right along with her pet doctor."

"Foolish man," Mickey muttered, thinking of his callous naiveté. He'd burned out her memory—maybe forever—and if he wasn't in the league of his employers, he still deserved everything that came his way.

The woman gave her a perceptive look, turning back to face her more directly if just as confrontational as ever. "You're ready to come in, then?"

To face her past directly? To see who she really was, as others also saw her? Mickey would have shuddered if she wasn't so wracked with the pain of the beating she'd taken. But Naia was safe and Mickey now understood the players of this game into which she'd been caught up. There was no reason to run any longer, aside from fear.

Not that there wasn't plenty of fear.

"Yes," she said. "I'm ready to come in."

CHAPTER 21

Steve swam out of the depths of a foggy, hallucinatory sleep to a foggy, hallucinatory awareness. The bed, he slowly realized, was jiggling. Tiny little bounces.

Totally atypical of his bed at any time.

"*Ise gaiduri*," he muttered at it.

The bed giggled. Just a little.

His eyes flew open. This time, he knew what he'd find.

"That door," he said distinctly, "was *locked*. And it was a new lock. A really spiffy lock."

"It was," she agreed.

He sat up with much more dignity than the last time this had happened, and figured she was perfectly well aware of what he did or didn't wear under the covers. Just the brush of the sheets woke him up with startling speed.

Or maybe it was Mickey, sitting cross-legged at the end of the bed in some lightweight yoga outfit, the single light by the door—which he hadn't left on—shining off the smooth lines of a new haircut. Shorter, spunkier, still framing her face and those bright, clear blue eyes. No bruises, no swelling. Healed and healthy.

"How's things with our new friend Anna?" Steve asked.

"Good enough to let you go, I guess." Weeks, it had been. Weeks during which he'd settled back into his routine here, weeks that included a certain amount of grilling by the CIA. The clean-up done by both the Irhaddanians and the CIA along the way meant there was no evidence of his involvement in anything but that last confrontation, during which he'd done nothing but fire a convenient gun in self-defense. Once the agency wars swooped into play, that little fact had pretty much been lost in shuffle. He'd been grilled by the CIA—an amazingly thorough process that went deep into his background—and turned loose. Back to build his classes up again, ponder how to juggle the disrupted cash flow, and explain to Dawnisha and the other ladies where he'd been, and why he hadn't come back with Mickey.

They'd liked Mickey, his neighborhood family had.

And here she was on his bed, making his heartbeat ratchet up as her presence truly sank in. He hadn't expected—he'd thought he'd gotten over—

He took a sudden deep breath, making up for moments of holding it.

She said, "Yup, I'm on the loose. They're going to keep me working in the background until I'm a little more solid, but I'm on the loose. And Naia . . . she's a hero to her country. She won't be working with us anymore, but . . . hey, now I can have lunch with her out in the open." She shrugged, tossing back hair that really wasn't long enough to toss any more. "And Anna . . . she's okay, as it turns out. Not a bad person to be. Works pretty hard to keep this country safe . . ." she hesitated, a thoughtful tilt in her head. "That woman . . . the Irhaddanians hired her when they thought Jane A. Dreidler would be an easy catch." She made a face. "Maybe I *was* an easy catch. I guess I'll never know."

"Somehow I doubt it." Steve hit dry tones in spite of the distraction of having her *right there*. "Jane A. Dreidler."

"My station name," she said. "Well, it *was*." She made another face, a wry one. "Maybe it's a good thing I had all that training to draw on after I escaped, and none of the memories that I hadn't actually been in a bad guy smackdown before. Lots of training, lots of scenarios . . . lots of clandestine stuff. But no smackdown." She straightened, her voice brightening. "But hey, I do have a cat—and a neighbor who feeds her when I'm gone, so she's fine! And I have the most amazing furniture. Turns out I'm pretty damn good at the antique thing. And I like it, too, which is a nice touch. I travel a lot . . . sometimes I play courier . . . sometimes I escort people from place to place. Never dull."

"You were never dull just being you," Steve said, rather fervently. "Even when you didn't know who you were."

"Oh, just wait," she said. "Now that I remember most of me—hypnosis is a wonderful thing—I'm sure I'll be even more fun than ever."

Look at that, he'd forgotten to breathe again.

"Speechless?" she said. "Or just waiting for me to break into song?"

"Waiting for you," he said.

"Oh, well then." She stretched, enough to lift her cropped top, to reassure him that she'd filled out to a healthy weight since her abduction and their big adventure. Sleek, toned, just waiting to be touched. "Move over. I'll teach you how to sing, all right."

ABOUT THE AUTHOR

Doranna Durgin lives in the high desert of Arizona with four dogs, with whom she competes in agility, rally, and obedience, and her Lipizzan, with whom she rides in the Ponderosa woods. She has no spare time.